Nancy Culver stared at the little being, then at the several other Whispers with him, in confusion. "I don't understand. What did Ben do now?"

Deem Sixteen, who was helping himself to sweets from Maude's refrigerator, turned and frowned at the girl. "Among other things, your brother has aided and abetted a monster, created at least twenty major anachronisms, subverted the entire technological basis of photogravitational temporization, and very nearly destroyed a working chronoloop," he snapped. "Not to mention the filching of a temporal effect focalizer from Leapfrog Waystop—which is now in the hands of the aforesaid monster."

"That is an exaggeration, Deem," Teal Fordeen hushed him. "It was all inadvertent. Unfortunately, the chain of events resulting from Ben's sleeptiming *has* become a can of worms. The worms were always there, of course, but they have become a factor largely because of your brother's somnambulistic excursions."

"I'd hardly call it 'worms' when two thousand years' accumulation of temporal theory and technology becomes abruptly obsolete," Deem argued . . .

By Dan Parkinson
Published by Ballantine Books:

The Gates of Time
THE WHISPERS
FACES OF INFINITY
PARADOX GATE

Timecop
VIPER'S SPAWN
THE SCAVENGER
BLOOD TIES

Author's Note

Eventuality is to the future as history is to the past: countless separate bundles of cause-and-effect sequences, occurring in parallel so that they cling and twist into continuous yarns of progression, each filament strengthening and binding the others in a uniform, progressive spiral. As these progressions coincide in time and place, they in turn spiral together in strands of trend. Through spatial limitation and chronological extension, continuing trends flow parallel and become spirals of spirals—a complex "rope" of separate filaments conjoined and interdependent.

Every event in some manner, at some point, is thus affected by all concurrent events, each the result of its own sequence of prior events and each a contributor to all subsequent events.

In history, this interwoven bundle of all occurrences—this rope from the infinite past to the present—consists of events remembered, reported, or presumed to have occurred. In eventuality, the elements of the rope are conjecture, expectation, speculation, and projection.

Yet history and eventuality are the same rope—the same bundles of sequence filaments twisted together into the same strands of trend that form the same cohesive spiral of progression.

The difference between history and eventuality—between past and future at any point of time—lies simply in the direction of the observation. At any point, a cross section of the entirety—a vantage gate for purpose of observation—reveals in one direction everything that has occurred before and in the other everything that will occur after. At any instant, the two directional sections revealed by the gate are exact mirror images of each other.

The beginning of the rope, which is the beginning of history, is a universal coordinate encompassing the entirety of each of the four prime dimensions. The end of the rope is the same universal coordinate—universal in that, since it includes all of everything, there cannot be another.

Thus the rope is eternal. It has no beginning and no end—an infinite circle of occurrence, the event filaments at every point determined by the events preceding it.

And being universal, a spiral of spirals within spirals composed of spirals, it contains not only every occurrence that is probable, but also every occurrence that is *possible.*

Within such a concept of time, the dissociation from the entire rope of any one filament or strand creates a paradox of paradoxes: being possible, the paradox is integral to the spiral. Yet to *be* a paradox, it must be separate from the spiral.

Still, within the matrix of universality, there can be no discontinuity. So, though separate for some duration, the paradox filament remains part of the whole. And a cross section of the whole must of necessity include a cross section—at the same point of section—of the paradox.

The vantage gate to paradox is the paradox that resolves conflicting paradoxes—that reveals them as mirror images of each other and thus, but for the gate itself, one and the same.

—Dan Parkinson

Preface

Glossary of Terms

Bichronism In Actualist physics, the view that time is two separate phenomena: Time1, or T1 (experienced duration), and Time2, or T2 (elapsed sequential duration along a line from the known past to the known present, infinitely extendable in the directions of past and future without variation of sequence; unidimensional time; "real" or "historic" time).

Gates and Bridges A general term for various significant temporal anomalies discovered by WHIS explorers in the extreme ranges of upstream time: the "time when time began." Almost invariably paradoxical in nature, these phenomena necessitated general reexamination of theories of temporal mechanics, including accepted views of relationships between probability and eventuality, and brought into question the view of T2 as a conjoined linear constant.

Paradox An occurrence, phenomenon, or juxtaposition of fact that is seemingly self-contradictory, absurd, or impossible but nonetheless exists or occurs in reality.

Photogravitational Spectrum Sequential spectrum based on the primal force of the universe, experienced at one extreme as gravity, at the other as light. Portrayed as a full-arc sequence, the p-g spectrum is a circle of graduation from pure gravity through accelerating stages of slow light to pure light, and from that extreme through decreasing velocities of mass effect—evidenced by free-fall inertia—to pure gravity.

Probability Warp A phenomenon in which a strand of probability becomes separated from general eventuality and veers off on its own T2 vector for an extended period, creating an independent cause-effect sequence. Though paradoxical from the viewpoint of T2 linearity, such phenomena might explain the bridges effect noted in primal reaches of the T2 continuum.

Slow Light The hypothetical point at which accelerating photation "captures" physical matter from the stasis of gravity, to push it ahead of the developing wave of "new light," thus achieving velocitation.

Temporal Effect Focalizer Electromagnetic device used to manipulate the photogravitational spectrum by the application of analogs. Essentially an energy exchange system, the TEF reverses polarity within the p-g spectrum and projects the sequence of reversal into three-dimensional space, resulting in a T1 shift by any physical body within the zone of projection.

Time One of the four prime dimensions of existence. Directions within this dimension are past and future. Primary measurements of time are duration, velocity, and sequence.

Timer A person capable of manipulating T1 time as it applies to himself or his surroundings, of altering the photogravitational spectrum by force of will or sentient resonance to create velocitation, to move at will within T2 without the use of analog devices; a natural time traveler. Some evidence indicates a correlation between this ability and conceptual exposure to altered gravitation.

Vector Focus Temporal navigation, whether through TEF quadrangulation or through innate perception in the case of timers, to "land" a T1 shift at a precise four-dimensional location.

Velocitation Alteration of elapsed T1 relative to T2 as an effect of velocity on mass. While T2 is a dimensional constant, T1 is subject to shift within the time continuum. Such shift is directly correspondent to the "velocity loop" represented by the p-g spectrum.

World History Investigative Society (WHIS) Organization authorized by the Universal Experience Bank of Pacifica in the year 2744, to conduct exploration of the past. WHIS developed the T1 conduit and the self-sustaining closed loop.

Participants in WHIS experiments and expeditions became known as Whispers.

From the *Paradox Addendum* to *The Quest for When*, an overview of the roots and development of bichronic time travel, compiled by Teal Fordeen (elscan 0-991-06ht. sm 103.11, trilev archives):

The first clear evidence of alternate probability sequence as a factor in the matrix of the T2 continuum was the "Lost Loop" message that led to conduit penetration of the Arthurian Anachronism at 2050. The message itself, conveying coordinates and vectors through the time storm, was a paradox. It was sent before the anachronism and received after the anachronism without encountering the anachronism.

This occurrence resulted in the research that eventually connected the bridges phenomenon hinted at by L-270 to probability warp theories, resulting in tangent investigations by WHIS volunteers.

Early charting of some of these tangent vectors had disastrous results. One such may have led to the ominous warning found in a ninth-century Scandinavian longboat crypt in Gotland. Identical runes, carved into a stone slab more than a thousand years earlier, were found in the early twentieth century, in a valley near Heavener, Oklahoma: GO WARILY IN FOREIGN TIMES. GO WITH SWORD IN HAND, FOR THERE BE DRAGONS.

A larger slab, also carved in ninth-century Swedish runes, apparently had been intended as a boundary marker. Its message said: THIS IS GLOME'S VALLEY.

∞

WHISPER GENESIS

In the time of the beginning they came to be, and were aware. And in all the world, they were alone. They numbered sixteen thousand on that first day, and the logics told them that this place—where vast resources of technical knowledge were theirs to use—was called Pacifica. The year was A.D. 2410, and all the accumulated learning of a vast world was theirs to use. It was theirs alone. There was no one else.

They multiplied and they learned, but as the years went by two questions remained mysteries: How did we come to be, and where are those who preceded us? With time, they became more and more focused on that greatest of mysteries, the past. With the past as their goal, they turned their attentions to time.

From the fluid crystal banks they assembled theory, and from theory technology. In the three hundred and second year, 1MgSOpm02 (Magnus Opum) perfected the equations of retrosynchronic penetration. Thirty-two years later the Universal Experience Bank (UEB) sanctioned conduit tests by the World History Investigative Society (WHIS). And in the year 2910 a Whisper expedition penetrated upstream time to the year 2050 before encountering the time storm later identified as the Arthurian Anachronism. More than seven hundred explorers were atomized in the collapse of that first exploratory conduit into the past.

Closed-loop technology was introduced in 2910, and in 2999 the powerful singularity designated as Closed Loop L-270 penetrated the time storm to reach the year 1947. One message made its way downtime from L-270. The signal suggested the existence of dimensional gates and bridges in the extreme past, and hinted at a paradox warp.

L-270, the "Lost Loop," was never recovered, but the erratic route of its single received emission became the pathway for a toraform loop, L-316, which sacrificed itself in the year 1951 to create a bypass conduit for others to follow.

The route of the conduit was never charted. Its path from the year 3006 to the year 1951 remained a mystery, eluding all explanation. UEB analysis suggested that the pathway was outside the known matrix of dimensions, and that it may have bridged a gap between alternate realities. This line of inquiry raised questions regarding the most fundamental axioms. Are there dimensions beyond the prime four? Is cause-effect continuity truly singular in all eventualities? Do alternate histories exist? Does evidence of variant sequences, suggesting the possibility of gates and bridges, indicate that all directions are—in some sense—parallel?

Nothing in UEB technology even addressed questions such as these. The route of the trans-anachronism conduit remained a mystery. But whatever the path, the conduit was there, and WHIS followed it.

The launch of L-383 into upstream time occurred sixty-two years after the first WHIS encounter with the Arthurian Anachronism. Following the unchartable path of L-270, along the conduit created by L-316, the exploratory loop emerged into real time in 1951. A primary task was to create acceleration boosters uptime, to facilitate exploration of the ancient past.

∞

From *The Journal of Time Loop L-383:*

We emerged into normal time in the year 1951, unscathed by anachronism except that we carried a passenger aboard—a backward-born stowaway named Edwin Limmer, whose situation was the direct result of Arthur's time storm. Edwin came into our care as a newborn infant and was ninety-eight years old and retrosynchronic when we finally managed to reinsert him into normal time. With his assistance, we undertook the development of booster accelerator points on the conduit, to facilitate Whisper expeditions into the distant past.

The first of these booster waystops was located in 1998, with a subsequent leapfrog booster in 1887. Through these accelerators, the Whisper expedition became a migration . . . back through upstream time toward those unimaginable reaches of antiquity when the dimensions were unstable. The time before time.

What began as a research goal has become the obsession of our race: the desire to see how it all began.

The Whisper conduit has been in place now for a time approaching fifteen hundred days, and millions of Pacificans have transported through the prime accelerator in that time.

Yet each day, it seems, we of L-383 learn more of the past and less of our own history. The riddles breed new riddles. Some of these are summarized in these notations of our First Volunteer, 1TL-0014, know as Teal Fordeen:

As we proceed with the primary mission of Closed Loop L-383, nearing this phenomenon's eight hundredth day in T1 durational time, riddles build themselves upon riddles:

1. Why, with all its resources dedicated to the exploration of the fourth dimension, did WHIS never suspect until our arrival in the pre-Arthurian eras that there were timers in the past—people able to do by act of will that which we do through technology?

2. Given that our race, the Pacificans, may be the result of genetic engineering during the Locked Centuries (2400–2600), what then became of our predecessors—the people we call "protomorphs," who are the human inhabitants of this planet during all the past centuries we have explored? Where did they go, as we were originating?

3. Assuming that our discoveries in retrosynchronic bioduplication are—as we believe—the ultimate breakthrough in practical time travel, why have we encountered no one except ourselves traversing the conduits of the past?

4. *Why, for that matter, have we not met others—from our own future—making use of our discoveries?*

—TEAL FORDEEN, L-383

To these, we append the further question:

Why, from the millions of our kind now streaming back through time in search of the earliest beginnings, have none returned except from the recent past? Where did they all go, in that ancient when, and what have they found in that chaotic dimensional morass of the universal creation?

—1LZY1PIR, NOTARIAN

∞

PROLOGUE

Sleepwalker

The South Platte
September 1869

Walks the Storm swam upward from sleep as a dove danced on his shoulder. Its little feet dug at him like urgent fingers, and its whisper was insistent. "Stand up, Cloudwalker!" it demanded. "Stand and see who is here!"

He shifted, felt the familiar soft fur of his sleeping mat against his cheek, and opened his eyes. It was dark in the lodge. Only faint embers lingered from the evening's little fire, and stars hung in a black sky above the smoke opening overhead.

The dancing dove vanished. The urgency on his shoulder blade was the fingers of Brings Water, prodding him from sleep. "Husband," she whispered. "Cloudwalker! Wake up! Someone is here!"

Walks the Storm turned his head and blinked in surprise. Just beyond the embers stood a fantastic figure, looking down at him. It was a man, but a very strange man. Beneath rumpled sunshine hair, the man's eyes were wide with confusion. Below a stubbled chin, his skinny torso was naked to the waist and as pale as the belly of a fish. His only garment was wrinkled pants of some thin fabric. They hung loose from waist to ankles, stopping short of bare, bony feet. His only adornments were a shiny bracelet on his left wrist and an ornamental ring on the middle finger of his right hand.

Throwing back his cover, Walks the Storm rolled upright, getting his feet under him. He came up holding a large knife in one hand, his war ax in the other. "Who are you?" he demanded. "Why are you in my lodge?"

The strange man backed away a startled step, tripped over

Brings Water's pole-and-hide sewing table, and sprawled backward, taking down hung pelts and a bundle of smoked meat as he fell. With an angry grunt, Walks the Storm tossed his ax aside and sprang across the fire embers to crouch over the fallen form, his knife at the man's throat.

"Who are you?" he growled again. "Do you want me to kill you?"

Beneath him the white man gasped, shrinking back from the threatening blade. His voice thin with panic, he jabbered words that to Walks the Storm were only sounds. Walks the Storm touched him again with the blade, just below the chin, and the man's voice became a plea. Behind Walks the Storm, the hide flap slapped as Brings Water darted from the lodge, out into the night. She was back in a moment, bringing kindling for the fire.

The white man lay sprawled among fallen pelts and bundles of wild rice stalk, still babbling—the same few sounds over and over again. Walks the Storm crouched over him patiently. His thighs straddled the stranger's gaunt chest, his knees pinned the pale arms to the ground, and the sharp knife in his strong, dark hand never wavered.

Not until Brings Water had a fire going and tallow wicks lighted did Walks the Storm move. Then he rocked back on his toes, came upright, and lifted the trespasser bodily by a handful of hair. The man yelled and struggled, but followed where his tortured scalp led him.

Walks the Storm looked him up and down, curiously—a skinny, pale-eyed white man, dressed only in flimsy britches. The shiny bracelet on his left wrist caught the firelight, and Walks the Storm grasped it, pulling it free. It was a metal thing, but it flexed and stretched in his fingers, tiny links spreading as he pulled at them. He slipped it onto his own wrist. Then once again, Walks the Storm grasped the intruder's scalp hair and asked, as politely as possible, "Who are you and why are you in my house?"

"Ben Culver!" the specter gasped, tapping himself on the chest with one hand while the other tried to persuade his host's fist to unclench itself from his hair. "I'm Ben Culver!"

"Bin'kofah?" Walks the Storm repeated the sounds, then gestured with his knife, nicking the man's chest with its point. "You are called *Bin'kofah*?"

"Ben Culver," the man agreed. Wincing, he tried to edge away from the blade, but Walks the Storm's grip was like iron.

"A white man," Brings Water noted, peering past the shoulder of her husband. "He has no weapons. How did he come into our lodge, Cloudwalker? The laces were still secure. Why is he here?"

"He doesn't know," Walks the Storm said. "I think he's a crazy man."

"Maybe Two Bulls would like to see him," the woman suggested. "Maybe you should take him outside."

"He came into our house while we slept," Walks the Storm growled. "I think I should kill him."

"Then go outside to kill him," Brings Water snapped. "Not in my house."

Still holding the pleading prisoner by his scalp, Walks the Storm half dragged him to the hide flap and pushed him through, following after him.

There was firelight among the lodges now, and men coming to see what was going on. Every man carried a weapon of some sort—a lance or war club, a bow with an arrow at its string, or a large knife. Women and children peered from open flaps of a dozen nearby lodges.

The white man stared around in panic and tried to crawl away, but Walks the Storm kicked his arms aside, rolling him on the ground. "Stop squirming," he suggested, kicking him again, in the ribs. With the trespasser subdued, Walks the Storm stood tall and raised his hand. A flicker of light dazzled his eyes for an instant, and he squinted. But it was gone. "I have a white man!" he shouted. "Someone should see if there are any others around! Redleg, please go to Two Bulls's lodge and tell him there is a white man here."

Men gathered around him, weapons ready, staring this way and that.

"Is the white man in your lodge, Cloudwalker?" someone asked. "I don't see him."

Walks the Storm blinked, looked down, and gasped. The white man had been right there, at his feet. But he was not there now. He was nowhere around.

Pleistocene Grasslands
800,000 B.C.

The beast was huge, far too big even to be what it most resembled, which was an elephant. Long, dark hair as lustrous as a horse's mane draped most of its massive body, and even the high, domed head, great bat-wing ears, and long, prehensile trunk of its nose were clothed in short, wooly fibers. The great tusks that curled upward on either side of its trunk were the size of willow boles.

Ben Culver crouched in tall grass at the foot of a waving slope and stared in fascination as the animal strolled along the fringe of a sun-dappled grove of trees, pausing here and there to select a succulent branch and strip it bare of leaves and soft bark.

He had seen pictures of such animals, photographs of drawings on cave walls—drawings done by ancient hands—and archaeological re-creations displayed in diorama scenes in museums. Mastodon or wooly mammoth? He didn't remember which. But the sheer size and vitality of the creature was something no drawings had portrayed, and most of all he was struck by the beast's majestic grace. It moved through the waving grass like a tall ship riding sedate seas.

In the distance he could see several others—a few scattered here and there near thickets and groves, and a parade of four ambling through the waving grass toward a sandy bottom where shallow streams of sun-bright water wound and meandered toward a mist-shrouded lower valley miles away.

Around and beyond them, other creatures moved here and there—grazing herds of antlered things in the distance, and occasional glimpses of solitary creatures rising to see above the grass. And everywhere were birds—birds of a hundred kinds, it seemed, some skimming low above the flowing grass, some rising on great wings to soar high circles in the sky.

Some distance from where he hid, grass rippled toward a rocky outcrop and a massive head emerged for a moment—a big, flat, feline head with down-curving fangs like white daggers. A lion, he thought, realizing at the same time that no lion was that big.

The fanged cat head disappeared and he saw the ripples in the grass as the predator moved away, angling downslope.

Culver watched until the ripples were gone, and found himself shivering. The breeze was cool on his bare back, the ground cold and moist under his knees. He wished he had a coat. He huddled there, low in the thick grass, feeling sorry for himself, then shrugged and straightened again to watch the browsing mammoths.

Some of them had shifted their positions, possibly alerted by cat scent on the breeze. The big tusker nearest him was facing outward now, its trunk held high, its ears spread wide. God, he thought, it is *huge*! Beyond and to his left, past the nearest fringe of the feeding grove, a female and calf had approached, to taste the offerings of the leaves.

The calf was playful, a giant little clown meandering this way and that, flinging its trunk high in imitation of its elders.

Then beyond the calf Culver saw something else. Just at the edge of the clearing, dark faces peered out—human faces, beardless and copper-apple dark under long, shaggy manes of black hair. Culver counted seven of them as they crept from the concealment of the tall grass, crouched and spreading like stalking wolves.

They wore crude garments of stitched hide and soft boots of the same material. Each of them carried two or three long, stone-pointed wooden spears, and their attention was on the mammoth calf nearest them.

Culver watched, fascinated, as they closed on the beast. At any instant, he expected one or another of the adult mammoths to turn and spot the hunters. But the animals stood now, facing the other way, their ears wide and trunks high. They stood as though frozen in place, pawing nervously but never once turning toward the hunters.

The men closed toward the calf, quartering from behind, each with a spear held level now, ready to hurl. Though only a tuskless baby, the mammoth calf was as tall as any of them and far more massive. Yet like its elders, it seemed blind to their approach. Then he saw why. A hundred yards away, in the other direction, were more of the primitive men, standing in plain view of the beasts, holding their attention.

The hunters flanking from behind were within ten feet of the calf when the first spear flew, thrown by a strong, sure arm. It lanced in from behind to sink itself deep into the animal's side, behind the ribs. Almost before the calf could react, other spears hit it, penetrating forward into its lungs and heart. It managed one cry—a desperate, high-pitched trumpet of sound—then staggered and fell. The hunters were on it instantly, raising spears and driving them home even as the adult animals trumpeted and wheeled around, finally alerted.

The nearest cow was the first to charge, a shrilling leviathan racing toward the attackers faster than Ben Culver could have imagined. Directly behind her thundered the lead bull and another cow.

But the men had expected this. At the last moment they scattered and ran, disappearing into the tall grass.

They had made their kill. Now they would hide and wait until the other mammoths wandered away.

His heart pounding, Culver crouched low and wished he were somewhere else. Behind him, something moved softly and he turned . . . and froze. Not fifteen feet away, the huge dagger-fanged cat stood half-crouched, its long tail twitching. It was looking directly into his eyes.

A moment only it hesitated, its lips curled up in a lethal cat grin. Then powerful haunches unwound like great springs released. The cat pounced—a sudden leap of fanged fury. The attack was so sudden, so hideously quick, that there was no time to duck or scream—only for a single act of will. Culver saw the world around him fade to slow dark as the cat's claws—gleaming scythes on huge, padded paws—reached for him and those chisel-ax teeth descended. What followed was a flash of light too intense to endure but too brief even to register on the senses.

Panhandle FFZ
April 2020

With a shriek he dived to one side and rolled, directly into the path of a striding boot. In the instant of realizing that both the pouncing cat and the tall grass were gone, he also realized that a cold rain was drenching him and that someone astounded was flipping over him, flailing and falling to splash headfirst into the water and mud beside him.

The impact of a boot against his ribs dazed him for an instant, and rainwater cascaded over him. He lay stunned for a moment, trying to recover his senses. Then when nothing else occurred, he pushed himself up on unsteady hands and looked around.

He lay on a sand path beneath a dark sky full of rain. Around him flowed runnels of cold water. Falling rain obscured visibility beyond a few yards, but in the gray nearness he could see a tall, chain-link fence with loops of barbwire running along its top, a gleaming tower of painted metal that rose into the mist above, and a businesslike automatic rifle lying in a pool of rain. Beside him a gray-clad figure sprawled facedown, unmoving. Most of the illumination came from bright little lights here and there—lamps like double-headed mushrooms that sat on pedestals and hung at intervals along the fence.

Culver rose to his knees, mystified. "Now what?" he muttered to himself. Squatting in the cold rain, he inspected the unconscious figure sprawled next to him. It was a large, tough-looking young man, clad in a sort of uniform of gray material with shoulder patches of black and yellow—the letters *ITR* and a sideways figure eight, like an infinity sign.

Obviously the man had tripped over him and fallen, and apparently he had landed on his head. The hat that lay beside him was a hard hat of some kind, like a metallic helmet, emblazoned with the same insignia as the shoulder patches: infinity and ITR.

He was out cold, but he was breathing. Culver retrieved the fallen rifle from the puddle and stood, trying to get oriented. He had no idea where he was or how he came to be here. The rain slacked momentarily and he saw silhouettes of buildings nearby—long, low buildings with dark window openings. Beyond them he glimpsed other, larger buildings.

At his feet the young man stirred and groaned, and Culver stood over him, wondering what to do. He shifted the rifle to his left hand.

The rain eased again and suddenly there was more light, larger lights beamed at him from somewhere above.

"Who goes there?" a voice in the mist demanded. Culver

looked up, stepping aside, and another voice shouted, "Intruders! Here's one! Crap, he's killed Ferguson!"

Culver raised his hands. "Wait!" he called, "I didn't do it. He fell . . ."

"Revivalists!" a voice shouted. "They're inside the perimeter!" Sirens wailed and more lights pierced the mist, seeking out the trespasser. Somewhere close a shot rang out, and something zipped past Culver's face. The wire fence behind him rattled and sang.

"You're making a mistake!" he shouted. "I didn't—"

More bullets spat past him and he ducked, pivoted, and ran, still carrying the retrieved rifle. "Holy shit!" he breathed. "Indians and tigers and now this!"

He dodged around the corner of a building, found a door, and tried the lever. It swung open and he ducked inside, closing it after him. He was in a long, low room, dimly lighted and quiet. Tall banks of electronic instruments stood along the walls, flanking a central area where faceless people lay motionless on a dozen linen-covered tables. All of them wore things like helmets and had their faces covered with dark fabric hoods. Most were draped with sheets but a few—all women—lay naked.

Culver paused at the nearest one—a young woman, trim-bodied, flawless, and naked from the neck down. The "helmet" on her head was an electronic device—black plastic with little switches and dials ranked on both temples. Wires led from the helmet to a console beside the table, where tiny lights flickered in intricate, repetitive patterns. Other wires led to electrode bands at her wrists and one ankle. Little cups between her breasts and on her belly held other sensors.

He hesitated, then touched her carefully, his cold fingers resting on her throat just above the collarbone. She wasn't dead, only in a deep sleep. Gently he raised the hood from her face. A soft, pretty face, young and vulnerable-seeming in sleep. Little movements of her closed eyelids told him she was dreaming.

Sounds beyond the door brought him around, and he scurried across to a wide, closed double door with a gold nameplate: JOHN JACOB ROYCE, DIRECTOR. Beside the doors was a shallow cloak rack, and he hid there as people came into the big room.

"Damn it, Maggie!" a man's voice snapped. "Why aren't these people covered?"

"Security," a woman said angrily. "Those—those goons have been through here again. We've filed a dozen protests! There are sheets in the cabinet, George. I'll see to it."

"Please do," the man said. "These are volunteers, not lab samples. Can't those louts respect their dignity?"

Culver waited until they had passed by, then opened the door behind him and ducked through it. Beyond was a smaller room, dimly lighted and apparently empty except for a big desk and great banks of instruments around the walls. Rows of monitor screens displayed corridors, laboratories, and bright, rain-shrouded exterior views where people with guns hurried here and there. A separate bank of screens—about a dozen of them—showed pulsing chart-lines, apparently from the electrodes attached to sleepers in the outer laboratory. In one corner was a stack of speakers, and a soft female voice was saying something in what might have been Latin.

A shadow moved—a high-back chair turning—and a heavy-shouldered, hard-eyed man looked across the desk at him. "Who are you?" the man asked. "Why do you have that gun?"

"I'm—I'm Ben Culver," he managed. "What is this place? Where am I?"

"Maybe you really don't know," the man rasped. "Well, Ben Culver, I'm Arthur Meeks, head of security. This is ITR, and since you don't belong here, it's too bad you came."

"What . . . why am I here?" Culver heard the confusion in his own voice and saw the hard eyes before him turn to ice.

The man just looked at him, the way a chess player might look at an insect on the board. "If you don't know why you came to ITR," he rumbled, "then who does? But I can tell you why you're here." The man raised a nasty-looking little weapon to point at him. "You're a trespasser, so you're here to die."

It wasn't a gun, exactly. Instead of a muzzle to launch bullets, its tip was a bright little bead of blue crystal. But there was no doubt at all that it was potent, and lethal. The weapon steadied, the man's knuckles paled, and Culver willed his mind to do that . . . that "flicker" thing, the thing it had done before, without knowing how. He concentrated on the sensation from just moments before, when the dagger-tooth cat attacked. He willed it, desperately . . . and time seemed to freeze for an instant. The area around him slowed, darkened, and there was a sudden, intense flash of light, gone even as it flared.

The place he found himself in was like no place he could ever have imagined . . . except that it was oddly familiar. In some dream, sometime in the past, he had been in a place like this, and he had known terror.

A maze, he thought now, seeing what was around him more clearly than that old dream recalled. But a maze of *what*? Everywhere he looked were brilliances and patterns—incredible sweeps of unbelievable scenery interspersed with scrolling columns of figures, like numbers and mathematical equations, that stood and danced in segments of nothingness. There were wide, moving dioramas everywhere, contour maps of vast areas, cross sections of planetary mass, breathtaking starscapes where galaxies swam in regal splendor.

And among all this were banks of strange, busy-looking instruments flanked by consoles on little pedestals barely higher than his knees. Not of this world, he thought. Not of any world I know. Awed and dazed, he wandered there for a time, seeing everything and understanding nothing.

Dream memories returned like tatters of dread—a place like this, yet not so bright or so clear. In the dream there had been deep shadows—shrouded figures on bloodstained tabletops, rows of fluid-filled translucence where things floated, and everywhere the smell of death. Ancient stone and dark shadows, and within the shadows something small and evil lurked. Something monstrous, with big eyes. He saw nothing like that here—no shadowed recesses, no sense of ancient death. But the majestic scrolling of equations in infinite fields of display, the swirling starfields and rolling landscapes all around him, brought back the nightmare.

That had been the place of the cone—the little, translucent-metal cone that had rested on a stone surface there, as though it were waiting for him to find it.

Something from another world had been in that old dream—something alien and evil—and its lair was a place like this. At a standing starfield he slung the rifle at his shoulder, rubbed his eyes, and stared in wonder at the display before him, picking out the components of it. Hologram, he thought, fascinated by its perfection. It seemed that wherever he focused his eyes, the three-dimensional scene zoomed in to show him detail.

Tentatively, he touched the starfield. His fingers entered its deep-space blackness and disappeared there, then his entire hand. He withdrew it and touched the scene again, at a different point. He felt nothing. It was only a picture—a display in three perfect dimensions, without substance.

Then, at the sound of surprised voices, he turned. There were people all around him—little gray-clad people with huge, inquisitive eyes and bald heads, hurrying toward him from all around, crowding in on him.

"Aliens!" he hissed. "Space creatures!" He turned to run, but all the avenues were closed, crowded now with the little creatures coming toward him. With a cry of desperation he dived headlong into a miniature galaxy, flinging numbers and equations aside. The starfield closed around him, flickered, and all the lights went out.

Pauls Valley, Oklahoma
The Present

He awakened abruptly, in his own bed with its own walls around him, and for a moment he was sure he had been dreaming. But only for a moment. Those had not been dreams, any more than the other times.

The telephone was ringing and the clock on the dresser said eight thirty-six. He ignored them both. He sat up, felt the aches in his ribs and the bruises that seemed to cover his body, and forced himself to look. Then he wished he hadn't.

His pajama bottoms were ragged, stained, and torn, his wristwatch was gone, his bare feet were covered with gray mud, and he was bleeding from several nicks and scrapes. The assault rifle lying on his bed was an ugly, lethal-looking machine, sort of like an AK-47 but more streamlined, more meticulously equipped. He suspected it was no weapon that had yet been designed.

"Oh, God," he muttered. "I guess I've done it again!"

With a groan, he stood, picked up the assault gun, and carried it through the little kitchen to put it in the pantry closet with the other mementos there—a jade dragon, a bronze short sword, a cut-glass bowl, a matchbook advertising "Tony's Grill, Cicero, Illinois," an old hat, a translucent cone of eye-confusing colors, a wooden belaying pin, a Texas Rangers badge, a straw doll, and some other things. Some of them he couldn't even identify. It was becoming quite a collection.

In the shower he soaped and rinsed, wincing at a dozen little wounds. Then he dressed, made his bed, and stepped to the window. Outside, lazy morning sun climbed a cloudless sky, and the routine activities of a small town were in full swing.

He felt sleepy—exhausted, in fact—but he was afraid to lie down. He was afraid it would happen again.

"God," he muttered, "if only I could get a little rest." He tried to imagine true serenity, and the image became a green valley among gentle peaks. A valley of joy and serenity. He stifled a yawn and turned from the window as the telephone rang again.

It was Nancy, and Nancy was angry. "Ben, where the hell are you?" she demanded. "Our appointment with Hofstetter is at nine!"

He sagged, feeling tired and defeated. "You handle it, sis," he said. "You don't need me."

"Don't *need* you? Ben, you know Hofstetter's a royal twit. He thinks women are for fetching the coffee. Get your lazy ass over here!"

"I can't, sis. I had a bad night. You just handle it, okay? Remember, he needs that acreage as much as we need to sell it to him." Without waiting for her objection, he broke the connection. I've got to do something about this, he decided. I can't stand this anymore.

It had been happening now for a long time, it seemed—this crazy thing that came in his sleep, that happened to him over and over again. At first they had been only brief, random episodes, unexplainable little occurrences that he kept to himself because he knew no way of explaining them to anyone.

And because they *happened to* him. Always he felt helpless, always the victim, never in control.

It always started with a feeling. Like when he was a kid and running through the open fields for the sheer exhilaration of running. Out beyond the cotton and cane fields east of town there was a wide, smooth prairie of short grass, sloping gently down toward the Washita. And when he ran that prairie, with the west wind behind him, sometimes he felt he could almost fly. He would lengthen his steps, trying to make each leap last indefinitely. And with each stride there was the delicious sensation that if he could—somehow—not complete that next step, he might sail on, suspended there above the ground.

It seemed so tantalizingly near, that tiny understanding that would let him do what he felt he could do. But each time, reflexes took over and he completed that step, then sailed into the next one.

This thing happening to him now was like that. Often he felt that—if he could look at it the right way—all limits would disappear and he could go anywhere he wanted, anytime, just for the joy of going.

Just, somehow, see the world from a different slant. Sometimes he almost did. Almost—but never quite. Then the dream things began, and they weren't dreams. As though to prove themselves to him, the dreams left tangible evidences. Evidences like the collection of oddities in his pantry closet.

He went there again now and opened the door, gazing at the odd collection. He was closing the door when a faint shimmer caught his eye. The little metallic cone, sitting on the floor beside the butt of the newly acquired firearm, was glowing faintly. The iridescent gradations of its surface seemed to flow and blend, and there was a tiny sound—like a hum barely within audible range, except that it did not seem to register to the ears as much as to the bridge of the nose.

He picked it up, squinted at it, and that old feeling came back, the feeling that there was something he could do—something he *should* do—if only he knew how.

The place it came from—a big, old-fashioned loft above a railroad turntable—had looked like something out of a history book, but the cone had not fit the scenario.

He paced the kitchen, staring at the thing in his hand. It was only a thing, an inanimate object of some kind, but there seemed an urgency about it now, as though it wanted to tell him something.

Anger drifted through his mind. I don't even know how to find out what I'm looking for, he told himself. Whatever is in control here, it isn't me . . . but, by God, it's time it was!

Maybe the "dreams" had been trying to tell him how.

Summoning all his strength for intense concentration, he leaned against the kitchen sink and pictured the sensation he had felt in his dreams—that sense of things slowing and darkening, down and down to an intense nothingness.

He concentrated, not really believing that anything would happen. It was just the stuff of dreams, that beckoning flicker. Yet those had *not* been dreams. People don't bring souvenirs back from dreams.

He concentrated, and the room around him seemed to darken. He felt abruptly heavy, and dizzy as though he might fall. He clutched the sink's steel faucet for support. The curtain at the window, stirred by breeze, hung frozen in its graceful billow, and everything around it faded to a tangible darkness . . . down and down into void. The intensity of the void closed down, then exploded in an unbelievable flash of pure, blinding light. It was all so abrupt that all he sensed for certain was a flicker, gone even as it occurred.

Abruptly there was bright, hazy sunlight through the windows. The whole house seemed to teeter slightly, one way and then another, and he felt dizzy. I missed, he thought angrily, then wondered what the thought meant. It had the feel of someone else's thought, occurring in *his* head. A hot, dry breeze wafted through the vents—a breeze that carried strange odors. Try again, the unwelcome thought nudged him, as though commanding.

Again he did the concentration thing, this time with more assurance. The feeling of heaviness, the focus on light . . . and with them an angry, commanding urge to focus a certain part of his attention in a certain way.

"I will not!" he muttered, reacting to anger with anger. "It's *my* insanity! I'll do it *my* way!" For the pure hell of it he twisted his concentration this way and that, randomly, and exerted his will.

And again it happened, that flicker of enormous, barely noticeable powers. The air billowing the curtain was suddenly cool air, carrying the tantalizing scents of pine and wood smoke. Where there had been sunshine, now there was darkness. Beyond the window moon-bright slopes rose against gentle, forested peaks under a clear, starry sky. Again the whole house shivered atilt.

Culver stood dazed, gawking at the changed room around him. It was still the same room, essentially—his kitchen, in his own little house. But he knew instantly that it wasn't where it had been before. It wasn't even *when* it had been.

The house now was slightly aslant, and timbers creaked as though its foundation were settling into uneven ground. There was the sound of water pipes draining, and a stillness that took a moment to register. There was no subliminal hum around him. It was the stillness of blackout, the sound of having no electric power. Even the heavy little cone in his hand was still now. Outside was night, but the only lights in the house were a couple of little FIRElights his sister had given him. The self-energizing devices had recently appeared at Willy World and on megamart shelves all over the country, and Nancy was a sucker for anything new.

One FIRElight was still sitting on a nightstand. The other had fallen and rolled against a wall, but continued to shine. There was no electric light, and he knew that the switches would not work. There was no electricity.

But there was moonlight through the windows, and it was still his house. It was the same as it had always been. But where it was—or when it was—wasn't.

It was just too much to cope with right now. Ben Culver choked off the FIRElights and went back to his bed, not much caring where he woke up next time.

∞

Anyplace you go seems strange at first, until you get used to it. But the strangest places of all are those you can never go to, because you're there already.

—HARRY COYLE, *The Incompleat Visitor*

∞

I

Anywhen, Inc.

Eastwood, Kansas
The Present

Lucas Hawthorn had seen missing-persons posters before, but never one quite like this. HAVE YOU SEEN THIS PERSON? the big print demanded. OR THIS HOUSE?

The two photographs below were of excellent quality, printed in full-color graphics on 20-pound rag bond: a head-and-shoulders of a young man with unruly blond hair and startled blue eyes, and a good-quality snapshot—like a Realtor's-book presentation—of a neat, small house on a town lot.

Maude peered over his shoulder, studying the pictures thoughtfully, then raised her eyes to the young woman across the kitchen table. Nancy Culver might have been in her twenties, a pretty girl with blond hair and skeptical blue eyes. "I suppose you've done the usual things," Maude suggested. "I mean, like talk to some of your brother's neighbors about any unusual activity, or maybe if they noticed which way the house went? Houses generally don't move around very much."

Nancy Culver nodded. "Of course I have. They're just as baffled as I am. Ben has always been a little weird, and he's disappeared before—a time or two—but this is the first time he ever took his house with him. The people next door are pretty upset about it."

"Sudden disappearance can be upsetting," Lucas assured her.

"They aren't upset about Ben," Nancy corrected. "They're upset about the hole where his house was. The whole house is gone, right down to the flashing under the foundation, and the water main ran wide open for two days before they noticed it. It filled the hole with water, and their cat keeps jumping in. They've filed a complaint with the city, I think." She sipped her coffee, gazing around at the interior of the Hawthorns' house. "This is an unusual arrangement," she said. "What did you do, replace the front wall?"

"That whole corner of the house," Maude indicated. "There wasn't anything left so we just restructured the whole thing. Do you like it?"

"Storm?" Nancy asked.

"Zen-gun attack," Lucas said. "A rogue time loop from a thousand years in the future tried to wipe us out."

"Lucas short-circuited it with a harpoon gun," Maude added. "So it left us alone and burned a warehouse in Topeka instead. That was in 1887."

Nancy Culver blinked at them. "Yeah," she said. "Sure."

"Try explaining all that to an insurance adjuster." Lucas grinned. "They finally put it down to storm damage from lightning. Anyhow, we changed the roofline and put in bay windows. So, anyway, you're looking for your brother. How did you happen to come here?"

Nancy stood, frowned, and moved around the table to peer through the open double doors adjoining the kitchen. There should have been a dining room there, but it didn't look like any dining room she had ever seen. "What's that?" she asked. "A steel floor?"

"That's the TEF chamber," Maude explained. "The thing on the tower over there—like a cone in a rat's nest—is a temporal effect focalizer. It's what bumps things around from time to time."

"Bumps things . . ." Nancy glanced around at them. "You mean like it—it *jostles* things, now and then?"

"That's another way of putting it," Lucas agreed. "It's future technology. It uses electromagnetic analogy to reverse gravity and light. That's what makes time travel work. This one's primarily an accelerator for Whispers migrating to the past. A booster waystop. But we use it for historical tours. How did you happen to know about Anywhen, Inc., Miss Culver? Did someone refer you to us?"

As though making up her mind, Nancy pulled a business

card from her purse and placed it on the table. "I guess this was a referral," she said. "It's your card, isn't it?"

Lucas picked it up. It was one of their own cards—ANYWHEN, INC. with a ∞ logo, fax and phone numbers, and the cheery slogan, HAVE A NICE TIME. He turned it over. Scrawled on the back was a handwritten note: "When you see Ben, tell him Molly said hi."

He read it again, then looked up. "So?"

"So, that note was in my mailbox yesterday morning. Somebody left it for me when I was out, I guess."

"Who's Molly?" Maude asked, reading the card.

"I haven't the vaguest idea. But whoever she is, she left your card in my mailbox, referring to Ben, two weeks after Ben and his house disappeared. That's why I came here. I'm hoping you might know what's going on."

Lucas and Maude looked at the card again, and at each other. Both of them shrugged. "Not a clue," Lucas admitted.

"Do you suppose her brother went some*when* instead of some*where*?" Maude suggested. "We might be able to get a handle on that, if he did." To Nancy she said, "Tell us about Ben."

Nancy shook her head impatiently. "To start with, he's thirty-two years old, going on maybe fourteen. He's irresponsible, unreliable, and unpredictable, and lately he's been almost impossible. He misses appointments, goes to sleep in sales meetings, and acts like his mind is a thousand miles away. He's been like that for months, and I can't find out what's wrong. And he collects the strangest things! His broom closet looks like a closing-out sale at a museum."

"What kind of things?"

"Just . . . things. Weird things. Swords and statues and vases, some kind of a spear, a little coneybob thing like that one you have . . ." She indicated the dining room that wasn't a dining room.

Lucas's brows went up. "A TEF? He has a TEF? Where'd he get it?"

"Where does he get anything?" Nancy shook her head. "I don't think he goes anywhere, and I know he hasn't spent any money on mail order. But things just keep showing up in his house and all he'll say is he hasn't been sleeping very well."

"Where would anybody get a TEF?" Lucas muttered.

Somewhere a little bell sounded. Nancy glanced toward the open doors of the steel-floored transfer chamber, and her eyes went wide.

In the empty room, something was happening. It grew perceptibly darker in there, and abruptly it was full of people . . . or almost people. They were more like shadows, dozens of them thronging together, almost filling the room—little, bald people with very large eyes.

The room grew rapidly darker, seeming to slow as it darkened until for the barest instant there was no light or motion at all. Then in that same instant a blaze of unbelievably intense glare filled the space, gone almost before the senses could register it.

And the room was as it had been before—an empty room with a gleaming steel floor and a little tower in one corner, supporting a maze of electronic components and a semitranslucent cone of all colors and no particular color.

Again the little bell rang.

"What—what was *that*?" Nancy gasped.

"Whispers," Maude said casually. "They were just passing through."

Lucas sat staring at the TEF chamber. "I know where we might get a lead on your brother," he said. "How do you feel about four-dimensional transference?"

"What?"

"Time travel. How do you feel about time travel?"

She looked at him with cynical blue eyes. "Look, I don't judge anybody's fantasies. If you folks sell time travel, that's fine with me. But don't try to sell me. I don't believe in things like that!"

"That's all right, dear," Maude said soothingly. "Most people don't, until they've tried it."

"Our best bet is L-383," Lucas decided. "The Whispers are pretty careful in accounting for TEFs. If anybody can help us find your brother, Teal Fordeen can."

Time Loop L-383

Though the Hawthorns had tried to explain to her what was about to happen when she and Lucas entered the room with the steel floor, Nancy Culver was unprepared for it. She knew there would be a light show or fog machine or something, but she wasn't a gullible kid. Special effects didn't impress her at all.

Not until now.

The first shock was the sheer suddenness of temporal transference. It just . . . *happened*, so quickly that her senses barely noted the shift. The second was what lay before and around her when it did.

A closed temporal loop isn't easy to describe, because there is nothing to compare it to. It is unlike any other phenomenon. A closed loop is, essentially, a section of duration brought around to meet itself, thus forming what in three-dimensional topology would be either a simple closed curve or a torus. These terms are analogous, of course, because the essence of a durational phenomenon is not spatial. It is temporal. A closed loop—like a T1 conduit—occupies fully all four of the prime dimensions.

As related to its fixed-sequence—or atemporal—surroundings, a closed time loop isn't exactly anywhere, except for its intervals of passage from one time vector to another. Nor does it remain anywhen, in normal circumstance. To exist at all, a temporo-spatial phenomenon must be in constant motion along the linear coordinates of at least one dimension.

At "present," L-383 was hovering in 180-second resonance in the vicinity of the southwest Kansas high plains. This temporal rhythm—from a minute and a half ago to a minute and a half from now—was the normal idle mode of the loop. It wasn't going anywhere. It was just being there, instant by instant in 180 seconds of real time.

If there had been such a thing as an ordinary loop in durational time, L-383 would have been it.

But what confronted Nancy Culver a moment after entering the TEF chamber at Waystop I was not ordinary by any standards she could ever have imagined. If it was a room, it was like no room she had ever seen. It seemed endless and boundless, even though no large, open spaces were visible. Nowhere did there seem to be any vertical partitions, yet the area she found herself in was enclosed on every side by displays—magnificent, mind-boggling displays of all sorts of things, all in minutely detailed three dimensions and most of them in motion.

Somehow Nancy knew that what she was seeing in the displays was not reality, but virtual reality, though nowhere was there any hint of distortion, discontinuity, or even pixel grain. Starfields flowed and turned in deep space, mountain ranges and oceans rolled by, planetary orbits traced their elliptical paths, lava crept along stone chimneys in deep, layered strata lighted here and there by pressing magma, and grid patterns appeared and revolved, displaying coordinates and vector relationships. Some displays were of phenomena she couldn't even guess at. And among them all, scrolled columns and patterns of figures, equations, and arrays of characters and runes.

It was dizzying and it was breathtaking . . . but no more so than the people who scurried here and there through the virtual mazes—tiny people, none approaching her own height of five foot one, and all of them completely bald, with eyes twice the size that eyes should be.

"Kind of boggles the mind, doesn't it?" Lucas Hawthorn grinned at her. "Mine, too, and I've been here before. This is Time Loop L-383, and these people are Whispers. That means World History Investigative Society. They're from a thousand years or so in the future."

She gawked at the little people hurrying here and there. "Are they . . . ah . . . human?" she murmured. "They look so strange. And so busy!"

"They're as human as we are," Lucas assured her. "And they *do* seem busy, don't they? Must be something unusual going on." He took her hand and led her toward a group of Whispers gathered around a bank of what looked like electronic equipment grown up. A moment later he was making introductions. "Nancy Culver, this is Zeem Sixten . . . and Toocie Toonine and Peedy Cue. That's Forel Embee over there, and KT-Pi. This is Deem Eleveno, and this gentleman—" He led her through a gathering throng to where a wise-looking Whisper perched on a translucent stool in front of a console. "—is the head honcho in charge of L-383, Teal Fordeen. Teal, Miss Culver is looking for her brother."

"It is a pleasure to meet you, Miss Culver," Teal Fordeen said distractedly. "But I'm quite sure we don't have him."

"Didn't think you did," Lucas assured him. "What's going on? Something new?"

"We're just a bit distracted, I'm afraid," Teal said. "We have encountered a sequence of random anachronisms, all centered on the present era."

"Something serious?"

"We don't know. It seems random, but these are definitely anachronisms, and *something* is causing them. We're trying to find a pattern. So far, all we've determined is that they seem to come in pairs. When one occurs, another happens somewhere else." He shrugged, a shrug that was surprisingly eloquent and expressive in a person barely four feet tall. "What was that about Miss Culver's brother? Should we know something about him, Lucas?"

"I thought you might be interested in him, since he may have a TEF in his possession."

"That isn't possible," Deem Eleveno declared promptly. "Every TEF that ever was or will be extruded is accounted for. There are no strays."

Nancy Culver hadn't said a word. She simply stood there, clinging to Lucas Hawthorn's hand, her dazed blue eyes shifting from one to another of the small, bald creatures gathered around them. She felt as though she had fallen through a hole into a Mad Hatter world of playing cards and flamingo croquet.

"Maybe you'd better check your inventory," Lucas told the Whispers. "Miss Culver has seen our TEF at Waystop I. Her brother and his house have disappeared, and she says he has a TEF like ours."

"We're in the real estate business," Nancy blurted out, then blushed at the sound of her words. "God," she muttered, "what an inane thing to say!"

The one called Teal Fordeen rubbed a small hand across his bald head thoughtfully. "Puzzles and oddities today, Lucas.

Unreconciled anachronisms . . . and we've found a spatial alteration in the T1 conduit, apparently centering on the anchor vectors of L-316. We can scan the change but we don't know what it means. And now you come with this puzzle." He gestured with graceful little fingers, and several of the Whispers scurried off to various consoles and data bank pads. Nancy felt a tug at her sleeve and glanced down into the big, searching eyes of a pretty little bald creature.

"I'm Toocie Toonine," the Whisper reminded her. "Tell me about your brother, dear. The missing one, I mean."

"He's the only brother I have," Nancy said. "Thank God for small favors."

"I'll be glad to, if we encounter Him," Toocie assured her.

"We've charted only about fourteen percent of known time so far," another Whisper—a male one—explained, stepping close to Nancy, his eyes speculative. "We haven't yet discovered a definitive phenomenon that we can identify as 'God,' though there are some tantalizing consistencies in the references we've encountered. Ah, would you mind if I—"

"Leave her alone, Peedy!" Toocie snapped. "She didn't come here to have her topography investigated!" To Nancy, she said, "Don't mind Peedy, dear. He has an obsession with primitive feminine contour. He can be a nuisance about it sometimes, when he has a tape measure in hand, but he's harmless."

Nancy blushed again.

"Ah . . . about your brother?"

"Oh, yeah. Well, his name is Ben. Benjamin Franklin Culver. He lives at 423 Oakhill, Pauls Valley, Oklahoma. But he's disappeared. And so has 423 Oakhill. There's just a lot there now, with a hole in it."

"She has a picture of her brother," Lucas said. "Show them your poster, Nancy."

Nancy opened her purse and pulled out a copy of the flyer. "This is him." She handed it to Toocie Toonine. "And that's his house. It's a three-bedroom, two-bath ranch bungalow with composition roof, weathered shakes over a gray brick facade. Two-car garage, of course, central AC and a formal entry . . ."

"You're rambling, Nancy." Lucas grinned. "We don't want them to buy it, just help us find it."

"Oh . . . yeah. Sorry. I . . ."

"First meetings with future beings take some getting used to, I imagine." Toocie nodded. The reassuring smile on her little Whisper face was at once childlike and very wise. She looked at the poster carefully, her eyes narrowing. Then she passed it around. One by one they studied the face in the picture.

Deem Eleveno in particular seemed to concentrate on the features of Ben Culver, then handed the poster to Teal Fordeen. "Look at this face, Teal," he said. "Isn't this—"

"I believe you're right." Teal nodded. "It certainly does resemble him."

"Resemble who?" Lucas prodded.

"We don't know who he is, exactly." Teal Fordeen shrugged. "But this resembles a person who came to L-383. But not through any transference of ours. He simply materialized here, momentarily. A timer, we assume, though he seemed quite startled at being here and left abruptly."

"That sounds like Ben," Nancy mused. "I swear it comes as a surprise to him every time his buttons match their holes. My brother is the most distracted person I know."

One of the Whispers fed data into a pad, and just beyond Teal Fordeen a virtual display winked out. The twice-life-sized hologram that took its place was a skinny, tousle-headed young man with startled eyes, crouching among virtual displays. He was naked to the waist, clad only in muddy, tattered pajama bottoms, and he had a dark thing like an assault rifle slung over one shoulder. For a moment he crouched there, turning one way and then another, then with a guttural hiss that sounded like "Aliens!" he plunged directly into a virtual starfield and disappeared.

"That's him!" Nancy exclaimed. "That's Ben! Where did he go? Did he have his house with him?"

"No house." Teal Fordeen shook his head. "Just that device at his back."

"It's a weapon indigenous to the early twenty-first century," Deem Eleveno elaborated. "Its basis is older—copper-encased lead projectiles propelled by a volatile carbon-nitrogen compound in a brass housing. The activating mechanism is a Sturn-Benning Model I gas-activated automatic rifle, circa 2002."

"We tried to trace him by resonance trace, after he penetrated the loop," Teal said. "But his transference was too quick. We surmise that he has the ability to catch slow-light crest somewhere below the true-light thrust. So far as we know, even Adam can't do that. If we're right, we have a new breed of timer here."

Nancy blinked at him. "Timer . . . you mean *Ben*? Are you saying my brother is a time traveler?"

"It's only conjecture," Teal assured her. "But we can assume at this point that it's a newfound skill and he hasn't the vaguest idea what he's doing."

"Well, that part sounds like Ben. Who is this *Adam* you talk about?"

"He's a timer," Lucas explained. "A very unusual person. He's a sort of . . . well . . . like a policeman sometimes. Not everybody traveling in time can be trusted, and Adam sort of makes it his business to keep history straight. He'd want to know if there's a stray TEF running around loose somewhere."

"But where would your brother get a TEF?" Toocie wondered. "And *why*? If he's a natural timer, he doesn't require analogous transposition."

"We've reviewed the focalizer data, Teal," Deem said. "Every existing TEF is accounted for—forty-six of them in present use or inventory, two destroyed, and the one Adam recovered from 1KHAF4. The recovered one went to analysis at UEB Sundome, then was reissued. And, of course, there is one focalizer beyond recovery. But it is documented."

Teal Fordeen nodded. "L-270's prime drive TEF. The scout loop's cone, embedded in stone when 1KHAF4 was entombed. So that accounts for all fifty."

"1KHAF4," Lucas muttered to Nancy. "That's Kaffer—the son of a bitch who shot out our front wall. He used to be a Whisper, but he went wild or something. They got him, though. Adam sealed him up in a pyramid."

"Could this fit into our current puzzle?" Teal asked Deem.

"I don't see how." The impatient Whisper shrugged. "We've found no traces of photogravitational reversal. A few blips, but no tracks. TEF activity leaves a finite wake. These are just random anachronisms . . . except that suddenly there are a lot of them."

"At least now our mystery visitor has a name," Toocie pointed out. "He's Ben Culver."

"We've been calling him Sleepwalker," Teal told Lucas and Nancy. "But we don't know where or when he is. I do think, though, that Adam might be interested. We'll try to get word to him."

"You already did," a deep, calm voice said, almost at Nancy's elbow. She looked around, gasped, and raised her eyes. The man standing there was tall—even taller than Lucas by an inch or so. Dark hair, dark eyes that had seen more than most eyes ever saw, and a sun-darkened face that somehow radiated irony, concern, and wisdom, all at once. He was dressed like an early-twentieth-century aviator.

"I was testing out a Spad at Somerset Aerodrome," he told Teal. "Mandy popped into the cockpit to tell me you had a problem." He glanced aside at Lucas, nodded, then lowered his gaze to Nancy. "Hello," he said. "I'm Adam. I'll see if I can locate your brother." He glanced at the others present and turned to Deem Eleveno. "Question," he said. "The temporal effect focalizers have been counted, but have they all been verified for authenticity?"

"Most of them are installed for use." The Whisper frowned. "Verification is a part of installation testing. The rest are in secured inventory. How could any not be authentic?"

"It's just a thought," Adam said. "Another thought is, what surety do you have that there are exactly fifty in existence? Couldn't there be more?"

"Nonsense," Deem bristled. "Extrusion of a polymorphic solid-liquid transformer attuned to pure light and pure gravity is one of the most exacting processes known, even to our culture. The raw technology behind it didn't even exist until the twenty-eighth century. And even in our home time, there is only one processing complex capable of making TEFs. It is within UEB Central. We know exactly how many there are!"

"George Wilson made the first ones in the twenty-first

century," Adam pointed out. "He didn't have UEB Central's technology."

"But he did have the Institute for Temporal Research!" Deem said. "Besides, his devices were the prototypes. And they are all accounted for."

"I'm sure they are." Adam grinned. "Still, what would it hurt to verify the inventory?"

Before Deem could respond, Teal Fordeen raised a hand. "We can and will run a verification, Adam," he said. "And we'll order tests of all that have been out of service."

Adam nodded. "Good. Why not start with the one I took from Kaffer's tomb. And look for modifications, while you're at it. I'll see what tracks I can pick up, while that's being done." He glanced again at Nancy, and his sardonic grin didn't hide the determination in his eyes. "Don't worry, Miss Culver," he said. "We will find your brother."

He seemed only to turn away, toward one of the holographic screens, then he was gone. As though he had never been there.

Nancy Culver's eyes were like liquid starfields as she gazed at where he had gone. "Jeepers," she said. Her hand brushed a console sensor, and above it a display screen spiraled crazily.

"Interesting," Peedy murmured to Toocie Toonine. "Females of this era evidence remarkable similarities in their reactions to Adam."

∞

To seek the beginning of time is to seek the limits of infinity, which has no limits. It is a paradox pursued. Yet as with any paradox, such pursuit is rational and valid from certain perspectives.

The WHIS T1 conduit, in effect a time tunnel, theoretically exists as an open bridge throughout T2 time, vulnerable only to massive anachronism and limited only by the extent of time itself. Time being infinite, the conduit also should be infinite. But in practice it has limits. Its distant upstream reaches, plunging back into the remotest past, become imprecise. The phenomenon loses definition, at a rate corresponding to the achronal discordance evidenced by time itself in the zones approaching universal origin.

The tunnel does not end abruptly. Rather, it simply fades into the swirling morass of conflicting probabilities and çeases to be a viable conduit.

It is this phenomenon that WHIS set out to explore initially—the temporal chaos of the "time when time began." But it was not what they found there that turned the exploration into migration. For what they found was a mystery far more startling than they could ever have imagined. In those furthest reaches of the universe's creation, a converging infinity where primal forces of gravity and light rampaged among empty dimensions, they found paradox. And they found the riddle of the gate.

∞

II

Anachronia

The North Sea off Kungsholm Fjord

A.D. 881

The storm struck with startling intensity, almost swamping the dragonship *Erethlyn* with its first wave. Like Thor's mighty hammer, the blow descended with no more warning than a little fog bank drifting downwind from Skjalling Point, to intercept the fleet of Raynar Invarsson just at sunset.

Fourteen ships there were, wide sails aslant on stubby masts for a fair cold wind—fourteen sleek hulls cutting the icy waves with Kungsholm behind them and the coast of Northumbria ahead. Though the fleet was financed and put to sea by Olaf Magnusson, chieftain of Vestfold at Hartzel, the complement of the venture was a mixed band of fair Norsemen, dark Danes, and cold-eyed Swedes, sailing under the emblazon of Kungsholm.

Sixty burnished shields lined the rails of *Erethlyn*, one for each man aboard. Behind the shields were broadswords and war axes and the strong arms to wield them. Sleek and proud, the longship took the swells of open sea like a coursing hound, its fanged-beast head proud and arrogant atop the high, graceful bow post and the curl of its stern post taunting the wind that swelled its great sail.

On the starboard quarter, stretching out ahead, were nine other proud longships, and aft aport four more. Like a javelin of doom, the fleet pointed its snouts at Northumbria.

The little fog closed in from directly astern, a swirling grayness that might have been a line squall except that it was the only one in sight. As it neared, bypassing the rearmost vessels and closing on the stern of *Erethlyn*, Harald Ericsson kept an eye on it and was tempted to veer aside, breaking line to let it pass. Yet it did not seem to be a true squall, or even an erratic waterspout. It was nothing but a fog, his eyes said—a little dome of harmless cloud walking across the waters.

At most, the cloud might hide gusting winds. With the true eye of a seasoned schold, Harald reckoned its course and made his decision. "Lash down the stores," he told his Vikings. "Lower the sail and secure. Vikings to the sweeps."

Erethlyn might buck a bit on crosswinds, he reasoned. But the weather would pass within minutes, and the sailing then would be fair. *Erethlyn* was built to handle the winter seas of Gotland and the ice reaches. No bit of fog would be more than a nuisance.

Beside Harald at the wide rudder, the flotman Glome Lodbrok gazed back at the grayness growing in their wake. "We'll be out of sight of the fleet," the Swede said needlessly. "People get lost in fogs like that, Harald."

"Half a league, no more," Harald said. "It is only a fog, Glome. All around it are clear waters and a clear sky."

A step away, young Invar Crovansson grinned through his blond beard. "It's always doom and disaster for the *Svenskr* folk," he chuckled. "Show a thirsty Swede fresh water and he'll see only the mud that's in it."

The skald Healfdeane raised a scarred, bearded face, glowering. "Someone's weird is in yon fog," he muttered.

"Close your mouths and open your eyes!" Harald snapped. "You, skald! You can pray! Stoke your pot and read the smokes! Everybody else, shut up and sail!" The little fog closed on them astern, its tentacles wrapping themselves around the ship like ghostly fingers. Then they were in it, and around them was nothing but grayness and cold mist.

Amidships the skald crouched over his tub of fire and prayed to Odin for safe passage. For long moments *Erethlyn* clove the icy waters in muffled silence, her sweeps out now, driven by strong arms. Then the sea around them seemed to rise abruptly, and the sky fell to meet it. In an instant of sudden darkness, the longship tossed like flotsam on a tide, and silent, intense lightning enveloped her.

Everywhere, men clung and shouted. *Erethlyn* leapt from the sea like a great fish, hung suspended for an instant, turning, then crashed down into dark waters.

In a dome of silence, the rolling fog thinned and receded, and startled eyes looked out from the longship's shield-capped rails. *Erethlyn* floated dead still. Dark water lapped at her hull, and around her a light, obscuring mist clung to the sea.

But it was not the sea it had been. The air was warm, fragrant with the scent of pine, and distant sounds came from all directions—sounds unlike any they had heard before.

Amidships, the tattered skald leapt to his feet, his gray beard whipping around him. Just for an instant he had seen—very clearly—the image of a little man hovering in the smoke of his omen fire. "*Wulkenfolket!*" he cried. "Odin, preserve us!"

"By the floes of Gotland!" Glome swore, pointing to starboard. "Look!"

Through the mist a mountain appeared—a moving mountain bearing down on them, cleaving the waters at a knifelike bow while the drums of Valhalla throbbed beneath it. Unearthly shrieks and trumpet blasts erupted from the vast apparition—the wails of Valkyries rampant on the storm. "Sleipnir's cry!" Glome hissed. "Odin rides the thunder!" All along *Erethlyn*'s deck, panicked Norsemen scrambled for their weapons. The behemoth towered above them, sky-tall and terrible. Waters surged and tumbled as the thunder of mighty hoofbeats echoed across the narrowing span. Harald Ericsson drew his sword and swung to the stern platform, baring his teeth as his voice rang out, "Man the sweeps! Bend your backs there, men of Gotland! Row! As Odin lives, row!"

Hampton Roads
Chesapeake Bay, Virginia
The Present

The frigate USS *Conroy* was a mile off Bandy Point when the weird little vessel came into view, hard-down and dead ahead on collision course. There had been no blip, no signal, no warning. The thing was just there, dead in the water two hundred yards ahead. For only an instant the bow watch hesitated, then pipes shrilled and sirens wailed as the vessel came to general quarters. "Steer aport!" Commander Timothy Craig ordered. "Hard back! All full back!"

"What the hell is that thing?" Officer of the Deck Paul Ferguson muttered. "Jesus! Who are those clowns?"

Fog lay on the water like smoke on a mirror, obscuring vision beyond 130 yards and muffling the distant sounds of shipyards, fish docks, and canneries. *Conroy* slewed and bucked, answering to the power of two gas-turbine engines driving twin eighteen-foot screws now backing water beneath her stern. The distance between the frigate and the obstruction closed to ninety yards, then seventy, then forty, and shouts came clear from the odd vessel ahead—a trim, elongated wood-hull with a single stubby mast between tall, ornate bow and stern posts. The forepost was capped with a man-sized wood carving like the head of a fanged beast, mouth open to attack.

"A Viking ship?" Ferguson breathed. "What is this, a reenactment?"

All along the little vessel's curving deck, men scrambled here and there, some breaking out long oars, others arming themselves with burnished metal shields and various hand implements—broadswords, axes, stout spears, and knobby clubs.

The men were a wild-looking assemblage, most of them bearded and all wearing garments of rough fabric and fur. Some wore burnished helmets of bronze or copper, a few ornamented with bands of bear claws or the horns of cattle.

"What the hell are they doing?" Ferguson wondered. "Do they think they're going to fight us with swords?"

"Load the forward fifties," Craig said. "Coms, raise GH. See if they know anything about this. And bring up the harbormaster's agenda. If there's a parade or something, why didn't somebody tell us about it?"

Dead ahead and closing, the little vessel had sweeps out now, clawing frantically at the water. For a moment it sat hull down, then it raised its beast-head prow and began to move. *Conroy* was almost on top of it when it skittered off astarboard, churning a wake across the FFG's bow curl.

A flung spear arced over the frigate's nose and disappeared into the water beyond, and a shout arose from the fleeing rowboat, deep voices raised in a battle cry. "Odin!" they shouted. *"Odin var Wikingr!"*

The strange vessel stepped up its pace, racing away into the mist, and now there was the unmistakable thud of drums calling its sweeps. Arrows rattled against the frigate's armor, and sailors on the open deck dived for cover. Another spear sailed high and rattled on the foredeck of *Conroy* as gunners danced aside from it.

"What the shit is going on?" a crewman hissed as the projectile came to rest at his feet. He picked it up. It was a stout stave, seven feet long, with a hammered, knife-sharp iron point bound to one end with sinews. "Jesus!" he muttered. "Are those people crazy? This thing could hurt somebody."

"Shall we open fire, sir?" Ferguson asked.

Timothy Craig shook his head. Off his starboard bow, the little wooden ship was fairly flying now, dodging a channel buoy as its jaunty stern post receded in the mist. "On what provocation? Throwing sticks at us? Just try to keep them under observation, Mister Ferguson. Someone is going to catch hell about this."

"Aye, sir." Ferguson turned, read the signals from the bow watch, and turned back. "Ah, we don't have observation anymore, Commander. We seem to have lost them in the fog."

"Radar?"

Ferguson turned to his chief on watch, conferred for a moment, then shook his head. "Nothing, sir. Too much clutter here. We can't track."

"File a report on this, Mister," Craig said. "And stow that spear we collected. Somebody's playing games in a restricted channel, here. The brass will want to look at it."

Near Prescott, Arizona
2023

Billy Bluefoot's ancient rover blew a valve above White Spar, and there was nothing he could do but climb down and walk.

"Think they'd build these things to last," he muttered to himself as he packed eighty pounds of .308 cartridges into a canvas duffel and strapped it on his back. "Claimed they did, back when they built 'em."

With the load secured high on his shoulders, he picked up his rifle and took a last, disparaging look at the patched-up old vehicle. "Pile of junk!" he grumbled, then shook his head. Twenty-one years of aggravation were in that pile of junk. Nearly four hundred thousand miles had shown on its odometer when the odometer quit working, and that was three or four years back. Salvaged parts and ingenuity were what sat there by the bend in the road. Every junkyard in Arizona had contributed to the rover's longevity.

An ironic grin split Billy's copper-dark face as he bent to remove the ignition key. Nobody was going to steal the rover. Nobody in his right mind would want it, even if it would run . . . which—at the moment—it wouldn't.

"Don't go 'way," he told the old car. "I'll be back eventually, then we'll get you going again."

Hitching his load higher on his shoulders, he set out walking. Four miles to Prescott, he thought. Four miles, and all of it uphill. Old Highway 89—a winding ribbon of cracked blacktop pavement mostly overgrown with vegetation—wound up and away ahead of him, clinging to a mountainside. Pine forest rose steeply to his left, and to the right open vistas ran across green miles. The snowcap of Towers Mountain dominated a hazed horizon thirty miles away.

"All hail to the red, white, and blue," Billy Bluefoot sang to himself as he walked. "Where a skunk may be somebody's bro . . . ther! All hail to the home of the brave, paper dollars to mark its grave!"

As he sang and walked, he kept his eyes moving. The ammo in his duffel, salvaged from the ruins of the National Guard Armory at Gila Bend, was worth good barter to the militia at Prescott . . . but only if he got it there. There were always scags hanging around any militia center, anywhere in the Southwest FFZ—scags who would gladly relieve a forager of his goods, without a second thought. But Billy Bluefoot knew the land, and he knew the signs, and the scags in these mountains knew him, too. Some—in the past—had thought he might be easy pickings. They knew better now.

They all knew Billy Bluefoot was one Injun who didn't take crap from anybody.

Coming around Eagle Bend he surveyed the road ahead and cursed softly. There was fog there! Right where 89 switched back toward Lookout, a gray cloud clung to the slope, obscuring the road.

"Shit!" he muttered. Angling across to the uphill shoulder he crouched, blending into the vegetation. For a time he waited, scanning the shrouded cove in the mountainside. His senses and his instincts told him that there was no ambush there. It was only a momentary bank of fog and would drift away. Yet as he watched and waited, the fog remained where it was, becoming more dense.

Trapped in the cove, in the shadow of the mountain above it, the cloud remained stationary. "Inverse thermal," he told himself. "Some scag notice that, there will be a waylay there as soon as he can round up his buddies."

The best bet, he decided, was to get past the cove before that happened. With a sigh he shouldered his heavy pack and set out, his senses alert to every nuance of the surroundings.

Coming up to the switchback, the road was obscured by mist—mist that intensified as he pushed onward. By the time he reached the curve, it was so thick he could barely see the far shoulder of the old road.

So far, so good, Billy thought. Damn stuff hides me just like everything else. Quarter mile, maybe, and I'll be past it.

Abruptly, he realized that his breathing was labored. The pack on his shoulders seemed to weigh a ton, and his feet ached. And it was growing dark. Suddenly, frighteningly . . . dark!

"What th' hell? . . ." he muttered, stumbling to his knees. The darkness suddenly was absolute, and the thought flashed through his numbed mind that this must be how death feels.

He gasped for breath. He felt as though he were being crushed. He felt the blackness around him seeping into him, closing in on his thoughts, shutting him down. And as suddenly as it had come, the darkness and the weight dissolved in a flash of brilliance too quick, too powerful to more than tickle his perception. Powerful enough to pick him up and carry him away . . .

Houston, Texas
The Present

The unearthly flash came, and it was gone, and he wasn't even sure it had occurred. He knelt on damp pavement on a muggy, vapor-arc-lighted street, too dazed even to move as oncoming headlights blazed at him, beginning to swerve as tires gripped wet pavement. Brakes squealed, flashing lights dazzled him, and a car came to a careening stop just yards away, sliding half-turned on the slick asphalt.

Car doors were flung open and beams of light played on Billy Bluefoot. "You, there!" a voice commanded. "Freeze right where you are! Just put the gun down. Put it down now! That's right, now push it away from you!"

Billy sensed more than saw the guns trained on him. Still on his knees, he did as he was told. He pushed his rifle away, then locked his fingers behind his head. Through dizzy eyes he saw impossibilities all around—curbs and gutters, fences and streetlights, traffic lights winking in the distance down a deserted city street, and above it all, tall buildings standing against a glowing, murky sky.

There were men on either side of him—one close, giving him commands and pointing a pistol at him, another beside a shiny white car with blue stripes and flashing lights on its roof. On its open door was an emblem and the words *Houston Police.* Beyond it, beyond the roadway, a lighted billboard proclaimed:

THE MILLENNIUM IS RIGHT AROUND
THE CORNER . . . AND SO ARE WE!
—FIRST ALLIANCE SECURITIES
FANNIN AT AMES

"Lie down, please, on your belly," the nearest man ordered. "That's right, keep those hands on your head, where I can see them. Do you have a name?"

"Billy," Billy said. "Billy Bluefoot."

"Bluefoot? What is that, Indian? Well, Billy, I want to know what you're doing out here, at three in the morning, with a high-powered rifle. Did you plan to shoot somebody around here? And what about the stuff in that bag? Do you want to tell me about it?"

". . . don't know," the other man was saying quietly, to a hand mike. ". . . just kind of sitting there, on his knees, out in the middle of South Fannin . . . Disoriented, maybe he's on something . . . No ID of any kind . . . No, it's a rifle . . . Weatherby Mark III, scoped, fully loaded . . . Sack's got about a hundred pounds of cartridges . . . Affirmative, rifle cartridges. Looks like maybe five cases, NATO issue, .308 caliber . . . Also has forty or fifty rounds of Weatherby .300 magnum in his coat pockets . . . Yeah, suspicion of stolen property . . ."

"I'm placing you under arrest now, Billy," the nearest one said. Billy's arms were pulled down, hands behind his back, and cuffs were slapped onto his wrists. "You have the right to remain silent . . ."

Rock Ford, Ohio
The Present

"Jerk!" Cindy shrieked as the screen door slammed, flapping on its hinges. "Horse's ass!"

She swung around the frame of the dining room door, heading for the back door, and heard his footsteps in the gravel outside. With a hiss of rage she picked up a frying pan from the stove, raised it to throw, then put it down again. He was already out of sight from where she was.

Through the open kitchen window she heard his pickup door slam, heard his motor start, heard his tires churning gravel as he fishtailed the old truck around the walnut tree and headed for the gate.

This time he wouldn't be back. She knew he wouldn't, because this time there was nothing left for him to take. Every dollar she had ever had—that he knew about—was gone. The emerald ring, the ring she had cherished since she graduated from high school, had been the last of it. She supposed it was in a pawn shop now, or in some dealer's pocket. Maybe it was already on another woman's finger, but when that thought occurred it was too much to stand so she refused to think about it.

For a time she stalked the old house, room by room, not really seeing it. She wanted to cry, but didn't. Not about him. She had cried enough about him. But she was frightened now. There were no bright prospects in her future, that she could see . . . just desperation. She sat for a while on the front porch steps, watching cars pass, out past the gate. Cars with people in them, all going somewhere.

Finally she went inside, showered and put up her hair, and laid out her best dress. In the bedroom mirror she saw a haggard young woman with honey-blond hair, still a pretty face despite the sad, angry eyes in it, and maybe a trace of the energetic little doll she had been ten years before. But those ten years were gone, and they would never be back. It was time to look ahead now, since there was nowhere else to look.

"I'm scared," she confided to the mirror. "I'm really scared. I don't know what I'm going to do now."

Wrapped in a towel, sloppy old thongs on her feet, she went through the closet and the drawers, laying out clothing, folding the items into a pair of battered old suitcases. Everything she owned—and everything Norma Jean owned—fit easily into the containers.

When it was all packed she glanced at the stove clock. It was three-ten. The school bus would be here a little after three-thirty.

Mrs. Coppel was a tired voice on a telephone line. "Hello," the voice said. "Coppels'."

"Mrs. Coppel, this is Cindy Bruce. Yes, ma'am, that's right. I called to tell you I'll be leaving. Yes, right away. No, he isn't here anymore. I don't guess he'll be back. Is it all right if I leave the key on the porch rail? Yes, I'll lock up and make sure everything is turned off. I didn't want to leave without telling you . . ."

That done, Cindy got dressed, fixed her hair and her face, and pried open the side panel in the kitchen cabinet. The oatmeal box was still there. She emptied it and put the money in her purse. It wasn't very much, but it would take them a little way.

When the school bus stopped out front, she was waiting there, suitcases beside her. Norma Jean started to get off, but Cindy stopped her. "He's gone, Raynelle," she told the bus driver. "He won't be coming back this time. Could you take us into town, please?"

Raynelle shook her head, sighed, and beckoned. "Sure, Cindy," she said. "Get in."

On the way into town, Cindy held her daughter close beside her. "We're going on a trip, honey," she said. "Maybe we'll visit Gramma for a while."

From the front, Raynelle glanced at them in the mirror. "He take your car, too, did he?"

"I guess he might have, but it wasn't there. It's at Fred's. He said he'd try to find a couple of tires to replace the ones that got slashed. I'm hoping it's ready."

"If it isn't, it will be right away," Raynelle said. "Either that or Fred Goyens can find somebody else to spend his Sundays with. Do you know where you're going?"

"Independence. Momma said come home if I needed to, and I sure need to now."

Coming into town, Raynelle glanced westward. Out there, Highway 12 headed for the interstate. Usually the big cloverleaf was visible from here, but now it wasn't. A low fog, like a drifting cloud bank, had settled in the valley out there, and the highway overpass was completely obscured. Strange weather, she thought, then shrugged. The weather was always strange.

The old Buick was ready. Fred had salvaged some serviceable tires from a totaled Caprice, and had thrown in hoses, belts, and a lube job. At a scowl from Raynelle he filled the tank and charged Cindy only for the gas.

Raynelle walked down to the corner and peered westward. Out on the interstate, the little fog bank still clung to the terrain, a quarter-mile-wide grayness hiding everything under it.

"The road to Independence is a long road," she said, helping Norma Jean into the Buick.

"Then the sooner we get started, the better," Cindy Bruce replied.

∞

For most practical purposes, the transmission interval of a nerve impulse from the axon of one neuron to the dentrite of another neuron—the basic tic of neuro-cerebral process—may be regarded as equivalent to the velocity of light. The elapsed time between an experienced occurrence and the perception or awareness of that occurrence, therefore, is the light-speed interval of a synapse times the number of such transmissions required to relay impulses from the sensory organs to the perceptual locus of those organs within the brain.

Thus the phenomenon of awareness is a constant, subject to variations in distance between point of sensation and point of reception and the acuity of the individual brain (the degree of perception required to produce conscious knowledge).

Response to an occurrence is an entirely different matter. A person can "see" instantly, "perceive" immediately, and "react" promptly, and still be slow in responding, due to the nature of sentient thought. It is both the blessing and the burden of intelligence to withhold response to a stimulus until we have thought it over first.

—D. W. KRCSJIESKI

∞

III

NERCs

Eastwood, Kansas
The Present

"We're from the government and we're here to help." Maude Hawthorn couldn't contain a grin as the old gag line crossed her mind. An oxymoron in statement form, she thought. The grin intensified as the two dead-serious young men standing in her living room raised slight brows, wondering what she was grinning about. Even their cookie-cutter expressions, she realized, were oxymoronic.

The pair wore not-quite-identical suits, not-quite-power neckties, and not-quite-harmless attitudes. Their names were Smith and Westin, which to Maude's mind was a nice polishing touch for the essence of clonedom they exuded.

Beware of sharks in business suits, Lucas had said more times than she could remember. She wished Lucas were here right now. He might have enjoyed this. So far, the FTC, the SBA, the EPA, the ICC, the FBI, the CIA, the IRS, and even the NSF had failed to notice—or possibly opted not to admit—that there was a full-grown time-travel agency located on a residential street in a placid extraurban area east of Wichita. But now somebody called the National Endowment Regulatory Commission had stumbled upon Anywhen, Inc., and had sent agents to get to the bottom of this mystery.

Everything about the two men said, We're from the government and we're here to help. They might as well have worn signs saying, Cover your ass, the sharks smell blood.

Actually, they hadn't said any such thing when she opened the door to them. What one or the other had said was, "Mrs.

Hawthorn, you and your husband have a business venture registered under State of Kansas charter, doing business as Anywhen, Incorporated. We're here to conduct an inspection of premises."

It takes two of you to look at a bare room? she had thought, but what she said was, "Come in, then. And it isn't *Anywhen, Incorporated,* it's *Anywhen, Inc.* We're registered as a venture, not a corporation. The *Inc.* is part of the business name."

Smith and Westin glanced at each other. "Isn't that just the least bit deceptive?" Westin suggested, like a cat ready to pounce.

"The Secretary of State's Office and the Kansas Corporation Commission apparently don't think so," Maude purred. "They both approved our d.b.a. And the Internal Revenue Service issued us a tax number under that name."

"I see," Smith said. He made a note in a little book. They both looked slightly deflated, but they pressed on. "You appear to be doing business in a place of residence. The zoning restrictions—"

"—apply to signs, parking lots, visible commercial paraphernalia, and retail displays," Maude finished it for him. "We don't have any of those."

"I see," Westin said. He jotted something in his own little book, then gazed across the living room at the rebuilt front wall. "Your recent building-permit application indicated that the damages to your property might be business related."

"We were attacked by a hostile time warp from the future," Maude said candidly. "He was hiding in one of the pyramids in Egypt, and he came out and blasted our wall."

The investigators looked at each other. "I see," they both said.

"But the insurance adjuster decided it was a lightning storm," Maude clarified.

They both scribbled in their little books.

"Are you familiar with the International Public Treasures Recovery Treaty?" Westin pounced. "Or the Documentation Act of 1981? What can you tell us about some jeweled eggs and a crown, resembling artifacts listed as 'people's property, unrecovered' in early archives of the Bolshevik Revolution in Russia?"

“Not very much,” Maude admitted. “They were pretty, though. The Fabergé nativity dozen and the crown of St. Peter. The last time I saw them, an officer of the tsar’s Imperial Guard was trying to take them to Vladivostok, for the monk Rasputin. He stopped here for a visit. The officer, I mean. Not Rasputin. I have coffee in the kitchen. Would either of you care for some?” She turned, leading the way. “By the way,” she said, over her shoulder, “is this going to take a while? I’m expecting a tour group about three-thirty. They want to see the parting of the waters.”

“We aren’t getting anywhere with this,” Westin whispered to Smith. “Let’s go for complicity, or illicit involvement.”

“How about sedition?” a honey-sweet voice behind them suggested. “I’ll bet Lucas would give you some opinions on mandate regulation that you could make a case on.”

They turned, startled. Neither had realized that there was someone else in the room. Both, in fact, would have sworn that there wasn’t.

The woman standing there was some years younger than Maude Hawthorn, a striking brunette with startling green eyes, and it was obvious that they were related. Maude herself was an attractive woman, pixie-cute and pleasant-looking, but this one—the one just discovered—was *stunning.* Graceful and thirtyish, she wore a short, apple-green dress and white lace-up boots. Rich, dark curls framed a heart-shaped face designed to increase pulse rates.

“Hello.” She smiled sweetly, shrewd green eyes dissecting both of them at once. “I’m Amanda Santee, and I’m here to help.”

In the kitchen, Maude called, “Hi, Mandy! Gentlemen, that’s my sister Mandy. Where you been, hon?”

“Nashville,” Mandy answered. “I saw Elvis. He was great! Saw Loretta Lynn at the Opry, too. Is your tour here, yet?”

The NERC agents glanced at each other. *“Elvis?”* one of them muttered. “Oh, yeah. My secretary’s mother saw him at Pigeon Ford. His name was Eddie Miles.”

Mandy ducked her head to hide a grin, then met Maude at the kitchen doorway. “I came to help you with these two,” she whispered. “They could be a nuisance.”

Maude glanced past her. "Oh? I thought they were just some more of those ICC people."

"NERC is a sham," Mandy explained, herding her sister away from the visitors. "It's a smoke-screen agency for some pretty big private agendas in Washington. A holdover from what's-their-names' administration. NERC's looking for business ventures with big foundation backing, and for anybody with new, noncontrolled technology. Started with investigation of CompNet and found a golden goose. Couple of years from now, they intend to unveil a divestiture mandate. No privately held technology, no trade secrets. Congress is being whipsawed now, to pass enabling legislation. The Treasury Department and the Attorney General's office are behind it. Just think what *those* people might do with the TEF!"

"Goodness!" Maude breathed. "Usually the Whispers catch things like that. Didn't they? . . ."

"It hasn't materialized as a probability. Probably because of something we'll do. I got wind of it from Adam, and—"

"How is Adam?" Maude interrupted. "Are you and he still . . ."

Mandy nodded. "He's fine. Anyhow, he and Ed Limmer have been watching this thing. Edwin wants to come here, to deal with these two. That's why I'm here, to bring him down from the 1880s. The waystop there isn't ready, yet."

"Maybe we should give these gentlemen a free sample of time travel?"

"I expect that's what Edwin has in mind." Mandy smiled sweetly. "He enjoys dealing with organized idiocy." Mandy glanced around. "These two—Westin and Smith—are zealots. True believers. The kind Edwin refers to as attack sheep."

With a glance into the living room, where the agents were making a surreptitious inventory of Lucas's gun collection, Maude set out coffee service. "Do you suppose they know about time travel?"

"You mean, that it really exists? Probably not. They probably think this whole thing—Anywhen, Inc.—is a hype of some kind. But they're hunting. When they find out about it, they'll want it, and the people they work for will try to take it."

"We could send them to meet Moses on the Exodus, then leave them there," Maude suggested.

"No, they'd just muddy the waters. Let's bring Edwin downstream, then you can go on with your three-thirty tour group. Edwin can tend to these two." Mandy picked up a tray of steaming coffee cups and headed for the living room. "Here you are, gentlemen," she said sweetly. "Just make yourselves comfortable. Edwin Limmer will be here in a few minutes to—"

"Limmer?" Westin blinked. "As in Limmer Foundation?"

"You don't mean the one who started the Limmer Trust back in the fifties, of course," Smith said. "He must have died years ago."

"Not so you'd notice it," Mandy assured them. "He'll be here in a few minutes."

Osawatomie, Kansas
1887

Faron Briscoe paused at the top of the catwalk stairs, gazing out across the busy, noisy arena of the roundhouse. He was thirty feet above the floor here, and the view impressed him as it always did. Out beyond the wide-open rail wall, where big doors on rollers were rolled back now, bright iron tracks extended westward on beds of oaken ties—first two tracks, then four, then eight, an expanding rail yard doubling its strands at staggered switches to become the MKT's Osawatomie rail yard, a great stepping-stone that each week assembled and flagged out more trains of cars.

On the wide arena floor below him, thumping donkey engines slowly rotated a rail table, turning an engine and tender. The 104 had come in eastbound, bringing passengers and buffalo hides to offload a mile away at Grady Switch. The cars had been shunted aside in the yards, and now 104 was being turned to repeat the run. Trainmen, oilers, swamps, and wheelmen scurried over and around her as she turned, fitting her up for a new haul of cars.

"Pretty," Faron said to himself. "Mighty pretty."

Pretty—and it was his. Not the railroad or the yards, not the trains that came and went. But the roundhouse itself and all that was in it, from turntable to crow's nest. Even the locked penthouse atop the east shops was his, though it dazed him sometimes to think of what was being done there. Travel of a different sort entirely, if Ed Limmer could be believed. Time travel, for people from the future.

"Truly a strange world, this," Faron muttered. "From urchin of war to kingpin of a fine roundhouse. Ah, the Land of Opportunity! Then to learn that all the luck was never luck but just part of a plan so that my penthouse could be a springboard for migrating Whispers!" He sighed, then grinned. There was no sense in arguing with fate—especially when that fate had served one so well.

Number 104 had completed her turnaround, and her firemen were feeding the boiler now, making up steam. At the end of the catwalk, Faron Briscoe unlocked his oaken door and stepped into the private penthouse suite that Ed Limmer had named Leapfrog Waystop.

The "nest" atop the TEF tower was nearly three feet in diameter, dwarfing and almost hiding the little iridescent cone of the temporal effect focalizer that was its focus. Ed Limmer shook his head as he walked around it. Artee Six assured him that a field circuit was a field circuit no matter what the gauge of its wraps, and they had determined before—back when Leapfrog was to be in a warehouse in Topeka, before Kaffer's zen-guns destroyed that plan—that while there was plenty of copper wire to be had in 1887, it was all *big* wire. Extruded filament as fine as hair was not an unknown thing in the second half of the nineteenth century, but its uses were limited and its quantities minuscule.

So, following the rule of WHIS that all possible materials be acquired by indigenous forage, they had devised a field circuit of telegraph line. The focusing-gathering mechanisms, by which the nest's electromagnetic impulses produced analogs for light and gravity, were homed on Sol and the Nordstrom Singularity. Like the coils of telegraph wire governing the impulses, these mechanisms appeared garish and crude. One was devised from a set of laboratory refractors and the guts of a mariner's glass, the other from bits and pieces of a box camera, a bell jar, a postage scale, and a surveyor's transit. Several fine prisms liberated from an antebellum mansion at Cutter's Haven, a pair of organ pipes, and several carefully milled lead ingots were included in the strange assembly.

The resultant complexity had all the charm of a steam-powered thrashing machine, but Artee Six was pleased with it. The Whisper, busily fine-tuning his coils with a stasometer and a magnifying glass, glanced around and grinned as Limmer snorted at the contraption. "It doesn't have to meet twentieth-century standards of appearance," Artee chirped. "All it has to do is work. Which it will."

"Rube Goldberg would have been shamed." Limmer shrugged.

"It looks all right to me," Faron Briscoe stated, coming in from the living quarters beyond the steel-floored chamber. "Strange, but no stranger than some other scientific marvels I've seen. Typewriting machines, electrostatic generators, electric lights . . . By the way, I read the entirety of James Clerk Maxwell's dissertation on electricity and magnetism. Is that how this thing works? Each force creates the other?"

"After a fashion," Artee said. "The coil field generates both, reverses them, and induces the TEF to repeat the procedure. But the electric and magnetic impulses are only triggers. Analogs. What the TEF actually reverses are light and gravity. That's what makes time travel possible. The reversal process 'captures' molecular matter and thrusts it into the sequence ahead of its created light. Slow light becomes true light, and the subject is pushed ahead of it."

Faron glanced at Limmer and winked. "So perfectly simple," he drawled. "Wonder somebody didn't think of it a lot earlier."

"Some probably did," Artee pursued, missing the irony of the primitive. Glass to his eye, he followed the stasometer along a curving loop of copper wire and climbed over a support bracket. His head and shoulders disappeared into the confines of the nest and reappeared below it, upside down. "But without the right technological infrastructure—solid-liquid stasis, subtopographic symmetry, paired extrusion of metals and molecular chain resins, resonance tuning, things like that—it simply wasn't possible to create a TEF."

"Ask a Whisper what time it is, and he'll tell you how to build a variation chronometer," Limmer noted.

Faron shook his head, glancing from one to another of his "tenants." A robust, energetic middle-aged man who claimed to have lived 145 years so far—two-thirds of it backward—and a big-eyed bald dwarf from the twenty-ninth century! Even for Faron Briscoe, who in his thirty-one years had seen more wonders than most men beheld in a lifetime, the creation of a booster waystop for travelers in a time conduit was often boggling.

Limmer stepped close to the nest of wires and whatsits and peered inside. "How much longer until we can test the accelerator?"

"I'll need visual readings on alignment of the solar system and the singularity," Artee said, somewhere within. "I can do that tonight if the atmosphere remains clear, then program the prime vectors and coordinate with Polaris for quadrangulation." His bald head popped out between organ pipes. "We don't have the advantages in this century that you did with the first booster. We're a hundred years too early to lock onto satellite signals for our reference coordinates."

"I know all that," Limmer said. "But how long?"

"Fourteen hours, possibly. Or maybe a week or two. I have to retest the nest resonances, for the substitute TEF. Does it matter?"

"Only to me," Limmer growled. "While I'm cooling my heels here, being useless, I could be at Waystop I, helping Mandy fend off ravening bureaucrats."

"You could go now, or next week, and still be there when you're needed," Faron mused.

"Easy as going from now to anywhen." Limmer shrugged. "You'll get the hang of it. Duration and sequence aren't the same. It's the difference between T1 and T2." He pulled a little gray card from a coat pocket. It was slightly smaller than a playing card, and tiny lights played over one of its surfaces. His thumb pressed a stud. "No sense waiting around, I guess," he said.

For the briefest instant, the space around them seemed to darken, a dimming slowness to frozen black, followed by a blaze of intense light so quick that it was gone before their eyes could transmit the image of it to their brains. An instant only, but in that instant Faron sensed again the enormous forces touched upon to create the effect—the primal forces of the universe itself.

And the chamber was full of little, bald people. There were six or seven of them, but they seemed a multitude as they scurried this way and that, depositing bundles, comparing notes, and converging upon the TEF mounting. Like Artee Six, they were all tiny—some barely four feet tall—completely hairless, and their deep, quick eyes were twice the size human eyes should be.

Faron nodded at a few of them, unperturbed. In recent months he had grown accustomed to the appearance and the abrupt comings and goings of Whispers. This crew had brought materials for the TEF's electromagnetic generator, which would be installed on the roof next to the "suntunnel" light refractor and the photogravitational receptors aimed at the North Star and at Nordstrom—the nearest stable interstellar black hole.

The installation would be done at night, and by morning the whole protuberance would resemble a chimney.

One of the newly arrived Whispers, a little female named Kaycee O'Fordie, tugged at Ed Limmer's sleeve. "We rode your beam upstream," she said. "Are you ready to trans to Waystop I?"

"Ready," Limmer said. He put away his gray card and took the little person's hand. "Be back directly," he told Faron and Artee.

Again there was that instant's flicker of forces beyond imagining—light to slow darkness to blazing new light—and he was gone.

"I'll never get used to that," Faron Briscoe muttered. Then he paced around the TEF tower, looking for Artee Six. He found the Whisper technician clinging to the base of the nest, calculating alignments. "What did you mean, 'substitute'?" Faron asked.

"What?"

"You said you had to retest for the substitute TEF. Why did we substitute?"

"Oh, that." Artee was attaching a device like a short fire hose with lenses to gimbals at the nest's base, using butterfly screws. "The TEF we're using is the one designated as spare. I couldn't find where the original was put. Probably over there among all those crates. But it doesn't matter. One TEF's pretty much like another."

Eastwood, Kansas
The Present

The blaze of light from the TEF chamber as a band of Whisper emigrants accelerated through was brighter by tenfold than direct sunlight, brighter than the brightest flare of any chemical reaction, bright enough to have blinded everyone in or near the chamber and the adjacent kitchen–living room segment of the Hawthorns' house . . . except for one thing. The TEF impulse that triggered a photogravitational reversal, creating pure new light from captured gravity, was instantaneous.

In two-millionths of a millisecond—barely more than the elapsed time of a single cortical synapse—the phenomenon was over and gone. So brief was the p-g reversal that by the time it could register on the nerve centers of the brain, a millisecond or so after it was completed, it seemed nothing more than the tiniest trick of the eyes.

Someone watching carefully might have imagined that he glimpsed several dozen little people who appeared and disappeared in an instant in the steel-floored vault that had once been Lucas and Maude Hawthorn's dining room. But Smith and Westin, hovering near the open doorway between living room and kitchen, weren't looking. Their attention had been distracted by the ring of the doorbell and Maude going to answer it.

Only Mandy Santee was watching the TEF chamber. As the acceleration boost was completed she thought, Fifty or sixty more. Must be close to a hundred thousand Whispers upstream by now, all on their way to the Great Paradox—the beginning of time. I wonder what they found there.

Whatever it was, they wouldn't be coming back. Her time-attuned eyes had noted that a lot of the transient Whispers in that instant's glimpse—maybe a third of them—were children. The exploration of deep time had become a migration. Whole families of Whispers were heading for the beginning of time.

A little bell indicated that the shunt was complete, and a moment later it sounded again, accompanying another instant of TEF activation. Ed Limmer materialized in the steel-floored chamber, saw her, and winked.

"We have Kallikaks," Mandy whispered. "They're right in there, helping Maude greet the Exodus tour."

If Smith and Westin, field investigators for the National Endowment Regulatory Commission, felt their quest for violators had led them into a funny farm, they hadn't seen the half of it yet. The NERCs gawked in amazement when Maude Hawthorn opened her front door and ten people filed in, all wearing rough-spun woolen robes, various garments of primitive flaxen weave, and closed sandals of rough-cut leather.

Five men and five women—five middle-aged couples dressed for a costume party. "We're ready to go." One of the men grinned at Maude. "I'm Sol Greenberg. We talked on the phone, remember? But Martin hadn't introduced us. Anyway, we've followed the tour-preparation instructions, and Miriam's sister Rachel did the costumes. So here we are. Which way to the Red Sea?"

"It's the *Reed* Sea, not the Red Sea," Maude corrected. She gazed at them critically. "I guess you'll all pass inspection," she decided. "Did you bring your personal gear?"

"Staffs for the men, waterbags for the women—they're actually vinyl but they look like goatskin—and blankets for everybody," the man said.

"And nothing bright-colored or shiny," a pert gray-haired woman added. "Don't worry, Maude, we've done our homework. We won't attract attention."

"We just want to see the waters part." Martin Herzog nodded. "They really did that, huh?"

"Yeah, they really did. You'll see it. Just stay away from Egyptian soldiers. And stay away from the livestock."

"We talked about that," Martin Herzog said. "I think that's probably what the Pharaoh's army was after—all those sheep and goats and donkeys and cattle that the Hebrews took with them. They may have thought of it as their tithe, but to the Egyptians it was grand theft. Moses wasn't wanted for escaping. He was wanted for rustling."

Some of the men went out and came back lugging rolled, rough-weave dark blankets, goatskin water pouches, and several cedar-wood walking staves. Maude herded her flock into the kitchen, glancing at Westin and Smith as they edged back from the doorway. "If you gentlemen will excuse me for a few minutes," she said, "we have a tour departing."

As the robed people filed toward the steel-floored dining room, Mandy Santee appeared at the kitchen entry, accompanied by a sturdy, smiling man of middle years. "Hello, gentlemen," he said. "I'm Ed Limmer. I understand you're investigating my foundation."

"Uh, yeah," Westin admitted. "Sort of. What are those people doing?"

"They're going on a trip," Limmer said. "Back to the time of Moses. Would you like to watch?"

"You mean . . . like time travel?" Westin stared at him.

"No, not *like* time travel. It *is* time travel. I'm sure you don't believe in time travel. Nobody does. But don't worry, you'll get the hang of it."

∞

T2 LOCUS: Waystop Accelerator Day 774
TO: WHIS Control
FROM: L-383, Teal Fordeen
SUBJECT: Priority III recommendation 0.09; ImAttReq

In light of the recent reports submitted as Paradox Events 91 through 133 inclusive, Closed Loop L-383 has undertaken study of relationships in paradox phenomena, tentatively labeled *Sleepwalker Events.* These seemingly sporadic events, occurring over a Time2 span of at least nineteen months, evidence certain remarkable consistencies:

1. Of the forty-three grouped occurrences, nineteen can be positively linked to the indigenee known as Ben Culver (whereabouts currently unknown). The remaining twenty-four identified episodes may be assumed to be directly or indirectly the result of this timer's activities.

2. Every *Sleepwalker* episode—while leaving a well-marked trail of typical photogravitational wake from origin to point of encounter and from point to point within each subsequence—ends abruptly in a simple disappearance of the subject without any telltale track that we are able to define. It is as though the timer—whom we suspect is not consciously aware of his skill—begins each adventure in typical time-traveler fashion, by exciting a reversal of the photogravitational field to accelerate himself past light speed, but ends

each episode in some other manner of which we are unaware.

All readings indicate that he simply drops out of the four-dimensional continuum, to reappear again in another time. Hence the designation of paradox: what he seems to do cannot be done, but still he does it.

3. The timer Adam, with whom we have had beneficial dealings, is presently searching for Ben Culver, but so far without success. This indicates that—while Culver's ability appears to be similar to Adam's—there is some other factor involved, beyond the known limits of the four dimensions.

4. The apparent possession of a temporal effect focalizer by Ben Culver is an added puzzle in two respects. As a timer, he has no need of—nor is there any evidence that he has actually used—such a device, and our records provide no clue as to how he might have obtained it.

In view of these circumstances, we recommend that WHIS and UEB review downstream records for any indication of Ben Culver's whereabouts at our present T2 placement, and further, that investigation be initiated into the question How can a person or object be relocated from one time and place to another without moving in any of the eight primary directions?

Submitted as Recommendation 0.09, priority status III.

∞

IV

The Exodus Tour

The Sea of Reeds, Southwest of Sinai
1274 B.C.

At its beginning, the Exodus was no more than three hundred people—mostly civil functionaries, clerks, vendors, and household servants slipping away from Pharaoh's city. But with each mile northward, across lush delta lands and along the stony heights to the east, the numbers had swelled. All through a long night, runners had spread the word. Saddened by the death of his newborn son, Pharaoh had abandoned his resolve. Let them go, he had said. Any who wish to leave, let them leave.

Where the land dropped away toward the vast tidal marsh known as Sus Papyrus—the Sea of Reeds—some four thousand people and their herds and flocks crowded into a neck of higher, arid land that thrust like a blunt spear point into the treacherous marsh.

But now Pharaoh had changed his mind. Rear guards on the high dunes spread the alarm. To the south, desert winds carried the dust of marching columns. Pharaoh's army was in pursuit.

The refugees milled and muttered, dark eyes darting from the menace behind to the miles of reed-grown muck and water ahead. Plying the Sea of Reeds was work for boats, not pedestrians. Out there were mires to bog the feet of man and beast, deep unseen holes below the murky stills, and hundreds of meandering tidal streams where swift currents flowed.

A man might cross the Sea of Reeds afoot, given time and great good fortune. But not a multitude. As one, the people prayed their various prayers and looked to their leader for guidance.

They were not a disciplined unit, no organized consort, but simply people—people of all ages, all conditions, a hundred diverse kinds and stations. They were all Egyptians, and considered themselves so. But they were not of the blood. In recent times, that distinction had become important. The get of Abraham had lost the acceptance their fathers had known. Now they filled the lowest strata of Egyptian life. They had become no more than slaves. They were farmers and craftsmen, vendors and herders, tanners and sweepers and laborers of every kind. Among them were ruffians and thieves, scribes and doctors, every level of skill and every level of education. But they were Hebrew, and thus all banned from privilege in Pharaoh's land. And the man they followed, though once a member of the royal household and a confidant of Pharaoh himself, was still no more than a fugitive.

Though once of high station, Moses was, like the rest, a descendant of the desert tribe of Joseph. And thus—like the rest of them—he was without status in the reign of the present Pharaoh. Rumor said he had killed a man of the true blood in a time past, then had fled Egypt and lived among the Midianites. But now he was returned, proclaiming the word of the old God Zhaveh. He had challenged Pharaoh, and lived, and now the tribe of Joseph came together again, to follow him out of the hopeless servitude of Egypt to a place of promise somewhere beyond Pharaoh's realm.

Beyond the Sea of Reeds was Sinai, and there they might be safe for a time. But the hills of Sinai were only low shadows on a distant horizon. They might as well have been in another world.

In a cove on the slope of an ancient dune, above the trampled ground where the fugitives milled, a little group watched with keen interest. "What will happen if the soldiers catch them?" Miriam Greenberg whispered to her husband.

"They didn't catch them," he reminded her.

"But what if they had?"

"Oh. Well, I suppose they would have killed a lot of them, as examples. I guess the rest would have been led back in shame and put to work in the copper pits or something."

"What copper pits?" Martin Herzog demanded. "They

didn't have copper pits around here, Sol. They sent slaves to the stone quarries."

"Stone quarries, then." Sol shrugged. "Or maybe they tended furnaces. What's the difference? They didn't catch them."

Sand and dust cascaded around them as the dunes seemed to shrug. A vast, deep rumbling sound rolled across the desert, almost below audible range.

"Another earthquake?" Hazel Bernstein chirped. "That makes what, six today? I never read anything about earthquakes in ancient Egypt."

Miriam was thumbing through the little tour booklet from Anywhen, Inc. "The concordance says there was a big interruption in the Mediterranean about this time. A vol—"

"Eruption," Sol corrected her. "Volcanoes erupt. They don't *interrupt*!"

"I'll bet they do," Hazel Bernstein giggled.

Miriam shook her head and sighed. "A volcano called Thera blew its top about now, it says here. An island in the Mediterranean. It just went bang and blew a whole big island right out of the water. Maybe these earthquakes are cosmic waves."

"Seismic," Sol said patiently. "Not cosmic, buttercup. *Seismic*."

"You know what I mean."

"Maybe that's it, over there." Cal Segal pointed. In the western sky beyond the sea's horizon, odd, dark clouds mounded, indistinct and far away. It might have been dark smoke, a very long way off, or it might have been only the hazing of sunlight across hundreds of miles of open water.

"Look!" Mabel Silverman hushed them. "It's Moses! Isn't that Moses?"

Atop a dune a hundred yards away, a solitary figure stood, leaning on his staff. Wind billowed his beard and robes, but even from here they could feel the intensity of his gaze. He, too, was looking to the west.

"He looks a little like Uncle Phil, doesn't he?" Miriam said.

Sol glanced at his wife. "Your uncle Phil is eighty years old and bald," he reminded her.

"Well, he looked kind of like that when he was a lot younger," Miriam declared. "You know, I expected Moses to look more . . . well, more *Jewish*. For that matter, hardly any of these people look Jewish, except maybe that bunch over there tending to those cattle."

"That's because those are Hittites," Martin said. "That's a different thing from Hebrew. But they looked Jewish. Probably the only people who ever really looked Jewish were the Hittites."

"I dare you to tell Howard Bloom that," Hazel Bernstein prodded.

"Why should I tell Howard Bloom anything? He tried to sell me time-shares in Florida."

"He told you about Anywhen, Inc., didn't he? After he and Naomi did the *Titanic* tour?"

"Okay, so maybe I'll talk to Howard Bloom. But I'm not moving to Florida."

"Moses is leaving," Miriam pointed out.

Atop the nearby ridge, the lonely figure had turned and was descending toward the waiting throngs. The tourists watched, fascinated—all except Miriam Greenberg. She sat as though frozen, staring at the top of the ridge where Moses had been only moments before. Just for a moment, as he turned away, there had been a house there. She was sure of it. A 1960s-style ranch bungalow, half-brick facade with gray clapboard and white trim! For an instant it had been there, ringwall foundation and all, teetering atop the rocky peak of an ancient desert dune. Then it was gone.

Below, the leader of the Hebrews joined his throng and there were shouts of "Ah-mose! Ah-mose!"

"I saw a house," Miriam whispered, to herself and the North African wind.

Straight and solemn, the man called Moses paced through the swirling masses of his followers and down to the lapping, murky waters of the reed marsh. Raising his voice, he spoke for a moment, then raised his staff above his head and brought it downward with force, smiting the shallow water at his feet. Again he turned and spoke, his voice rolling out across the multitude.

"What's he saying?" Mabel rasped. "Miriam, be quiet! I

can't hear Moses! Is that Hebrew he's talking? It doesn't sound Hebraic."

"It isn't," Martin Herzog stated. "He's speaking Egyptian. Most of those people probably don't understand Hebrew. They'll have to learn it all over again."

"I saw a house," Miriam said, to no one in particular. "Why would there be a house?"

Sol glanced around at her. "A what?"

"A house," she said. "I saw a house!"

Again the low, throbbing rumble came, and the earth beneath them seemed to quiver. Sand flowed down the faces of the dunes, and dust rose on the wind.

"Seven," Hazel Bernstein muttered.

It was like before, but this time it didn't stop. Gradually, implacably, the rumbling swelled in volume, and the earth shook in response. The tremble became a vibration, and the vibration became a series of nauseating heaves, as the entire landscape seemed to rise, fall back, and rise again.

The babble of the crowds below swelled to a roar, punctuated by screams and shouts. Animals milled and bolted in panic, and great clouds of waterfowl lifted from the marshes to beat away on thundering wings.

In the western sky, the strange, dark clouds had climbed higher, and now a huge, ropy cloud of smoke was plainly visible there—still hundreds of miles away and barely a dot on the Mediterranean horizon, but unquestionably smoke, rolling eastward on the prevailing winds of the sea.

Just to the south now, men appeared, running, scrambling, and sliding down the last wall of marching dunes. The Hebrews' rear guard—fleeing ahead of Pharaoh's army. They raced northward, down the narrowing pathway into the vast marsh, and behind them came the sounds of shell horns and copper drums. Dozens of silhouettes appeared on the skyline of the dunes, then hundreds and more hundreds. Horse-drawn chariots in the van, footmen with long spears flanking them, Pharaoh's army came down the slopes, gathering speed as they closed on the huddled refugees.

Again the prophet Moses slapped the water with his stick, and as the audible rumble of earthquake grew—punctuated now by the drums and calls of the advancing Egyptians—the earth seemed to respond. With a mighty heave, the land thrust upward. Beyond the refugees, water rolled away to both sides on great, curling sheets, exposing the sand and stone, the running, matted mud of the marshland's exposed base. Moses raised his staff, shouted orders, and as one the thousands of refugees crowded forward onto the high, exposed highway between churning waters.

Sol Greenberg got to this feet, swaying on the unsteady ground. "Time to go," he said. "The Exodus is moving!"

But Martin Herzog pulled him back. "No, let's stay," he urged. "Those people—our ancestors—they never saw what happened behind them. I want to see it."

"Me, too," Hazel decided. "Get down, Sol. We can see the Sinai some other time."

"But there'll be the Commandments," Sol shrilled. "God will speak to Moses on the mountain! We can be there!"

"That comes later, Sol," Cal Segal reasoned. "This is now. I want to see this."

As though in a trance, Miriam stared at the empty crest to the north. "What's a house got to do with anything?" she muttered. "Why was there a house?"

Outvoted, Sol subsided. Staying low, the little group peered over a sand rift as the first chariots of the Egyptian guard rolled by, flanked by footmen.

Burdened by their flocks, and by the old and the lame, Moses' refugees were no more than a thousand yards ahead when the army reached the reed-matted highway leading off through the rising marshes. For long moments the Egyptians hesitated there, letting the rearmost units catch up. Then at shouts from the charioteers, the horns wailed again and the drums took up a marching rhythm. Twenty by twenty, four columns abreast, Pharaoh's army went after the fleeing Hebrews . . .

. . . And the rumble of earthquake crescendoed. With a final slow heave, the wide, wet avenue pointing northward toward the tip of the Sinai raised itself another foot, then settled back. Tectonic shift or frontal thrust, the earthquake had spent itself, and the low bottoms of the marshes subsided, back to where they had been.

On both sides, the whisper of rushing water became a roar, as mountainous torrents descended—a mighty tidal wave from the Mediterranean side rushing to meet the backflow from the Red Sea basin to the south.

The Egyptian army was barely started on the Reed Sea path when the path was no longer there. For those in the rear it was too late to flee, and for those ahead there was nowhere to go. Howling both ways down a five-hundred-yard channel, huge flash floods crashed together in the middle—tidal wave against torrent—and nothing could have withstood such raw, violent force.

For long minutes the waters collided, lashed, and swirled, waters that turned as dark as night as the muck of centuries was stripped from the marsh floor and stirred into the mix.

When finally the seas subsided, there was no reed marsh there. Instead there was a wide, deep channel of dark, roiling water. In the silence the waters hissed and gurgled, and here and there men popped to the surface—dead men, floating and sinking in a cess of reeking mud, flowing tides, and uprooted marine vegetation.

With eyes as big as dollars, the little group on the dune stared out across the silence. Finally Martin Herzog tore his gaze from the scene and looked upward into smoke-hazed sky. "My God," he muttered. "Oh, my God!"

Far away now, still fleeing eastward along a corridor that remained upthrust, the people of the Exodus, the followers of Moses, made their way toward the distant horizon that was Sinai and freedom.

Through her tears, Miriam Greenberg watched them go and knew the glory and the tragedy of her own culture. Those were her ancestors out there, and they would survive. Bickering, faltering, querulous, and thoroughly human, they would make their way as they had done, toward a destiny that even in her time was not yet known. Through one cataclysm after another, down through history, the wandering people of Moses, the people of Joseph of the tribe of Abraham, would make their way the best they could.

Yet even through the grandeur of it, a bizarre question

remained. "Why was there a house here?" she wondered. "Of all things, why a house?"

Waystop I
The Present

The NERC agents watched the Exodus tour depart, then peered with dazed eyes into the steel-floored TEF chamber. "Where did those people go?" Westin asked finally. "Is this some kind of joke? Where are they?"

"The appropriate question is *when*, not *where*," Edwin Limmer corrected him. "They've gone to visit the Nile Delta region, spring of 1274 B.C." He grinned. "Nobody believes in time travel until they've tried it," he said. "We can give you gentlemen a sample tour, if you'd like."

Smith and Westin glanced at each other, and Limmer could see the wheels turning.

"Uh, I wonder if we might be excused for a moment," Smith suggested. His glance at Westin said, We have to talk.

"Down the hall, second door on the left," Maude said cheerfully.

Smith led Westin down the hall. Coming from the TEF control booth—a little room that had been a closet before the advent of the Whispers—Mandy watched them go.

"They've got the scent," Limmer said. "Right now they're 'seeing the big picture.' Either we have valuable, new, unregulated technology here—technology that certainly is in the 'public' interest—or we're committing some kind of a swindle that involves fraud and might have interstate ramifications. Either way, the source of capital is a registered foundation subject to endowment regulations." He grinned wolfishly. "Oh, they love it! Right now those gentlemen are unzipping their britches and looking at their career options."

Maude giggled.

"So what do you think they'll do?" Mandy asked.

"I expect they'll play cover your ass," Limmer decided. "They *are* bureaucrats, after all. But they smell blood here, and they're excited. They suspect fraud, but they need evidence.

Right about now, they're reporting in on Smith's pocket phone. They'll schedule a callback to protect themselves. Then they'll take us up on the free sample."

"So where and when do you want them sent?" Maude questioned.

"I'll book the tour." Mandy smiled a dazzling smile. She keyed in a data program on Maude's bookkeeping PC. For a moment she searched files, then brought up a meteorological chart. "What do you think, Edwin? Maybe a whirlwind tour?"

"Wonderful idea." Limmer looked over her shoulder. His grin was all wolf. "Let's start with Gustave, Nebraska, May 27 of 1944. Every ill wind should blow some good."

Working rapidly, Mandy programmed a TEF sequence and fed it to the main bank. Looking on, Maude raised a brow. "They won't be hurt, will they?"

"Of course not." Her sister glanced up. "That's what the pre-seek is for. Just like all the tours we've done. Fail-safe scan, downstream five seconds. That's as close as they'll come to real harm, before the skip throws them to their next scheduled visit."

"Five seconds? I thought we allowed a margin of five minutes."

"We do, on the usual package tours. But then, duration is relative. It doesn't take very long to look at a tornado." Her programming done, Mandy headed for the control booth behind the TEF chamber.

When Smith and Westin returned from the toilet, Edwin Limmer was waiting for them. "We have a few minutes free now," he said. "Would you like to see how time travel works?"

The NERC agents exchanged glances. Westin nodded. "This is as good a time as any. How long will this take?"

"How long would you like?"

Smith looked at his wristwatch. "Not more than half an hour. We have to call in, then."

Limmer nodded. "No problem," he assured them. "Right this way. The empty room with the metal floor is our TEF chamber, and that thing on the pedestal over there is the TEF itself. That stands for *temporal effect focalizer.* Essentially, the device responds to a reversal of electromagnetic fields, and reinterprets the analogies, producing an inversion of fundamental light and gravity. The light produces the drive for faster-than-light transfer. Hence, time travel."

Pausing in the open doorway, Westin peered at the room that had once been just a dining room. "Where's your power source?" he asked. "Do you have a license for high-voltage equipment?"

"High voltage?" Limmer chuckled. "There are more volts in a flashlight battery. The power sources are the sun and the Nordstrom Singularity, with Polaris as a triangulator."

"This I have to see," Smith muttered. Notepad and pen in hand, he stepped into the room. Westin followed. "What do we do now?"

"You just did it." Limmer smiled. "Have a nice time."

The transfer was too sudden and too brief for real perception. The NERCs experienced an instant of slowing darkness, followed by a flash of pure light far too intense for description, even if they had noticed it. In the blink of an eye, the two men were standing in a blowing field, where huge winds tore at them and thunder like a hundred speeding trains deafened them. As one, they fell and tumbled, rolling like debris in the impossible wind. A wall of swirling darkness marched down upon them, as notepads, pens, Smith's coat, and one of Westin's shoes hurtled away on the wind.

"Jesus Chr . . . !" Westin mouthed as wind like a giant's fist picked them up and tumbled them upward, higher and higher. A big, whirling object that resembled a barn's roof whisked past them, and an uprooted barbwire fence danced just out of reach. Small trees, a tractor tire, and a chicken floated past in a maze of debris barely visible in the murk of hurtling straw and topsoil.

Smith glimpsed Westin's trouser leg and grabbed it, but there was no one in the trousers. Half-disrobed, Westin spiraled by a few feet away, his mouth open in a soundless howl.

They both saw the thing coming directly at them—a grain silo bent double and hurtling toward them like a rampaging juggernaut. It was almost upon them when the slow-dark-light thing happened again and they found themselves sitting on the roof of a building in a little town.

With dazed eyes, Westin looked around. For an instant, vaguely, he wondered why Smith was sitting on this roof, his hair wild and full of straw, holding a pair of pants in one hand and a chicken in the other. Then, with a deep, bone-shuddering roar, the dark sky above dropped down on them and again they were riding the wind.

"Second stop," Amanda Santee called from the control booth. "This one's Woodward, Oklahoma, 1947. That's a good one."

"Hope they're enjoying their whirlwind tour." Limmer grinned. "How many transfers did you put in, Mandy?"

"About sixty." Mandy came into the kitchen. The TEF's program would handle things from here. "Just the storms that have been documented . . . and then I added a rest stop before retrieval."

"Rest stop?" Maude asked.

"The wind tunnel at Jet Propulsion Laboratories," Mandy explained innocently. "They might enjoy a breather after all that excitement."

Valley of the Washita
A.D. 1102

Inertial stress resonance, dubbed *stratance* by the ITR researchers who first noted its peculiar properties, is not a substance, nor is it a form of energy, exactly. Rather, it is a condition found in certain combinations of polymers and nonferrous metals, in which the catalysis of compounds not occurring in nature creates a molecular tension capable of emitting certain exotic energies at low, steady levels.

These energies can be encoded into messages, in which case the subject material becomes a "talisman," speaking in its own frequencies for anyone capable of hearing it.

The simplest example of stratance is the varying polarity of crisscrossing copper filaments embedded in polyurethane resin. Depending upon the size, complexity, and pattern of the filament design, some have claimed, such a talisman will attract anything from mosquitoes to fruit bats and certain species of domestic felines. It "talks" to them and they respond.

The sleaving material of an extruded temporal effect focalizer, or TEF, is vastly more complex than this simple example, but the principle is the same. In the same way that a time transference accomplished by a TEF field leaves residual trace patterns, the sheath of a TEF cone babbles in the range of telepathic awareness.

Or, properly encoded, it becomes a beacon . . . but only for those receptive to its call. The being known as 1KHAF4, or Kaffer, had experimented with the mechanics of the human brain, far more than any other researcher of his or any time. As a fugitive by choice and a psychopath by nature, Kaffer had none of the restrictions or hesitations that others might have. With all of the data of time loop L-270's banks at his disposal, he had discovered within certain brains a capability remarkably similar to polymeric stratance. Working alone, he had duplicated the stress patterns of exceptional human ganglia—that of known potential timers—in the only stratance artifact available to him—the TEF of L-270. For an encoding pattern he had selected, simply, L-270's vector loci.

It was not in the nature of Kaffer to trust in luck, but on this occasion he was lucky. The TEF he subsequently lost was, to all intents and purposes, a homing beacon attuned to the telepathic mind.

1KHAF4 was imprisoned now, in the vast impenetrability of the tomb of the Pharaoh Khafre. But L-270's TEF was not. The device at the moment rested in a slanted house on a brushy hillside not far from a little river that would one day be named Washita. And there its insistent psionic babbling—like a silent suggestion in a void—called out to any mind able to sense its message.

∞

To even suggest that anything man might discover, explore, or seek to alter is somehow out of bounds—that mankind in its enthusiasm might trespass on the sacred turf of God—demonstrates a low opinion of God.

—MAHLON BIRKHAUSEN, *Manifest Cause*

∞

V
The Time Tangle

Chesapeake
The Present

"It was the fog." The skald Healfdeane raised his eyes from the dancing firelight to gaze intently at first one and then another of those around him. Some of them shivered and looked away. Sometimes the eyes of a skald reflected more than a man wanted to see. "The fog was Loki's playful hand, grasping a toy," Healfdeane said. "*Erethlyn* is that toy."

The Swede Gladen Lodbrok, who was called Glome, cast a cold, baleful glare at Harald Ericsson. "I knew that fog was evil," he growled. "I told you we should stay out of it. I told you there was dire magic in such a mist!"

"You told me no such thing," Harald sneered. "You just said people get lost in fogs, sometimes."

"Well, if this isn't lost, I don't know what is!" Glome pulled his bearskin cloak tighter around his shoulders and looked upward at the glowing sky above the forest. "What place is this, where iron monsters thunder across the waters and the stars come down from the sky to light the way for men? Never in life or legend have I heard of such a place as this!"

Gathered around a pair of little fires in a forest beside a brackish stream, sixty Vikings muttered among themselves. They looked around nervously at the night shadows in their refuge, and up at the glowing sky, which silhouetted the shapes of oak trees standing above lesser growth. *Erethlyn* was bow-grounded on the grassy bank of the stream, her long, graceful dragon shape dwarfed by the trees above her.

The glow in the sky was cloud reflection from vast arrays

of bright lights—brighter than firelight—that seemed to be everywhere around the wide fjord just beyond their hiding place. In the mists of evening the Vikings had fled across those waters out there, using every shred of cover while the skald spoke chilling spells to hide them. Those had been fearful hours, dodging monstrous vessels that roared and muttered and laid vast wakes behind them. As darkness descended, the shores all around came alive with bright lights, and everywhere were strange people doing strange things.

Finally they had entered a river that flowed to the bay, and the sharp eyes of Invar Crovansson had found this secluded place, a little tributary stream screened by foliage. Here they hauled *Erethlyn* into the cover of deep forest, and Invar climbed a tree to look around. In all directions he saw bright lights, whole flocks and schools of them outlining the shores of the great bay, and trailing away in clusters across the surrounding countryside. Never in his nearly twenty years had the young Norseman seen or even imagined so many lights, so brightly shining, or so much human activity.

Now he arose from his crouch and stood tall, shaking back his shadowed sun-blond mane. Stepping away from the fire, he listened intently for a moment, his nostrils twitching. Then he grinned. Women! Out there somewhere, beyond the screening cove, women's voices laughed and chattered.

Invar turned, blue eyes glittering in the firelight, singling out the dour Glome. "I don't have your answers, *Svenskr,*" he said. "But I say wherever this place is, this is where we are. I would rather explore opportunities than reasons."

Harald Ericsson looked around thoughtfully and nodded. "Odin's dark sky will aid us," he decided. "Float *Erethlyn* and muffle the oars. We'll have a look around."

As *Erethlyn* crept from the stream cove into the open bay, Invar climbed her dragon figurehead and squinted. Miles of open water lay quiet now beneath the glowing sky, and a mile or so out a vessel floated at anchor—a gaudy bright cluster of lights on dark water. At Harald Ericsson's command the Viking ship arrowed toward it, great sweeps barely rippling the waves as the long, sleek hull closed in—a lithe, dark predator closing on a fat, grazing beast. It was from that prey that the fascinating sounds came. Loud voices and laughter. Lively strains of exotic music and the lovely, laughing tones of women.

"Odin's giftings come oddly parceled," Invar Crovansson told himself. His proud young beard parted in a grin of pure, savage Viking delight.

By the time anyone aboard the yacht *ParTTym*, Cozy Maselli's floating pleasure palace, noticed *Erethlyn*, the dragonship was alongside and setting grapples. By then it was too late for any meaningful reaction. A dozen Vikings had already stormed aboard the yacht, and more were coming over the rails.

Rocco Gianelli was just coming out of the forward salon when shouting intruders confronted him. As Cozy's top hammer, rash action had never been Rocco's style, but then Rocco had never before encountered howling wild men waving swords and axes. He panicked. The first shot from his little .380 went wild, the second ricocheted off a polished bronze shield, and the third took off a piece of Gunthar Crom's left ear. Rocco never pulled a trigger again. Gunthar's ax split him from collarbone to belly button, and his body was still twitching when it sailed over the port rail and into the water beyond.

Luca Corsini skidded around the forward bulkhead and ran headlong into Invar Crovansson. The Norseman grunted in surprise and backed away a step, and Luca's instincts took over. Fifteen years in the ring had left their imprint on "the Sicilian Bull." He crouched, sprang, and twisted, knocking the young Viking's sword and shield aside, then put all his weight into a straight-arm belly punch to the solar plexus.

It was like hitting a wall. For an instant, the blond intruder stared at him, looking perplexed, then his beard split and strong teeth glinted in a grin of pure glee. *"Var Wikingr!"* he shouted. He dropped his sword and shield, feinted to one side, and iron fingers closed on Luca's scalp. The Sicilian's head went down, Invar's knee came up, and cartilage crunched. Dazed and half-blinded, the Bull felt himself lifted, flipped and tumbling, then cold water closed around him.

"Invar!" Harald Ericsson shouted. "Tend to business! We're here to plunder, not to play!"

It was all over in a minute or two. Cozy Maselli's remaining muscle, along with every other man aboard *ParTTym*—crew, guests, and dealers—were herded together on the afterdeck, stripped of their watches, rings, and other shiny baubles, and thrown overboard. Their shouting and splashing annoyed Harald Ericsson, so he cut the lifts on a little boat dangling from stern davits and dropped it among them. Then the Vikings turned their attention to the yacht itself and its remaining occupants.

Harald strode the vessel from stem to stern, his eyes glowing with delight beneath his studded helm. "No sail," he muttered. "But a dragon in its belly. How does a man make a dragon swim?"

On the afterdeck Glome Lodbrok peered at a little mushroom of bright light, touched it carefully, then grasped it and grunted. It was small, but extremely heavy. Heavier than his sword, shield, and ax combined. Yet when he held it before him and turned the metal collar at its midriff, the light dimmed and its weight decreased. When it was fully dark, it weighed no more than a fling-stone.

"Magic," he growled, putting the thing down carefully.

Beside him the skald Healfdeane peered at the little device, then at others like it, shining brightly here and there. "No magic," he decided. "Only craft." He raised his bearded, scarred face, and his nostrils twitched. "There are people everywhere," he growled.

In the main salon, Invar Crovansson looked around curiously at the various meaningless furnishings of the place, then focused on a huddle of scantily clad women in one corner. They wore a variety of sheer, ridiculous little garments and adornments, and their perfume filled the air. They stared back at the strapping, bearded young giant, and the others crowding in behind him, and their eyes were as big as walnuts.

Invar's eyes narrowed, his grin widened in pure delight, and he cast aside his trapments and strode forward, singling out two or three of the lovelies for starters. "Valhalla!" he muttered. "Odin, I am here!"

Of them all, at that moment, only Healfdeane remained preoccupied with the question that had plagued him since the fog: Where are we and how did we get here?

Rock Ford, Ohio
The Present

Cindy Bruce was three miles out of Rock Ford, turning on the interstate ramp, when the fog closed around the Buick. She glanced at Norma Jean, beside her. The little girl had her seat belt snugged. Cindy completed her turn, accelerated, and squinted. Around her, the ramp seemed to fade away into a thick obscurity. Fifty yards up the ramp, she couldn't even see the merge lanes ahead. "Thick," she muttered, easing back on the accelerator. It wouldn't last long, she knew. It was just a wisp of fog, and the atmosphere beyond it was clear.

"It looks funny, Mommy," Norma Jean whimpered. "It . . . feels funny, too."

Cindy leaned forward, squinting. Abruptly, the fog had grown very dense and dark. "It's all right, baby—" she started. The car seemed to buck and spin then, and brilliant flashes lit the fog like chain-fire lightning. Beyond the windshield was only darkness, an impenetrable curtain. Cindy hit the brakes, and there was no response. It was as though the car was in midair, its wheels not on any surface. She gasped, and the air was cold as winter ice.

Suddenly there was daylight and a fury of abrupt motion. The old car crunched and shuddered, bounding over rough ground, and skidded as its brakes took hold. A tree trunk loomed ahead, and the car halted, its front bumper touching the rough bark.

Norma Jean strained upward, twisting to look out the windows. "What happened, Mommy?"

White-faced and shaken, Cindy pushed her door open, staggered from the Buick, and gaped at the world around her. Crisp morning sunlight bathed a rolling land of groves and meadows, and a light, spring-scented breeze tousled her hair.

There was no road! No on-ramp, no interstate ahead, no verge of fenced cornfields, no cable towers nearby—nothing but the open, rolling land and the colors of spring.

Norma Jean clambered from the car behind her and crowded against her, gaping at the surroundings. Her voice was barely audible as she gasped, "Mommy . . . where are we?"

Cindy turned full circle, dazed and confused. "I don't know, baby. I just don't know. Do you see anybody? Anything? . . ."

"No," the girl said slowly. "But there's a house over there."

Cindy turned again. Where Norma Jean pointed, the grove thinned and beyond it was a slope. Up on that slope was a house—an odd-looking, slanted house, but it was definitely a house.

"Where the heck are we?" she muttered. "How did we get here?"

Elsewhen

Ben Culver awakened to the sound of someone rapping at his front door. Half-awake, he stretched, yawned, rolled over, and pitched headlong out of bed. Shoulder and hip, he landed on a precarious throw rug, which skidded away down the incline of a slanting hardwood floor. Ben yelped and crashed into a dresser, grabbed a drawer handle in panic, and caromed aside, taking the drawer with him. He thudded against a wall, cursed, and looked around. The whole room was at a fifteen-degree slant.

Then he remembered. And wished he hadn't. Morning sunlight poured through his open south window, which obviously didn't face south anymore. Beyond he glimpsed the new spring leaves of cottonwood trees, and beyond them a blue, cheery sky.

"Shit," he muttered. The night was gone. The sun was shining. It was time to try to figure out where he was now and why he was there . . . if he could.

Again the insistent rapping sounded. What are they using? he wondered. A baseball bat? "Just a damn minute!" he shouted. "I'm coming!"

Negotiating the sloped floors carefully, he worked his way down to the front door and pulled it open. Bracing himself on the frame, holding the heavy door open against its will, he looked out. The front porch slab was a split ruin, bits of six-inch concrete dangling from bent rebar, and the ground was five or six feet below it. And on that ground stood a young woman and a little girl, staring up at him. The woman held a long, bent stick, which he supposed she had used to bang on his door.

He started to say something, then stopped, his eyes sliding to the left, along the slope beyond. He *knew* that slope. Holding the reluctant door open, he leaned outward, gazing around. "I'll be damned," he muttered.

Below him the woman with the stick called, "Mister? Hey, can you tell me where—"

"Just a minute," he said. He pulled himself back inside and turned. The door, released, closed with a resounding bang. Quickly he climbed the floor to a tilted dresser, found a ball of twine, and returned. He opened the door again and tied it open, then squatted on the stub of the broken porch. "Excuse me," he said. "Uh, did you happen to notice if there's a river over there, a mile or so away?"

"I don't know," she said. "I don't even know where we are!"

"I think I do." Ben cocked his head. "I think this is Pauls Valley, Oklahoma. South Oakhill Street, on the slope of Jackson Hill. This is where it should be, anyway. Doesn't look like Pauls Valley is here, right now."

He found a ladder, set it against the broken stoop, and climbed down. "Hi," he said. "I'm Ben Culver, and this is my house. Who are you?"

Norma Jean suddenly chirped, sidled around her mother, and pointed. Fifty yards away, a large, dark animal ambled from thickets into the high grass of the open meadow and stood tall on its hind legs, sniffing the air.

"It's a bear, Momma," Norma Jean said.

"Let's go inside," Ben suggested.

Cindy was already scrambling up the ladder, herding Norma Jean ahead of her.

"It's about time," Ben Culver stated abruptly, hauling his ladder into the living room. When it was in, he released his twine and the door slammed shut with a satisfying crash. Ben stepped to a window and peered out. The curious bear had seen enough. It was ambling away, across the hillside.

Norma Jean peered around curiously at the peculiar, tilted house, then knelt beside a little mushroom-shaped device lying against a downhill wall. Her fingers touched it, turned its midriff collar, and one end of it glowed brightly. "FIRElight," she mused. "Momma, he has FIRElights."

"What do you mean, 'about time'?" Cindy Bruce asked suspiciously.

"That's what all this is about." Ben glanced around. "It's about time. It *has* to be. My God, it might be hundreds of years ago out there. No telling *when* it is, but it sure isn't now anymore. That's what I did when I . . . when I did that thing."

"What thing?"

"A sort of flip of the mind. I—I tried to do something. I thought I could, and I guess I did, but maybe I missed. But I did figure out what this is all about. It's about time. I wasn't just waking up *there*, all those times. I was waking up *then*. The *where* sort of tags along with the *when*, if you see what I mean. But then I tried to do it intentionally, but I guess I haven't quite got the hang of it because I'm *here*, all right, but I'm not *now* anymore. Uh . . . how did you two get here? You weren't already here, were you?"

Cindy stared at the tousled, perplexed man standing dejectedly on the sloping floor of a slanted house in a wilderness where bears were, and hadn't the vaguest idea how to answer his question. The only thing that occurred to her to say was, "We have a car. It's down the hill a ways. It was so foggy, I don't know where the road went."

Norma Jean had wandered into the kitchen, scrambling up the slope of the slanted floor. She returned, but now she was chanting—rhythmic, monotonous syllables in a voice unlike her usual childish chatter. Steadily, slowly she approached them, staring sightlessly like one in a trance. Cradled in her arms was the lustrous cone, which now glowed faintly with a pulsing radiance.

"Nine-six-six-three," the girl intoned, "east nine-six-six-three, spinward nine-six-six-three, *adjust*. Nine-nine distant, nine-nine far, nine-nine, *adjust*. Fall two-four-zero-zero. Down two-four-zero-zero, *adjust*. Tee plus two-eight-nine-eight, two-eight-nine-eight, tee return, tee adjust to zero . . ."

"What—what's she saying?" Cindy whispered.

Ben's eyes were tightly closed, his head down in concentration. "Vectors," he said. "It's vectors!" He shuddered, staring now at the little girl. "She hears it, too!" With a lunge, he snatched the cone from Norma Jean, yanked the front door open, and threw the thing outside.

Norma Jean seemed to snap out of her trance. She staggered on the sloping floor, then rushed to her mother and clung to her, wide-eyed.

Culver turned, visibly shaken. "Did you ever see a—a cloud that reminded you of a song?" he asked. "Or maybe smell something that made you think of colors?"

Cindy shrugged. "Of course. I—"

"Well, it's like that. Those numbers the kid was saying, they were like a compass, or a road sign, or a map. They made me think of motion . . . like the instant you fire a rifle at a range target . . . it's so far away and so small, but in your scope it's close, and you just sort of 'think' the bullet toward the bull's-eye."

Cindy stared at him, bewildered.

"Vectors!" he repeated. "Don't you see? That thing . . . that cone thing, it's like a scope, in your mind. It says point this way—Aw, hell! You can't understand unless you know about it." Shaking his head, he plopped into a chair, which immediately slid down the floor to thump against the front wall.

"That thing talks to you?" Cindy gaped.

"Well, yeah. It sort of did, when I did that mind thing, like I dream about. It was sort of like it wanted me to go this way, and this way, and this way and some other way, all at once. But I didn't want to, and then here I was."

"It said numbers to you?"

"No. But when the kid said them, they . . . well, they sounded . . . they *felt* like what it wanted me to do. Only I didn't want to. I—I think I've been there before. It's where I first saw one of those cone things—then I dreamed about a railroad roundhouse and came home with that one out there. But the place it wants me to go . . . it's a really bad place. I don't want to go there again."

Without municipal utilities, nothing worked in the house. Appliances, faucets, toilets—everything was dead except the two little FIRElights. They made a meal of cold, canned chili and corn chips, then went exploring. Because it was a wilderness, Ben carried the assault rifle he had brought back from his latest sleepwalk. His old shotgun had only quail loads, and he doubted bird shot would deter bears.

Cindy got her old car started, and Ben blazed a trail for her to bring it up to the house. They found the Washita River and Rush Creek, and Ben knew for sure where they were. This would be Smith Paul's land some day. Paul's Valley. But it wasn't yet.

They stood atop Jackson Hill, and Ben said, "Jackson School will be right here."

"Will there be a lot of children?" Norma Jean wondered.

He nodded. "Lots."

"I think you'd better do something about this," Cindy decided. Her tone said, You got us into this mess, now you get us out of it.

"I guess I can try," he said. "Later."

"Why later? Why not right now?"

Ben watched Norma Jean scampering off toward his slanted house. "Scares me," he said. "Maybe if I hang on to both of you, I can do it again, get us all somewhere else . . . or some*when* else. But some whens I've seen, I don't want to see again. One especially. That cone thing . . . I had it when I went there. I don't want to go there again."

"Why are you so afraid of that place?" Cindy glared at him. "I mean, if you've been there before—"

"I have," he said. "At least in a dream. First I was in a railroad place, and I guess I picked up that cone there. But then I was somewhere else. It was a tomb, or a mausoleum or something, and there was someone . . . something there. Something that kills . . . that enjoys killing. Something angry. I've never seen such anger."

"What kind of something?"

"Like a short, malevolent person with no hair. But what I remember is the rage it had. That's why I'm afraid of it. I feel like that was a real place, and that thing is still waiting there. It wants me to come back. Somebody . . . or something . . . Do you believe in good and evil?"

"I guess so. Why?"

"Well, I believe now, because I've seen evil."

Houston, Texas
The Present

There were no reports of missing or stolen .308 rifle cartridges. There were the usual stolen-gun reports, thefts from pawnshops, and inventories of property stolen by burglars, but no one was presently missing a Weatherby .300 magnum. And there were no wants, warrants, or even outstanding traffic tickets against Billy Bluefoot. No match was found for his fingerprints, and no posters matched his face or his description.

The place where he was picked up was in the Astrodome area and thus an accepted pedestrian zone. The loaded rifle in his possession was a legal, full-length sporting weapon, carried in plain view, and he had not fired it.

He wasn't inebriated, he hadn't resisted arrest, and even though most of his answers made no sense, he had willingly submitted to interrogation.

In short, there was no reason to detain him beyond twenty-four hours, so they let him go.

"If I were you," Sergeant Larry Jones suggested, returning Billy's belongings to him, "I'd take all that stuff to a gun dealer and sell it, then use the money to get back to wherever you came from. Houston's a tough town, for outsiders. You keep carryin' all that around here, somebody's going to take it away from you one way or another."

"Thanks," Billy said. "I've dealt with scags before. Where's the nearest gun dealer?"

Watching him go, Jones grinned at two off-duty patrolmen still hanging around the booking desk. "Indian," he said. "Bet you ten he's off some reservation out in New Mexico, and some chief back there is wonderin' what happened to the tribe's ammunition supply."

"They let Indians keep guns on those reservations?"

"Don't know why not. They got their own governments, they can do anything they want to."

"Well, if he might have stolen that stuff there, why didn't we check Bureau of Indian Affairs?"

"They don't know anything." Jones shrugged. "Those Indians don't tell them anything. An Indian reservation is like a foreign country, Jim. They don't report anything they don't want to, and that includes felony warrants. Reservations are outside of state jurisdiction. The city of Houston and the state of Texas have nothing on Mr. Bluefoot, so he's free to do whatever he wants."

Billy had never seen paper money, but he had read about it. Back before he was born, in the time he seemed to be in now, it had been the common medium of exchange. It had even been referred to as "the greatest of accepted lies."

Now, stepping out of Lone Star Sporting Goods, he had several specimens of 1990s currency in his pocket. He walked around for a time, looking and listening, letting his senses test the surroundings—Houston, Texas, premillennium. It was a huge city, still viable and bustling—a monstrous beast spinning global webs, luring to itself all the commodities generated by global resource and human effort. Like a great spider it worked at luring people and their valuables to its lair, where it consumed everything and excreted money.

No one of Billy Bluefoot's time had ever seen a functioning big city. With the paper panics and the world trust collapse, such monstrosities had lost their means of survival. But he found it fascinating—dozens and hundreds of little, integral towns all crammed together, bound and interwoven by great networks of expressways, feeder roads, park corridors, utility systems, and a brittle, suspicious social order serving as a binder.

Where the expressways went, people afoot did not. Meandering the paved pedestrian paths, away from the whining herds of vehicles on the main roads, he found himself in less and less elegant surroundings. Gates and barred windows made little fortresses of dwellings and commercial places. There were people everywhere, their aura that of endless desperation. Furtively, suspiciously, they shared the limits of common space. Some of them smiled on cue, few displayed open hostility. But Billy sensed that amiability in this place was paper-thin, as though the natural rhythms of city life were set to a discordant cacophony of snare drums and clashing cymbals.

Billy had no inkling of how he'd come to be here, but life was full of mysteries and he was pragmatic about it. Finding himself in south central Texas, in the long-ago world of the late twentieth century, he accepted where and when he was and went sightseeing.

Still, as a long day wore into evening, he felt homesick for his own, familiar surroundings. Sure, the mountains out there were full of scags and rebels. There were predators and scavengers and occasional sudden, deadly sorties by the king's AATVs. But still there was a serenity about it that he missed.

Here there was no serenity. These people, he suspected, lived out their lives in high stress. The emotions he sensed around him were narrow and overlaid by secrecy, hostility, and fear.

Like caged rats, he thought. Too many rats, too little space. It was a wonder they didn't all go berserk and kill one another. They did that, of course. It was the normal weeding process of an urban environment. The vicious weed out the vulnerable, the ruthless prevail, and only the strongest survive for any length of time. But there was a sort of order about the process. Random acts of violence were of no benefit to the beast. Bloodletting was condoned only when it aided the digestive process or provided an entertainment for the public.

The mechanics of urban life.

Billy found food at a small restaurant in a decaying strip center, and sensed the keen attention of some around him when he displayed his currency to pay the bill. As he left the place, he knew that a signal had been sent and predators were watching.

Scags, he thought grimly. Yes, there are always scags.

He walked to the end of the strip center, noticing that the illumination dimmed with each few steps. Not hiding his movements, he turned, stepped into a trash-littered cul-de-sac alleyway, and waited.

It didn't take long. He saw three and knew there were more. They entered the alleyway furtively, assured yet cautious, analyzed the situation, and spread, facing him. They were young, dark-skinned, and bug-eyed arrogant, and there were little similarities in their garb. Gangies, Billy thought, remembering something he had seen on an old tape. There used to be gangs in cities, and sure enough, here were some gangies.

"Gots us a booter," the center one said, grinning. "Hey, man, this Poley turf. Turf got tolls. That be some fine green you got there, but it ours, now."

"You're probably right." Billy shrugged. Slowly, showing no menace, he pulled out his currency and held it toward the robber, stepping forward. As the kid's hand lashed out to take it, Billy ducked and spun. His sudden move swept the gangie's feet from under him, and Billy's boot took him full in the face as he fell. Without losing momentum, he ducked to the right, kicked the one there in the kneecap, and sprang like a panther at the third. As he expected, the startled robber swayed to the side, ducking—directly into a solid fist whose swing had begun three yards away.

All three were down, but the one with the broken knee was not out. Cursing and spitting, he pulled a gun from his coat. Almost casually, Billy Bluefoot stepped across and broke the tough's wrist, relieving him of his handgun in the same motion.

"You boys were born too soon," he muttered. He took a step away, then dropped low. Gunshots echoed as bullets chipped a brick wall above him.

Scuffling sounds and a solid thud came from the cover where the shooter was, and he saw a gangie pitch from the shadows at the alley's entrance. Nose down, the thug skidded across a yard of wet, filthy concrete and lay still. Behind him a tall, laconic figure in a long coat stepped into view and gazed around. "That was all of them," he said. "Hello. I'm Adam. Obviously you aren't Ben Culver. So who are you, and how did you get to this time?"

"A fog." Billy Bluefoot stood. "There was a fog."

"Well, that's a lead." The newcomer shrugged. He was taller by a head than Billy, but of about the same age. Dark, shaggy hair, piercing eyes, and an ironic half smile. A formidable man, Billy felt, but not a hostile one.

"How did you know that fourth one was there?" Adam asked. "You couldn't see him."

"I . . . I felt him. Same way I knew you were there. You've been following me, just like they were."

Adam raised a brow, studying him. "Handy skill, that," he said.

"Sometimes it's useful. Helps to know who your friends are. But why don't *you* tell *me* how I got here. You seem to know more about it than I do."

Adam stooped, picked up a gun one of the robbers had dropped, and handed it to Billy. "Keep this one," he said. "It's a Glock nine millimeter. Better than that piece of junk you picked up."

The punk with the fractures was writhing and crying now, and Adam glanced down at him. "You boys should have stayed in school," he said casually. Then, to Billy, "You're not a timer, are you! But you're not from now. How did you get here?"

"Wish to hell I knew." Billy shrugged. "I went into a fog, and came out somewhere else."

The punk with the fractures was groaning and whimpering piteously. "We'll talk someplace quieter," Adam suggested. He extended a friendly hand and Billy took it, sensing no enmity there. Strong fingers clasped his, and suddenly the alleyway and everything in it seemed to slow, to darken toward oblivion. It ended as abruptly, in an instant of pure, brilliant light.

The one hoodlum still conscious, the one with the shattered knee and broken wrist, lay moaning and gasping, his pain blending with his outrage at his victim's retaliation. They weren't supposed to fight back. They— He gasped. The two men had been standing directly over him. He was sure of it. They had been right here! But now they were gone, as though they had never been there at all.

∞

What is it that makes man human? Certainly we are not so different, physically, from the other creatures who share our world with us. We are blood and bone and transient flesh. We are born, we struggle, we mature, we reproduce if we can, we nurture and teach the young, we spend diminishing resources of vitality on increasingly tenuous survival and—inevitably—we die.

We seek, and never truly find, a reason for it all.

The creationist asks, If we are in God's image, then why are we so imperfect? Why did He leave us so? The evolutionist asks, Why are we so acutely aware of our shortcomings, yet not improving ourselves to resolve them? Why are we not what we know we could be?

These are both the same question:

Why aren't we better than we are?

How, then, are we different?

It is not in any physical ability that man excels. We are not fast, or strong, or graceful. We lack wings, fangs, talons, stingers, and hooves. We have no inherent specialties, no special skills or weapons or camouflage. We possess no exceptional characteristics at all that are not equaled or exceeded by a myriad of other living things.

But the mind! The mind of man! In that, we are unique. Alone on this earth, we question the unseeable, consider the unthinkable, and quantify the intangible. Of all creatures sharing this biosphere, only mankind can and does wonder, *Why am I not better than I am?*

The mind that can ask this question is the mind that can become better. The only obstacles are those imagined, those believed, and those we ourselves create for one another.

To master the universe is to master one's own mind. They are, for each of us, one and the same.

—JOHN THOMAS WOLF, *Gateways*

∞

VI
The Unleashed
Time Loop L-383

"This is remarkable!" Teal Fordeen paced before a vivid virtual-reality screen, oblivious to the wonders of its holographic display—revolving cross sections of a stellar galaxy. Less than five feet tall and totally bald, the chief Whisper fairly radiated concentration as he paced. His large, thoughtful eyes glowed with un-Whisper-like excitement. "Fog, you say? Fog, as in condensed atmospheric moisture?"

"A fog," Billy Bluefoot repeated. "Plain old wet, cold fog, thick as sheep's wool." He gazed around him at the "place" Adam had brought him—a place like no place at all. And people like none he had ever seen. *Yunh'wi tsunsdi,* the old ones might have called them. The *little people* of old legend. But these weren't legends. These were busy, big-eyed, hairless little people, and the place that was no place was full of them.

Billy liked the Whispers immediately. They fairly radiated a warm, quick intelligence—an intelligence that blended curiosity, unabashed wonder, and shrewd calculation in a mix that had no taste of meanness about it. And, once he got used to the bald heads and oversized eyes, he found them quite pretty.

Whispers, Adam called them, and Whispers they were. The *yunh'wi tsunsdi* were Whispers. Billy would have bet his boots that somewhere back there, in the time of the old ones, his own Cherokee ancestors had known that.

He sensed a presence and turned, glancing down. One of the Whispers, the little female called Toocie Toonine, was beside him, looking up at him curiously. "You're perceptive," she said. "Do you sense thoughts?"

He shook his head. "I don't think so. Wish I could, though."

Another one, Deem Eleveno, turned from a console of some kind. "We've tracked his event, Teal. In A.D. 2023. It shows as an isolated atmospheric condition, one-ninety-one degrees at three-point-one to point-three miles, plus gradient, southwest of Prescott, Arizona."

One of the screening virtual displays went blank and was replaced by a vivid, three-dimensional aerial view of pine-clad mountains where an old, once-paved road snaked toward a cluster of structures. Symbols that Billy took to be coordinates blipped in midair above the scene, and he stepped closer, squinting. "There's my rover!" He pointed. "That's old Highway 89, and there's that pile of junk, right where I left it. See, I went up the road here, around Eagle Bend, and the fog was— There it is, there in that cove. See it?"

"I see it," Adam said, moving to stand beside him. "I see something else, too. A time transfer. You went to Houston, just then." He turned to Deem Eleveno. "Can you do a meteorologic search, for other fogs like that?"

"We already did," the Whisper said, slightly offended. "We are not simpletons, Adam. We found sixteen similar incidents, scattered all over the globe and all over time. No apparent relativity in T2, but they all involved an anomalous salient thermal change resulting in fog, and a spontaneous photogravitational reversal."

"How do they relate in T1? Is there a pattern?"

Deem's little fingers danced on a console pad, and symbols scrolled across a display. "Random, but with a certain symmetry," he mused. "What do we match it to?"

"Sleepwalker," Teal Fordeen suggested.

Again Deem tapped the pad, and the scrolling symbols suddenly became orderly columns. "That's it!" Deem said. "There are four . . . no, five . . . six obvious matches!"

They moved around to peer at the Whisper's monitor device, and Billy squinted. The arrays of columns, graphs, and sequence spirals displayed there were dizzying. But there did seem to be a pattern within it, and he found he could almost grasp its meanings.

"Here, here, here—" Deem pointed, indicating intersecting spirals where tiny scrolls of figures and symbols danced. "Here are the atmospherics, and here are the quadrations of episodes. In durational time, each of these atmospheric anomalies coincides with a Sleepwalker episode. The terrestrial and temporal locations are different, but the occurrences match."

"Ben Culver has left some interesting tracks," Adam mused. "What of these other anomalies? They have similar characteristics."

"They don't all match." Deem shrugged. "A few of them are obviously separate phenomena, by durational proximity." He pointed at the monitor again, selecting phenomena. "This event, for instance, could not have been connected with the same source, because these two—this and this—form a durational sequence that excludes it.

"By the way," Deem said, "we completed the verifications you suggested, on all existing TEFs. They are all authentic, according to inventory."

"There was one thing, though," Teal Fordeen added. "The TEF you took from 1KHAF4, the original drive TEF of Time Loop L-270, was thoroughly inspected after you retrieved it. It had been tampered with. UEB surmised that Kaffer had attempted to modify its molecular resonance. Traces of the attempt were found in the structure of its shell. Certain long-molecule resins were realigned to radiant strands, like a sensory transmitter. But it was only a stratance effect and didn't get past the shell. The TEF has no sensory attunement.

"UEB believes Kaffer was trying to make a beacon of his TEF . . . a carrier. They suggest he may have tried to infuse it with some sort of psi-factor command. But obviously he failed. It remains as it was, only a TEF. It has since been tested again, and reassigned."

"Psi?" Adam muttered thoughtfully. "You mean Kaffer tried to give it *mentalist* powers?"

"It seems so." Teal nodded. "UEB thinks he may have toyed with some sort of telepathy. Kaffer was, after all, probably the world's foremost authority on the workings of the human brain."

"I know." Adam's eyes narrowed. "I saw the remains of some of his experiments. Where is that TEF now?"

"Leapfrog Waystop, 1887," Teal said. "1RT6Beta—Artee Six—is installing it for the indigenous operator there, one Faron Briscoe."

"Telepathic resonance in a TEF?" Adam muttered. He glanced across at Toocie Toonine thoughtfully, then turned his attention to Billy Bluefoot, who was still exploring the virtual-reality holograph of the mountains around Prescott. Billy had located the old White Spar campgrounds. He leaned close, peering at the exquisite detail of the display.

"Scags," Billy muttered. "So *that's* where they base."

Without looking directly at him, Adam concentrated on Billy, calling up feelings of intense hostility and focusing them on the unaware man. Instantly, Billy turned, backed away a step, and braced himself, defensively. Adam nodded. "Did you see it, Toocie?"

"He is obviously a percept," the little Whisper said. "What did you do?"

"I thought about killing him." Adam shrugged.

Billy gawked at the taller man. "Why? What did I do?"

"I just wanted to see if you'd react to intent," Adam said. "Those street punks in Houston, how did you know about them? And about me?"

"I don't know," Billy admitted. "I just know things like that. In my business, it's handy. There are always scags."

"I can see how it might be useful. Teal, I'd like some sensitivity testing on this man. Telepathy, telekinesis, teleportation, precognition . . . range of perception, proximity sense, hostility-empathy awareness, the whole ESP battery. Can you people do that? And maybe a catalog of characteristics of ESPers in general?"

"I suppose we can provide that." Teal Fordeen shrugged. "Extrasensory perception was widely researched in the period leading up to the second millennium, so I'm sure there is a substantial body of knowledge on record. Is this to help you find Ben Culver?"

"Partly," Adam said. "And maybe more than Culver. I have a feeling about those atmospheric blips. I think Ben Culver is part of something a whole lot bigger than just being lost. And I have a hunch. You may have been right about Kaffer, Teal. It might have been better to kill him than to imprison him. There's something about this Ben Culver thing, this whole Sleepwalker business . . . I keep having the feeling that Kaffer might still be around."

"Who is Kaffer?" Billy Bluefoot asked, sensing the revulsion of those around him.

"I want to check out some of those other 'fogs,' " Adam told Teal Fordeen. "Mandy might be interested, too. Let's run your ESP tests, then I'll take Billy with me. Maybe it's time for two pairs of eyes."

The Great Pyramids
Giza, Egypt

In a place of silent shadows, surrounded by stench and impenetrable stone, the creature lurked, waiting. Though imprisoned within the massive stone of an ancient tomb, 1KHAF4 was not without resources. Time Loop L-270, the first devised phenomenon to penetrate the Arthurian Anachronism and explore upstream time prior to A.D. 2050, had been well provisioned for a crew that numbered nearly a hundred people—Pacificans from the year 2999, members of the World History Investigative Society, and a few observers from the sponsoring Universal Experience Bank of Pacifica. Now these provisions were at Kaffer's disposal. Most of the time loop's contents were beyond his reach—embedded now where they had materialized, within the porous stone of the pyramid itself—but he had enough to last him for a long time.

L-270 no longer existed. An indigenous timer known only as Adam had lured Kaffer into a trap—the Pyramid of Khafre—and used steel cable to disrupt the integrity of the temporal loop.

It was ironic, in a way, that it was a primitive who destroyed the great mastermind's plan to create an infinity with himself as its creator and beneficiary. A *timer*! One of those rare individuals of antepoluvian time who had the gift of dimensional insight. 1KHAF4 had devoted extensive energy to finding, analyzing, and exterminating timers. They did not fit his plans for the future.

But then it was one of *them* who foiled him! Kaffer's own contemporaries—Pacifican scientists from the trimillennium era—had exhausted their technology in their attempt to neutralize the rogue historian. Using their own time loop, the torus L-383, they had threatened to encase and engulf L-270. A futile attempt. There had been a way out, and 1KHAF4 found it. The Pyramid of Khafre was Kaffer's shield.

But then that timer . . . that Adam . . . had made a trap of the shield, and L-270 was no more.

Now Kaffer paced the shadowed floor of a concealed crypt, deep within the massive stone monument, and waited. They had imprisoned him, humiliated him! But they had underestimated him. His researches into the phenomenon of four-dimensional autonomic transference had fallen short of their goal. He had not managed to equip himself with timing ability.

But his tireless studies—the numerous dissections he had done, submicroscopic examination of the brains of infant temporal adepts—had given him other knowledge. He had learned the cerebral mechanics behind some of those abilities the ancients called extrasensory perception, and he had made use of those. The source of such energies was in the brain, and its activation had a measurable range of resonance patterns. A perfect receptacle for such resonance codes, he found, was the surface substance of a temporal effect focalizer. He had experimented with L-270's own TEF, before it disappeared, and the implanted resonance he had chosen—the TEF's own locational alignment—was the quadridimensional coordinates of this very place. To any percept exposed to that TEF, its hull would emit a command—a command to focus vectors to this point—the King's Chamber inside the Pyramid of Khafre. Maybe—just possibly—he could draw a timer to him, and maybe he could make that timer return his TEF.

It had been only an experiment, not a plan. He had used the

TEF because its casing was the only material he had at hand that could accept resonance imprint. He had not really hoped that its stratance would lure a fish.

But it had proven itself dramatically. Almost before 1KHAF4 had realized that L-270 was gone, a man had appeared, standing dazedly in this very vault. The man was a primitive, and obviously a timer, yet he appeared to have been walking in his sleep. And under his arm he carried a TEF. Before Kaffer could reach him, though, the man was gone again, and with him the TEF. But Kaffer knew then what had occurred.

And now he knew the answer to the question that had eluded him before—the power that natural timers had, the ability to travel at will along alternate time-place vectors. It was a variation of the ESP trait.

Timing was teleportation—the ultimate psi power, the mark of the fully evolved extrasensory percept. And because of the peculiar variant skill of the natural timer, it was four dimensional! Certainly not all ESPers were timers, but all timers were ESPers! It explained everything Kaffer had tried to learn through research. Like the psychic abilities found among some protomorphs—empathic touch and precognition, telepathy and telekinesis—the timer's ability originated in the neurological structure of the brain itself—the evolutionary extension of the sympathetic nervous system to the environment.

Studying dissected brains under his microscanners, Kaffer had seen the physical mechanics of it. Now he knew what it was that he had seen there. And now he knew his path of escape.

A timer had the missing TEF, and would sense the TEF's command. The TEF—L-270's TEF—was Kaffer's, and he knew it was in the hands of one who was capable of returning it to him. Kaffer could not regenerate L-270. But with a TEF in the old time loop's empty electromagnetic nest, Kaffer could escape this place. He had already cannibalized L-270's drive module and rebuilt the components into a workable photo-gravitational analog chamber. And he had programmed a comlink. With a TEF, he could go anywhere. Anywhere and any*when*!

He knew the TEF would come back to him. All he had to do was wait. The timer carrying it—who would deliver it to him—

was no problem. Kaffer had killed timers before. Counting the Pacifican crew of L-270, the infant timers whose deaths he had arranged through his Deltas, and all those indigenees who had fallen before L-270's lightning and zen-guns as he rampaged across the world and across history before being trapped, Kaffer had killed hundreds of people. Maybe thousands, he thought. They meant nothing to him. That timer Adam had called him a psychopath. The simpering Whispers of old L-270 and his nemesis loop, L-383, had said Kaffer was a creature without feeling—without remorse, devoid of empathy. They had declared him not human!

They had cost him his Deltas, too. Those indigenous people he had implanted with cerebral controls, they had been useful to him. But now they were gone—all dead but Delta Four, and she probably was dead, too. It had been her task to trigger the events history would record as the Asian Apocalypse. And she had done her job, in the T2 time vector 2001. Relative to the current now, that time was still a few years in the future. But it had occurred. Kaffer himself had seen the confirmations of the Asian Abyss in 2003. And there had been no way out for Delta Four. Kaffer had no further use for her, beyond that.

Monster, they called him. Remorseless and inhuman. Psychopath.

All of this brought a grim satisfaction to 1KHAF4 as he awaited his ESP-implanted TEF and planned his plans. They hated him, of course. They feared him because he had none of their weakness. In their eyes, to be human was to be hesitant about inflicting pain on others. Kaffer had no such hesitation. Pain was pain only if he felt it, and the pain of others meant nothing to him.

They feared him, and that pleased him. He would show them fear! Once free of this ancient stone, he would show them all! No one on earth understood better than he the intricate webs of history. He would use history as his road to power, and power as the means to subjugate *everyone*. Everyone who had ever been or ever would be.

Let the Whispers dither about the directions of dimensions and the nature of the universe. In their weakness and their stupidity, they settled for studying phenomena, rather than taking it for their own. Kaffer had no such weakness. Whatever this universe might be—intricate weave of dimensionality, delicate balance of forces of light and gravity, or simply a cosmic accident still happening—it would be *his*, and he would use it as it suited him to.

They didn't know what fear was, yet. But they would. Kaffer would see to that. He would escape this prison, then he would attack them where they were most vulnerable—the sequence of historic events from which time travel—*their* time travel—grew.

Let him once get free, and he would alter history to suit himself.

Valley of the Washita
A.D. 1102

Structurally, Ben Culver's house was a disaster. A stick-built residential structure on a concrete foundation of poured portland cement and gravel aggregate, the house might have lasted a hundred years, sitting where it belonged in a residential lot in Pauls Valley, Oklahoma. But it was only a house. It was not built for travel.

The ringwall foundation was cracked in a dozen places, and the concrete-slab garage floor hung from its sagging rebars beneath a stressed and parted roofline, eighteen inches above the stony ground.

They had brought Cindy's old Buick up to the house, as near as possible, but had not even tried to put it in the garage. "I might lay a ramp up there and get it inside," Ben mused. "But it would collapse the floor and that would bring the whole roof down right on top of it. I guess we'll just have to leave it."

"Leave what?" Cindy Bruce demanded. "You mean the car?"

"Don't see any other way." Ben shrugged. "I know I can move the house and everything in it, but I'm pretty sure I can't move anything that's outside."

"Then leave the house," Cindy decided. "We'll take the car. I'm not leaving without my car."

Fifteen or twenty minutes later, Ben conceded. "I've never

met such a stubborn woman in my life!" he grumped, sliding in behind the Buick's wheel.

Cindy got Norma Jean stowed in the backseat, then joined him in the front. "Here are the keys," she said.

"I'm not exactly driving," Ben growled, even as he obediently inserted the key in the ignition. "I'm just going to sit here and try to make something happen."

"What do you mean by that?" she demanded.

"I don't know what I mean! Just hush up and hang on. Here goes!"

He closed his eyes and concentrated, the way he had done before. As it came back to him, he noticed the fantastic intricacy of the patterns that formed in his mind—visions of place and time as though scrolled through a loom, but the loom seemed to extend in all directions and some of the directions weren't directions at all. Latitudes and longitudes rolled by, like exquisite colors interlaced with senses of altitude, terrain, and the flowing motion of points on the face of a spinning globe streaking through nothingness.

Abandoning logic, he let the feelings of the visions control his thoughts, and felt all the latitudes, longitudes, and altitudes combine into a perfect pitch. The vectors of destination blended with the vectors of present location and became one. Now only one dimension remained, and he focused on the now of his orderly life in Pauls Valley. When it seemed all in place he nudged the trigger, that intense, ready sensation in his mind that made things happen.

Even with his eyes closed, he knew the world around was going dark, slowing to absolute, black stillness.

In that instant an unwelcome, uninvited thought penetrated. Like a child's voice, the thought prodded his mental vectors: "Spinward nine-six-six-three, *adjust* . . . fall two-four-zero-zero, *adjust* . . . tee plus two-eight-nine-eight . . . adjust to zero . . ."

No! he thought, but it was too late. A sensation like enormous white light, surging light, driving light, and the Buick bumped as though it had fallen into a hole.

Ben Culver opened his eyes. All around the car were shadows, and a feeling of ancient immensity. Stone walls! Stone all around, stone above and below . . . a vaulted place like a stone box, in which shadows hung. And in the shadows a shadow moved.

"No!" Ben screamed. Swiveling around, he stared at Norma Jean. The child sat as though dazed, cradling a pulsing cone in her arms.

Behind the Buick, a small shadow rose and a flicker of ruby light touched the Buick's window. With a hiss, Ben ducked, hauling Cindy down with him. Where he had sat, a blue beam of pure energy sizzled through the car from rear to front, and beyond the car ancient stone erupted into sparks and magma.

Ben turned the ignition key, heard the engine catch, and shifted into reverse, gunning the engine. The Buick lurched backward a few feet and slammed into a stone wall.

"Take that thing away from her!" he shouted at Cindy. "Get rid of it!"

Again there was a sizzling blue beam, this time from one side, and part of the Buick's roof disappeared.

Cindy wrestled the cone from Norma Jean, and Ben grabbed it. With an oath, he flung it out of the open driver's-side window, then shifted gears and gunned the old car again. As it lurched forward, toward solid stone twenty feet away, he put all his concentration into the panic call, "Away! Away!"

In a rush of frosty air, lightning flashed and thundered. The Buick careened toward stone, then seemed to be spiraling into nothingness—a dense, suffocating fog of eternity.

Crashes and thuds, roars and bumps, and abruptly the old car was on its wheels, tortured rubber howling as it spun sideways, barely missing the flanks of a speeding truck. Other vehicles were approaching, horns blaring, and Ben slewed the car into a quarter turn, narrowly avoiding a gaping culvert and heading for the ditch.

Cars and trucks flashed past as the old car wallowed to a stop, axle-deep in mud. Uselessly, Ben turned off the ignition, then looked around. They were in a wide median between parallel lanes of pavement. A major highway—an interstate—extended away in two directions, shrouded by a deepening fog. The air was cold and growing colder.

"Everybody all right?" he rasped.

"That was pretty." Norma Jean's muffled voice came from behind. "Like before."

"Uh, yeah, we're okay." Cindy's voice was thin with shock. "Th-that thing tried to kill us! Who—what *was* it?"

"Evil," Ben breathed. "The mind thing got us away, I guess, but now that creature has what it wanted." He wrenched the car door open, staring out at the unfamiliar surroundings.

Cindy assured herself that Norma Jean was all right, then stood upright in the car seat. The Buick was a wreck. Parts of it were gone, including most of the roof. "Where are we?"

"I haven't got the least idea," he admitted. "But we're sure not in Oklahoma anymore."

By the time they got out of the car, there were people coming toward them from the roadway—people who had seen the Buick hit the ditch. In the thickening mist, the people seemed remote and vague, even as they hurried toward the Buick. But before any of them arrived, someone else was there. The fog seemed to swirl, to intensify for a moment, and a small man stepped into view as though stepping out of a cloud.

Bright, inquisitive blue eyes and a trimmed gray beard framed the impish features of an irritated leprechaun. The man was short, bowlegged, and sturdy, and his attire—a gray cloak, thrown back from a soft, dove-gray weskit with bright buttons in abundance, a belted, plaid kilt above soft, knee-length boots with buckles at the ankles, and a floppy tam-o'-shanter cap atop his mop of graying hair—was of some other time and place.

He might have been fifty, or seventy, but his keen eyes had a youthful sparkle and there was a quick, cocky air about him that was almost tangible.

"What have you done to my bridge?" he demanded, glaring up at Ben.

Ben gaped at him. "What bridge?"

"My bridge to Convergence," the leprechaun snorted. "Getting so a man can't step through a gate without being shunted aside. Are you the one who's been muddling around with the bridges? I knew there was someone. You must be him. A shifter!"

"I—I haven't seen any bridges," Ben stammered. "Or any gates, either. I don't know what you're talking about."

"It was like a little cloud," Norma Jean chirped, peering from behind her mother. "With sunshine holes in it."

"Aha!" the leprechaun snorted. "The child is my witness. She knows of gates. So it *was* you who interrupted my bridge, with your blasted fogs."

Ben shook his head, completely baffled. "Look," he said, "I'm sorry about the bridge, wherever that is. I don't know what's happening, but it happens a lot. I keep waking up somewhere else. I've been to some of the damnedest places . . ."

The little man cocked his head, as though finding the answer to a riddle. "Unaware," he said. "I might have known. Do you have a name?"

"Ah . . . sure. I'm Ben Culver. This is Cindy, and that's Norma Jean. We've been . . . well, you wouldn't believe where we've been."

"Ben Culver." The small stranger cocked his head, looking upward. "Well, what goes around really does come around, doesn't it? When there's an after, there has to be a before. I'm called Zephyr. I suppose you really *are* a shifter. Someone around here is, and I know it isn't me. I just do bridges." He glanced around at the people approaching from the highway. Lights were flashing on the road, and there was a sound of sirens. "I guess I'd better do one now, since I obviously already did."

Ben gawked at him. "What are you talking about?"

"About bringing you to Convergence, of course! We'll go now, unless you want to try explaining this mess to those people. Just stay in touch, and we'll cross the bridge."

"What bridge?"

"This one." The little man's hand closed on his, and the other hand touched the shoulder of Cindy Bruce, who was holding Norma Jean in her arms. Suddenly the fog was wool-thick, a shrouding mist that hid everything beyond a few yards' radius. The dimness flared with reflected lightning—a chill, blinding fog that seemed to lift them all and carry them away.

Then the fog was gone, as though it had never been there. The approaching people were gone. The highway was gone.

The Buick was gone. In their place were pleasant meadows rippling under a soft breeze—vistas that might have sloped away toward pretty valleys, somewhere beyond the mist of middle distance. They stood on a footpath road, and not far away were wide-spaced buildings—odd-looking, low buildings that seemed mostly roofs with only suggestions of walls. But they were recognizable as types. There was a big barn with shed wings, several cottages, and a large, comfortable-looking house that seemed to be mostly roof and open windows.

Beyond, scattered here and there, were other houses and structures of various kinds. Horses grazed in a distant field, and birds sang overhead. The view was a curving crescent of pastoral serenity, rolling away around the perimeter of a standing fog bank that seemed to occupy all of the center portion of a mist-bounded panorama. The fog was bright, glowing, and immensely high.

It was like being in a fish bowl, Ben thought. The suggestion of limits, and a riddle in the middle. Beside him, Cindy gazed around wide-eyed. "The light's weird," she said. "Like sunlight, but there's no sun. Where does it come from?"

A few people were in sight in the distance, and one of them—a young girl with bright button eyes and a mane of dark, reddish hair—came toward them.

As she approached, Ben decided she was not much older than Norma Jean—a bright, grinning sprite of a girl, twelve or thirteen, sizing up the newcomers with wise eyes. He felt as though he knew her, then realized that it was instant acquaintance. The girl had a presence about her—an almost visible aura—and as she looked at him he felt as though she saw every nuance of his being.

"Travelers, aye?" Her speech was almost song, thick and lyric with something resembling—but not quite—a Gaelic brogue. " 'Ello, I'm Molly, be names like to matter." She scampered around Ben, a little bundle of bright energy, scrutinizing him.

"I think I've brought the first shifter, Molly," Zephyr said. "He must be. His name's Ben Culver. A late developer, and unaware."

The girl's bright eyes seemed to measure Ben, and in his mind he had the sensation of curious, exploring fingers touching the surfaces of his thoughts—feather-light touches that startled him, and taught him. Without knowing how he did it, he returned the touches and felt glimmers of a bright, intense curiosity that was not his own. Intertwined with his own intelligence was another intelligence, and he realized it was the mind of the girl. Recoiling with a blink, he rejected the eerie sensation, and between them a little mist of chilled air appeared.

"You've the right of it," Molly said. "He *is* the one. He's like me, the one who was here before me. Frosters, th' both of us!" She touched Ben's hand, dark Gaelic eyes boring into his. "I'll call ye Ben," she said. "I'm Molly."

Before he could respond, her attention left him. He felt it, like quicksilver slipping away. She glanced at Cindy, nodded her approval, then focused on Norma Jean. "Come with me if ye want to, lass. We'll ride the ponies, an' maybe I'll make us a rainbow."

Norma Jean gazed somberly at Molly, then grinned. Like bright, flitting birds they were gone, two little girls skipping across the field toward the barn.

"It's all right," Zephyr told them. "Molly's a good soul, even if she is a pest. She's the first shifter I brought over after you, though that will be years ago after you show me how. Very few can cross between the probabilities alone, without a bridge. You're the only one I know who reached the verge without an escort, even from our side." He gestured toward the glowing fog that stood like a monolith in the middle of this place. "Pulls you here like a magnet, you told me . . . or maybe you'll tell me that another time, earlier."

Cindy stared at both of them, mystified. "Didn't you . . . *didn't you bring us here?*"

"Eventually, yes." Zephyr shrugged. "Though I wouldn't have if your friend hadn't found the verge like he did. I don't know how he managed that alone. It isn't exactly there at all, for most folks."

"Managed *what* alone?" Ben demanded.

"Finding the interface." The little man frowned. "Pay attention! I just told you, you're the first! And since you found it, I had to bring you into Convergence. Otherwise you might have stumbled in anyway, and brought half the population of Oklahoma with you."

"But the girl, Molly . . ."

"Oh, I see, you're obsessed with sequences. Well, don't worry about it. I don't understand it, either. I'm minding my own business, trying to make a bridge to observe the other side. You're the one who's juggling eventualities. Just don't expect hard sequence here. Duration occurs sideways in the interface."

Ben gaped at him, blinked, and gaped again. "What?"

"You're in the interface!" Zephyr snapped impatiently. "The gate. Sequences don't apply to the gate. It's contrary to sequence, because it's sideways! You probably don't even realize that you're a timer, do you?"

"A what?"

"I didn't think so. A timer's logic would balk at the gate. But you do it unaware, so you're not hobbled. So you're a shifter. It's as good a term as any. A timer, like some others of your era, but more than a timer. There are more ways than one, you know, to span eventualities. Anyhow, welcome to Convergence. Maybe somebody here can explain it all to you. I've other things to do. Good-bye." Fog swirled for a moment, and the little man was gone.

Feeling dazed, Ben took a deep breath. "Convergence?" he muttered. "That's the name of this place?"

"Not so much a name as a condition," a flutelike voice piped, behind him. He spun around. Zephyr was gone, but now there were two other little people there, a male and a female. "Z-4 confuses everybody," the female explained. "Hello. I'm Gambit, and this is Jaeff. We're the ones who tell you about all this, so you can tell us about your side."

"This is full circle for us," Jaeff added. "We've done this whole conversation before. But don't worry, we'll get you synchronized. Yes, this is called Convergence. That's what it is."

"What *what* is?"

Jaeff sighed. "This is a place," he said. "A place and a frame of reference. The interface is here. The prime gate, right where we found it nearly fifty years ago. It's the interface. The span of convergence between your reality and ours, and you've crossed it."

"Reality?" Ben felt as though he were swimming in a whirlpool. "Are you telling me we've gone to another world?"

"Well, hardly." Gambit shook her head, and little curls of dark hair danced across her bright eyes. "It's the same old world, of course. The very same planet. How could it be otherwise? We just have different versions of it. You don't know a thing about alternate strands, do you!"

"Alternate . . ."

"Thought not. Well, we'll take it a step at a time, but no history lesson just now. First, let's sort out the sequences. You're the first people Z-4 brought over. Molly came later, with your help. But she arrived first, so the sequences are a bit off. Z-4 isn't very much concerned with sequence. To him it's one thing after another."

"He found you because you were where he linked his bridge." Jaeff took over. "He'll insist you muddled his bridge by being there, but we're not sure of that. Maybe you *were* the bridge. At any rate, he collected you, and later he collected Molly because of you."

Cindy Bruce was tugging at Ben's sleeve. "Let's get the hell out of here," she whispered. "This is crazy."

"Oh, hear us out," Gambit urged her. "This man's a loose kite right now. Until he understands it, he's not safe to have around." She turned her gaze to Ben. "When you understand the alternates . . ." The pixie eyes narrowed. "You really *don't* know what I'm talking about, do you?"

"I haven't the vaguest idea," Ben admitted. "Alternates? What kind of alternates?"

"Alternate *tempora*," Jaeff said. "Parallel histories! By normal standards, eventualities should never coincide. But because of the gate, they have. And with shifters like you running around loose, there must be some order observed."

Cindy was clinging to Ben's arm now, looking dazed. "Do something!" she demanded. "What's this all about? Where are we?"

Gambit had turned away, looking toward the tall, distant wall of fog that hid the nearby hills. Now she turned back and looked up at Cindy with something like sympathy. "You're caught up in a dilemma, eh? As I recall, you are ordinary. An innocent bystander. But Ben knows what's happening here, even if he doesn't quite realize it. Your little girl does, too. She has the latent perceptions. Please don't be alarmed, though. You're safe here. It's easier to understand than it is to explain. You're right where you were. And right *when* you were, when Z-4 found you. In your eventuality, this place is a stretch of Highway 12, about 1999—which is what you call now there. But this is outside of that eventuality. Your world is just past the gate."

"What gate?"

"The gate." Jaeff spread his hands. "The splice. Interface. Convergence. It's a probability breach. We encountered it forty-eight years ago. Before then it wasn't here. Now it is. Eventually it won't be, again. We've tracked its linear future with kites, and recovered them, so we know it doesn't go on forever."

"The gate, you mean?" Ben hazarded the question, prompted more by intuition than by logic. "The gate is a meeting of different world histories?"

"Exactly." Jaeff grinned, his whiskers and round cheeks giving him the appearance of a chipmunk. "What it amounts to is, you can go everywhere from anywhere, but nobody can go anywhere from nowhere. The gate simply sprang into being in what you would call the year 1951. We don't know why, but we think it had something to do with our ancestors . . . or maybe yours, or both. There were shadows here then, for a brief time—shadows who spoke to some of us, then disappeared . . ."

Gambit pointed at the high, glowing cloud bank off to their left. "They left the light, you see? That wall was dark when they went into it. Now it's bright."

They walked toward the group of buildings, and Ben noticed that the distance was deceptive. What seemed a mile was only a few hundred yards, yet the smaller spans of distance proved longer than they seemed. The very dimensions in this place were puzzling, giving the entire view a surreal quality.

Gambit noticed his confusion and muttered to Jaeff, *"Sur tero kiel akvo orbiatas."* Jaeff answered amusedly, in words the newcomers couldn't make out.

Cindy frowned. “What are they saying, Ben? It’s a foreign language, isn’t it?”

“It is our own speech,” Gambit assured her. “I was only commenting that this must all be confusing to you. This language we use with you is one we’ve learned in Convergence. It was the language those shadows used. We didn’t know what they had said until later, when we analyzed it phonetically. But we learned it, and it’s your language, just as we suspected.”

“Shadows,” Ben muttered. “Yes, I’ve seen shadows.”

“What they told us,” Jaeff said, “was all very puzzling. They said we might be their descendants, coming back. They went into the *staniu* . . . the cloud, then, and disappeared. In linear time, either way, that was in your 1951. The splicing of continuities began then. We haven’t reached the end of it yet.”

Both Cindy and Ben stared at him blankly.

“It’s hard to explain.” Jaeff shrugged.

“It’s like a gate built on a road,” Gambit suggested, “but the road doesn’t run through the gate because the gate is sideways. It *blocks* the road. The open gate leads only from one edge of the road to the other. The pillars of the gate are roadblocks. The road is sequential time, and the section between the pillars is an island in time. The only way to get from here to there is sideways.”

“Sideways . . . ,” Ben muttered.

“That’s one way to look at it,” Jaeff agreed.

Beside Ben, Cindy turned, stopped, and gasped. Some distance away, toward the structures, Norma Jean and her new friend had scampered to the top of a little rise where wildflowers bloomed. Now they stood there, entranced, as sparkling colors danced and cascaded above them—a mist of tiny clear-ice crystals catching the sunlight, breaking it into its primary colors. “Look at that!” Cindy gasped. “What are they doing?”

“Molly’s made a rainbow,” Gambit said. “Pretty, isn’t it?”

∞

The phenomenon of velocitation—the shifting of Time1 loci relative to Time2—occurs at a transitional rate of 299,793.10001+ kilometers per second (670,217,454.36+ miles per hour). This velocity is the *minimum* speed for velocitation propelled by raw, primal light (new light) with no measurable wavelength.

In practice, velocitation has no known maximum rate. As primal light produces wider ranges of radiance, velocitation is affected by these variations. Research indicates that mass propelled by new light actually increases its speed as the propellant radiance spreads across the light spectrum, and wave intervals shorten, producing broader, slower wavelengths. The increase in velocitation can be likened to a surfer racing a curl. The higher the wave crest (or the wider the wavelength of the driving light), the faster the surfer riding its frontal slope moves away from the crest. The surfer is propelled both by the velocity of the wave and by the pitch of the slope.

Such considerations acquire more than academic significance in application to the paradox gate phenomenon, in which multiple dimensional factors accelerate initial propulsion. In context of gate transit from one probability sequence to another, *instant* must be viewed as a self-contained eternity within which infinite subinstants occur.

—UEB Archives

∞

VII
The Raiders

Sand Harbor Marina
Bridle Point, Maryland
The Present

Fancy DeLite, Honey Bunn, and their dozen or so "sisters" aboard Cozy Maselli's gaming ship might have considered themselves experienced career women—right up to that fateful night when the displaced Viking rover *Erethlyn* came along.

Cozy's party girls were all carefully selected, and those assigned to *ParTTym* were the cream of the crop—all young, all beautiful, but all as seasoned and cynical as they were sensuous. The girls were a key part of Cozy's operation. They knew men, and how to part them from their money.

The fact was, though, that not one of them had ever encountered a Viking. The taking of *ParTTym* had become a life-altering experience for all of them.

"He's just . . . just magnificent!" a starry-eyed Fancy had confessed to the other party girls after two or three hours of serious Viking business in the main and after salons. Her ruby-sequin dress—or what was left of it—barely covered even the parts of her that it had originally draped. It hung in tatters when she tried to put it on, but its demise was more than balanced by the gold Rolex watches on both forearms and one ankle, the heavy string of gold eagle coins resting like a crown on her tousled hair, and the ropes of gold chain on her shoulders.

She gazed across the salon, where Invar Crovansson was happily demolishing a roulette table. He had removed the wheel and was playing with the bearing on which it had turned. To Fancy, he looked like some big, barbarian god-child playing with toys. She shook her head in wonder. "Can't understand a word he says, but God! I won't never be the same, ever again!"

"Same as what?" Maggie Dupres purred. "I don't believe I remember anything about how it was before Olaf showed up. Heard there was studs in this world, but I never believed it till now. Lordy, what a man!"

"Can't hardly believe none of this," Honey Bunn agreed. She drew what was left of a silver lamé evening dress around her and stroked the sunshine beard of Gunnar Leifsson, studying his sleeping features with adoring eyes. "Lord a'mercy, if I'm dreamin', just let me sleep."

A few of the invaders were drowsing, catching a moment of well-earned rest. The others, satisfied for the moment, were prowling the yacht, amused and amazed by each magical thing they found.

"What you s'pose they want to do next?" Honey wondered languidly. "Whatever it is, I'm for it. God, it wouldn't s'prise me none if my tubes come untied an' I was pregnant this minute. With twins!"

Invar tired of the roulette wheel and wandered away, glancing back at them with a grin and a happy wink. Tagging after him, Fancy found him on the bridge. He had discovered the yacht's controls and was studying them carefully.

"You want to make this tub go?" she asked. "Is that it? You want to drive the ship?"

He regarded her thoughtfully, trying to find meaning in the words and the hand motions that went with them. Then he grinned, tousling her hair with a large, gentle hand. *"Oh, ja!"* he said. *"Trife . . . den yip!"*

"He wants to trife the yip," Honey murmured, coming in from the port promenade. "Isn't that adorable?"

"Prob'ly a good idea," Fancy agreed. "Cozy's boys, they'll make trouble when they get ashore. Prob'ly report straight to Cozy. Best if we was someplace else."

While Invar and several other furred giants watched admiringly, Fancy and Honey started *ParTTym*'s twin diesels and put the yacht through a few paces. Then, with lights doused and *Erethlyn* in tow, they headed for new adventures elsewhere.

The last place Cozy and his friends were likely to look for

his missing yacht, Fancy reasoned, was at his home base on the Maryland side of the bay. And it was a place where the girls knew their way around.

While Fancy instructed Invar in the handling of modern yachts, Harald Ericsson and some of the other, older Vikings gathered on the foredeck and made their plans. The young bucks had had their fun with a conquest at sea. Now it was time for some serious pillaging, and the skald Healfdeane agreed with Harald that the place they were headed for—a place some of the strange little women showed them on a chart—was as good a place as any.

Through it all, Gladen Lodbrok remained dour and withdrawn. The Swede had a bad feeling about all of this. He had the feeling that his own weird was at work here in some way, and he wasn't sure he would like the outcome. Odin was behaving irrationally, it seemed, and men suffered when gods were in a playful mood.

As Glome prowled the strange ship, the little women they had found there skittered away from him in dread, as they did when Healfdeane or old Hagar passed. It was always so. Women taken as prize always shrank from the dire, mysterious scrutiny of the skald, while Hagar's numerous battle scars and his missing arm seemed to frighten them.

With Glome, it was different. Like a big, dark cloud, he awed and intimidated those unaccustomed to him, simply by his presence.

Lacking the sunny disposition of the Loki-blessed Norwegians in the crew, or even the sharp, searching wit of the Danes, Gladen Lodbrok—the one they called Glome—was precisely what he was: a Swede. Big, powerful of arm, and quick of eye, he was probably the most deadly of all *Erethlyn*'s warriors. But unlike the playful *Norsk*, or even the shrewd, methodical *Dansk* among them, Glome rarely had much fun.

Still, it was to him that Harald Ericsson turned when the charts were deciphered and the stronghold of Sand Harbor singled out. Unlike the shadowy Healfdeane, who sometimes saw what was not there, Glome usually saw precisely what *was*.

The iron boat, he advised Harald, was useless as a strike vessel. It was too big, too visible, and too noisy. For taking a port by storm, *Erethlyn* was far better. The dragonship was designed for speed, for stealth, and for head-on combat.

This ungainly thing, though, might make a nice diversion, where a narrow channel must be navigated to reach the goal.

The old bell tower chimes at Bridle Point struck five as a lithe, dark hull powered by twenty wide oars skimmed across star-dappled ways and into Sand Harbor Marina, unobserved by either the few late stragglers along the piers or a distracted night watchman at the harbor entrance.

Such blissful serenity in a normally busy yacht basin existed because it was five o'clock on a Sunday morning. The distraction was provided by a brightly lighted gaming ship cavorting wildly just beyond the anchorage buoy. While Harald Ericsson brought the dragonship *Erethlyn* into the sheltered harbor, Invar Crovansson and several other young Vikings remained in the fairway channel, playing with their new toy.

The diversion was Glome's idea, but Maggie Dupres had elaborated on it. To a woman, the girls aboard *ParTTym*, starry-eyed from a night such as they had never known before, had become enthusiastic accomplices of the Norsemen. Among them, they had instructed the Vikings in how to drive and steer the yacht, and had helped plan the invasion of its home berth.

They knew Cozy Maselli's operation. They knew where the goods were kept and where the bodies were buried. They had seen Cozy's goons put casually overboard by these barbarians who came out of nowhere, and they had learned, firsthand, about *real* men. True to the best instincts of civilized femininity, the girls switched sides without hesitation. Visions of great wealth, great adventure, and great, indefatigable studs danced before them as they planned the *blitzenkrok* of Sand Harbor Marina.

"Cozy's gonna go crazy mad about this." Maggie grinned as Bridle Point came in sight. "Anybody know if he's home?"

"Didn' he go to New York?" Sugaranne Hayes said. "I think he had a meeting there. But if he ain't home, Mario will be." She giggled. "Can't hardly wait till Mario sees these here Vikings runnin' through his club. Friggin' pimp's gonna want to kill somebody."

Honey Bunn smiled serenely, gazing at the broad shoulders,

massive arms, and big, ready blades of the bearded young giants around them. Several of them had added handguns to their personal arsenals, and at least two now had short-barrel, pump-action shotguns slung like axes at their shoulders. "He'll play hell doin' it, too," she purred. " 'Specially since Maggie showed these boys how to use ol' crazy Rocco's gun collection."

Fancy had a map of Sand Harbor spread out on the charting table, going over it with Invar while other Vikings gathered around. "This is the main channel." She pointed. "That's where we're headed for. Now, inside, this whole basin is full of little channels, piers, and charter berths. Here on the point, this is headquarters. Offices, game rooms, party rooms, bars, dance floors . . . the whole shebang. Mario runs this south wing, where all the girls sleep . . ."

Invar didn't understand a word of it, but he got the drift and followed along avidly, muttering explanations to the other Vikings.

"Now, all these back sections of piers, they're just charter stuff," Fancy said. "People lease berths for their boats. We'll leave all that alone. But this T-head pier, it's Cozy's business associates. Everything along it is mob stuff. Block this off from headquarters, and most of the muscle is out of the picture."

The skald Healfdeane leaned close, studying the map. He put a finger on the drawing of the headquarters club. *"Nu er den lukket,"* he muttered, *"og last mod al magi."*

"Oh, we can get in," Fancy assured him. "I know where the master key is."

Towering over most of them, Glome reached across to touch a pattern on the map. *"Hvor forer den hein?"* he demanded.

"That's Cozy's private airstrip," Fancy explained. "He's got an executive jet there, an' some other crap."

"Krapp?" Invar glanced at her, puzzled. *"Vas bit den krapp?"*

"Airplanes," she said. Spreading her arms like wings, she rose on tiptoes and looked toward the sky, then pointed at two or three mechanical contraptions around them. "Flying machines. You know."

"Flyinge . . . flettermaksin?" Glome shook his head.

Fancy shrugged, gesturing at the entire boat. "Think of a flying ship," she suggested.

"Flyingge . . . fletterflot? Krapp!"

"Yeah, it's crap, all right. Cozy thinks that jet plane of his is the finest thing there ever was. But it's just like Cozy. Twenty million dollars' worth of crap."

"Krapp." Glome nodded. *"Fletterflotwerken . . . krapp."*

In the dark, quiet time of a Sunday morning, while *ParTTym* cavorted beyond the channel—brightly lighted, festive, and its rails lined with naked women—dark *Erethlyn* slipped into Sand Harbor Marina, rounded the clubhouse docks, and made for the main T-head past sleeping ranks of cigarette boats, assorted business boats, and various pleasure craft.

When the dragonship was in place, *ParTTym* ceased its cavorting. Fancy took the con, gunned the yacht's engines, and took the entry channel at eight knots—lights blazing, horns blaring, and deck speakers blasting out "When the Saints Go Marching In" at full volume.

It was twelve minutes after five on a sleeping Sunday morning. Fifty miles away, fourteen angry, bedraggled men with two small lifeboats had just made shore and were breaking the lock on a closed bait-and-tackle store in search of a telephone. They would place a call to Cozy Maselli's headquarters and find the phones there out of order. Then they would try Cozy's closely guarded cellular number, and get no answer. Cozy Maselli's private Gulfstream 4 was airborne, en route home to Sand Harbor.

On the roof of the clubhouse, two shadows watched the activity below—the brightly lighted yacht rounding the point while in the distance, at the end of the darkened T-head pier, Vikings swarmed from their longship.

"What are they doing?" Billy Bluefoot rasped. "Is this a raid?"

"Wait here," Adam said. "Be right back."

An instant's glare, and the timer was gone. Billy watched in fascination as the bright yacht put in at the lighted pier just below the building, shattering timbers as it crunched to a halt. On its foredeck, big fur-clad figures bearing shields and axes leapt ashore, racing toward the building.

Again the instant brilliance, and Adam was beside him. "It's a raid, all right," he said. "Those are Vikings, the same ones we traced from the fog." He grinned. "The original scags, Billy. But these others, the ones they're raiding, are something worse. In my time, they're called gangsters."

"Yeah." Billy nodded. "Outers. Guess there's always parasites."

On the manicured lawn before the main building, two gunshots rang out, then a man screamed as a broadax severed his arm. From the dark roof, Adam and Billy watched with interest as the invaders spread and flanked like drilled, seasoned troops. One of the Norsemen was bleeding from a thigh wound, but it barely slowed him. There had been two guards, lounging near the entry. Now they lay on the ground, not moving. From their pockets, some of the women produced key rings, and headed for the heavy, barred door.

"Tidy," Billy allowed.

"Watch the Vikings," Adam muttered. "One of them is like you . . . an ESPer. Can you tell which one?"

Billy concentrated, turning slowly. Directly below them, several big Vikings gathered at the gate, almost hiding the flock of scantily clad women there. Other bearded giants had gone around the sides of the building, establishing a perimeter. In the distance, sounds of violence grew as Vikings from the longship made their way up the main pier, swarming the craft berthed there, boat by boat. Between the main building and the club dock, a group of five Norsemen was clustered, back to back in a tight ring, watching the harbor entrance, the access roads, and the turning basin. Two among them were distinctive, even in such a group. One wore a hood of rough fabric, hiding the face behind a grizzled beard. The second was a giant even among these giants—a big, hulking figure wrapped in dark furs, legs like oak trunks bound in fur and leather. The shield he carried was dark and scarred, and the great ax in his hand—forty pounds of dark, honed iron on a stout shaft—looked small in his grasp. This one focused his attention toward the lighted airstrip on the rise beyond the basin.

Billy pointed toward that group. "One of those is a far-seer," he said. "He . . . knows things. But I can't tell which one."

"Stay with him, Billy. Try to pinpoint him. He got to this

time the same way you did, and maybe he knows what happened. He might be our lead to Ben Culver."

The moment *Erethlyn* was secured at the T-head, Harald Ericsson led the main force onto the pier. The T-head was a wooden dock on anchored pilings, ninety feet in length at the end of a much longer pier leading to the landscaped grounds of the club. The long pier was shed-roofed, and lined on both sides with boats of a hundred varieties, all snugged aft-in and two-by-two. Little lights at fifty-foot intervals gave the scene an eerie quality against the surrounding darkness. Forty-four Vikings gathered at the T-head—big, savage men with fur-and-leather garb, horned helmets glinting in the dim light, shields at arm, and swords and axes ready. At Harald's command they funneled onto the docking pier, spreading both ways to swarm along the assemblage, boat by boat. Most of the boats were vacant, but in a few they found cabins where people slept. Methodically, systematically, they hauled the people out, passed them back, and assembled them—terrified and huddling—on the T-head pier under the guard of Gunnar Hyrdahl and Varl Jurgensson.

With military precision, the invaders advanced up the pier—a surging, leaping wave of big, dark figures heading for the lighted clubhouse ahead. On the next pier over, two or three startled heads appeared at cabin ports, then ducked out of sight. Those boats, Invar's prize woman had impressed upon them, were innocent bystanders, and Harald's men accepted that . . . for the moment. First things first. They could loot and pillage the neutrals later.

Inner defense of the clubhouse evaporated when the big doors slammed open and a flood of rampaging giants burst into the dimly lighted mezzanine. Fleeing thugs inside were overtaken, disarmed, and thrown outside, and Invar Crovansson's raiders spread and took the ground floor room by room, while Fancy and her girls headed for the stairs, scurrying ahead of their striding giants.

At Cozy Maselli's private office, double doors exploded from their hinges and Invar led the way in. Two bug-eyed little men, napping on couches, offered no resistance. Fancy headed for the wall safe as an inner door popped open and several young women in flimsy nightgowns clustered there, sleepy eyes huge with wonder.

"Hey, Honey!" one said. "Hey, Fancy! Who y'all got there?"

"Barbarians!" Fancy grinned, looking around from the exposed safe. "Come join us. There's plenty to go around. Anybody know the combination to this thing?"

Behind the women at the inner door, a man's gruff voice shouted, and women scattered, some of them falling. The man who shoved through was barrel-chested, beer-bellied, and bowlegged. He wore only black stockings and a sweaty T-shirt, and the little, close-set eyes beside his bulbous nose were those of a brute. "Damn whores! What the hell's going on here?" he demanded, then tripped over one of the fallen women and clung for an instant to the door frame. With a hiss of anger he kicked at the offending female, sending her tumbling.

Invar Crovansson stormed around a file cabinet, his greatsword ready. *"Hvor Krot?"* he demanded. The man in the doorway seemed to freeze, his mouth dropping open.

At the safe, Fancy DeLite gestured. "Gentlemen, this is Mario Carasco. He's a pimp and a creep, and he runs this place when Cozy's gone. Mario, what's the combination to this safe?"

Like one in a trance, Mario gawked at the big barbarian advancing on him, noticing vaguely that the room was full of others just like him. For a moment he stared, then he gurgled, squeaked, and bolted, back the way he had come. Invar caught him halfway down the hall and dragged him back, dangling from his soiled T-shirt.

"Pay attention, Mario!" Fancy demanded. "I said, what's the combination to this safe?"

"You stay out of there!" Mario roared, trying to break away from Invar. "You crazy whore! That's Cozy's private—"

The girl who had been kicked was just getting to her feet, bleeding from a cut on her head. With a shrug, Invar upended the hoodlum, slammed him to the floor, then stepped back and kicked him. Screaming, Mario tumbled across the floor like a grotesque, limp puppet.

"Trold!" Invar scolded. *"Ilchen bondesdottre! Ni samfundet stotter."*

Casually, Sigurd Haarfager grabbed a handful of the gangster's face and lifted him upright. *"Ondesfolket."* He shrugged, flinging him back to Invar.

"Mario," Honey Bunn purred, "I 'spect you best just help Fancy open that safe."

Healfdeane was first to give the alarm. Far out on the waters of the bay, bright lights were moving, converging toward Sand Harbor. Haakon's trumpet sounded, its three-note signal rolling clear through the night.

Gladen Lodbrok, though, was preoccupied with something else. Lights were moving in the sky, too, and he watched them with fascination. The motion he noticed was lateral, from north to south, but after a moment it became obvious that the beacon in the sky was drawing nearer, descending as it came. When he was sure what he was seeing, he raised his ax to point. *"Krapp,"* he said matter-of-factly.

"It's Cozy's jet," Maggie Dupres said. "The son of a bitch is back!"

The others in the perimeter guard watched the lights for a moment, then muttered and began a retreat. Healfdeane pulled his dark hood close around him, lowered his head thoughtfully, then looked up. "The weird closes upon us, Glome. I taste destiny here. It is *your* weird, Glome. The next step is yonder." Dark and shadowed, he raised a commanding arm, pointing westward. With a shudder, Glome looked to the west. There, a few hundred yards away, were the neatly patterned lights of Cozy Maselli's private airstrip.

Maggie Dupres was startled when the somber giant looked down at her and laid a huge, gentle hand on her shoulder. His deep voice gone soft, he spoke words she did not understand but which she knew to be a salute to her. His hand dropped away from her shoulder, and he shook his head. You are beautiful, the gesture seemed to say. You make me wish I were not alone.

It was an astonishing moment for Maggie—that a man so big, so dour and terrifying, could seem abruptly so tender. Yet the sight of him—the huge, formidable bulk of him—frightened her. She drew away, repulsed. Just for an instant his gaze lingered on her. In that moment she saw moisture in his eyes—moisture that pooled and became a tear.

The other scary one—the tall, sinister barbarian with the hooded cloak—glanced at her, looking puzzled. Then both men turned and headed toward the airstrip, long legs carrying them rapidly away. And suddenly Maggie Dupres, whose twenty-three years had been devoted to survival, rejection, and scathing cynicism, found herself following them, running as fast as her bare legs would move, trying to catch up.

Somewhere above, there was the roar of twin turbofans winding up, to provide thrust to landing flaps.

Cozy Maselli's Gulfstream 4 touched down just as the first of the boats at the main pier went up. In the third berth, a party of Cuban smugglers had seen the Vikings coming and decided to put up a fight. Two Norsemen fell to automatic weapons fire before Haakon Krom and several of his companions broke out Rocco Gianelli's scatterguns and swept the vessel stem to stern with double-O buckshot.

Then, because it seemed the thing to do, they torched the yacht. Continued gunfire carried the flames to the after fuel tank. It was the first time any of the Vikings had ever seen a gasoline explosion. The mounting fireball lit the sky for miles around, and was echoed as other associate craft up and down the line ignited.

Gladen Lodbrok and Healfdeane were at the verge of the airstrip when Maggie caught up. Panting, she grabbed a handful of the big warrior's fur cloak and tugged. Glome halted and turned, towering over her.

"What . . . what is your name?" she gasped.

He tilted his head, not understanding. Maggie tapped herself with her fingers. "Maggie," she said. "Maggie Dupres."

Behind Glome, brakes sighed as the Gulfstream rolled to a halt. In its cockpit windows, the pilot and copilot gaped, lighted by the rising flares from the harbor. The main hatch thumped open and two nattily dressed men emerged, gawking at the fires beyond.

"What the shit is going on?" Cozy Maselli wailed. "That's my club!"

He began to run, and the man with him followed, carrying a briefcase in one hand, a .45 automatic in the other.

In the shadow of his hood, Healfdeane's good eye slitted. He sensed malevolence in the two men approaching, and took a firm grip on his blade.

But Glome was not watching. Tall and massive, he looked down at Maggie Dupres and his full beard split in a startling grin. "Gladen," he said, indicating himself. "Gladen Lodbrok."

"Well, I'm very pleased to know you, Gladen Lodbrok." Maggie smiled.

In that instant, someone collided heavily with Glome's backside. Cozy and his accountant-bodyguard, their eyes full of the fireballs rising above Sand Harbor Marina, had failed to notice—in the predawn darkness—that there were people in their way.

It was the last thing the accountant ever failed to notice. Healfdeane's broadsword impaled him through the sternum, protruding nearly a foot from his back.

Cozy, though, ran headlong into the mass of Glome and bounced off. As he fell, a huge ax hummed through the air above him. Quick as a cat, Cozy rolled and got his feet under him. Without hesitating, he scurried around Glome, wrapped a stout arm around Maggie Dupres, and held her before him as a shield. Half dragging her, he headed for his jet.

Glome was only a step behind, but the long, thin knife at Maggie's throat held him at bay. Behind them all, the skald Healfdeane planted a fur boot on the dead bodyguard's chest and heaved upward, freeing his sword.

At the boarding ladder, Cozy Maselli climbed up backward, dragging Maggie with him. "Get back!" he shouted, waving his knife. "You goddamn monster, back off!"

His meaning was clear, and Glome hesitated, backing away a step. At the hatch, Maggie braced one arm against the aircraft's sleek skin, flailed, and tried to break free. Cozy struggled with her for a second, then rasped, "Shit!" The knife turned, sliced deep, and bright blood spurted from Maggie's opened throat. With a heave, the gangster flung her away, turned to the cockpit hatch, and pulled it open an inch. "Get us out of here!" he shouted. "Now!"

Beyond the hatch, the pilot and copilot gaped at him, dumbfounded. "You heard me!" Cozy shrieked. "Take off, right now! Climb and head west!"

He slammed the hatch and turned the bolt. Then, half-blind with panic, he hauled the gangway up and slammed it home. He lurched as the slender Gulfstream took thrust and hurtled down the runway. For a moment, Cozy Maselli leaned against the closed hatch, his eyes closed. He didn't know what he had just escaped from, but it had been close. Damn close!

His hands were wet and sticky with blood. Catching his breath, he felt the Gulfstream lift off and begin its turn westward. Then he sighed, straightened, and looked around—around and up, directly into the ice-blue eyes of Gladen Lodbrok. The big, melancholy Swede seemed to fill the luxurious cabin. And directly behind him was the skald Healfdeane.

Cozy Maselli's scream went on and on, lost in the sealed, pressurized opulence of twenty million dollars' worth of soundproof luxury as the Gulfstream 4 climbed into the dawn sky and headed due west.

Billy Bluefoot watched the Gulfstream take off, and shrugged. "It's one of those two," he told Adam. "I still can't tell which one."

"Well, they're still together," Adam said. "We'd better stay with them."

"Stay with them?" Billy squinted, watching the airplane diminish in the brightening sky. "Up there?"

"There are four dimensions," Adam said. "They're only moving in three." He grasped Billy's hand, and the instant of slow-dark-thrusting-light occurred.

Below where they had been, Vikings and reborn party girls swarmed from the looted clubhouse. The Norsemen were laden with paintings, draperies, jewelry, gold statuettes, crystal ashtrays, bits of furniture, plumbing fixtures, oriental rugs—anything that glittered or otherwise caught their fancy. The women carried bags and cases crammed with currency, negotiable bonds, deeds, and titles, and Fancy DeLite cradled a stack of ledgers in her arms.

As *Erethlyn* rounded the turning basin and came to meet them at the dock, Fancy told Honey Bunn, "Got to find some wrapping paper and tape, and some stamps. First mailbox I see, I'm gonna do the rightest thing I ever did in my whole life. Th' Feds been real interested in Cozy's operation. Well, they ought to have a field day with these books. Names and numbers! Dates and places! Hot damn, there's gonna be a bloodbath!"

∞

Analogy is, at best, only a facsimile of reality. It is the comparative elucidation of known phenomena as a means of understanding what—for lack of semantic basis—cannot be directly explained. Analogy is to actuality as the blueprint to the structure, the score to the music, the intention to the action. Analogy is a likeness, not a duplicate.

Yet in certain circumstances, as with an onion and its peel, the difference between analogy and actuality might be no more than a matter of perspective. The onion and the peel are not the same, but each *is* the other.

—ELDON HAAS, *Comparative Semantics*

∞

VIII

Gate-Maker

University of Oxford
Oxfordshire, England
September 2, 1996

High in the three-centuries-old Tom Tower, built by Sir Christopher Wren to reign over Wolsey's gateway, Great Tom had commenced its evening serenade when Hideo Ikebata closed his books in a secluded atrium of the old Ashmolean and put away his reading glasses.

In his three years of graduate study at Oxford, it had become Hideo's custom on lonely evenings to "stroll to the bell." The span of minutes of Great Tom's 101 strokes, he had found, was precisely the time it took for him to walk from the Ashmolean's arcade, at St. Giles and Beaumont, to the Bull and Staff, from which he could see the pillared entry of Rhodes House. The leisurely strokes of the seven-ton bell set a nice pace for a pleasant stroll before supper.

This evening, though, he lingered, listening to the measured tones of the bell. For three years, the tones of that big bell had been part of Hideo's life. In the past two years, they had developed special meaning. If there was a thriving heartbeat within that sudden, living insight into the nature of sequence that had become his direction and his obsession the past two years, it was Great Tom. The bell measured a span of elapsed time that was precisely the same each day. Yet just out there in the quadrangle, twenty-four months ago, Hideo had seen the drama of duration enacted as though on a Kabuki stage.

Now he listened to the bell toll, and on the eighth stroke he bowed his head. "*Yukio,*" he murmured. "*Watashino tomodachi, Yukio.*"

There had been eleven Japanese scholars here then. Eleven, counting Hideo and his *tomodachi*, his childhood friend from Osaka, Yukio Tanizaki.

"The Nippon Twins," some called them, not unkindly. It was because they were often together, chatting in Japanese while perfecting their English, and because—to the occidental eye—they looked so alike. They might, in truth, have been brothers, so similar were they. Both were small, wiry young men with the distinctive, hirsute appearance of Ainu ancestry. Both were exceptional scholars and both wore thick, corrective eyeglasses. Their associates at Oxford—even the other Asians there—often mistook them for each other.

The resemblance ended at physical appearance, though. Where Yukio Tanizaki was a gifted artist, imaginative and intuitive, with a curriculum heavy in the semantic expression of form and abstraction, Hideo Ikebata was a theoretical scientist.

More precisely, Hideo concentrated his studies on mathematics as a means of bridging the theoretical and practical aspects of the physical sciences.

The Nippon Twins looked alike, but their personalities were opposite in most respects. Yukio, the extrovert, was like a bright butterfly. Gregarious and effusive, his quick laughter and ready wit were almost tangible. Hideo, on the other hand, was studious, reserved, and socially timid. Except for Yukio, he had no real friends.

Yukio's insights came, it seemed to Hideo, as great, unbounded leaps of intuition. Hideo's understandings were more cumbersome. He was meticulous, thorough, and always precise.

"If those two were one," an exchange counselor had remarked, "they would be a rare genius."

Yet, alike in appearance and unalike in every other respect, the two—Hideo and Yukio—had been fast friends since their childhood in the Osaka district of western Honshu. Formidable scholars, each in his own way, they had received their appointments to Oxford during the same week in their twenty-sixth year. Hideo came to England as a Rhodes scholar, Yukio as artisan-designate of the Emperor Hirohito.

Counting Great Tom's tolls now, Hideo remembered—as he often did—a conversation with Yukio almost three years ago, following their enrollment at Oxford. Yukio had been in a playful mood, chiding and teasing Hideo about his compulsive punctuality. "Be late sometimes, Silkworm," he had urged. "Or be early. Regard lifetime as the time of your life. It belongs to you, not you to it. You have watched orcas feasting on a school of mullet in Suruga Bay. We swam together there, remember? Didn't you notice which fish always escaped the whales? It was always the first and the last who got away, never those in the middle."

"I am neither impulsive nor slow," Hideo had defended, as he always did. "And I am not a mullet. What use is it to lead, if one loses his followers, or to trail if one loses his pack? If mullets had clocks, there would be no first or last. They would all arrive at their destination at exactly the same time."

Yukio had laughed at that, and his infectious laughter made Hideo smile with him. "What a sight that would be!" the artist chortled. "A million mullets side by side in perfect rank, all wearing wristwatches on their tails! If they moved inshore, their line would stretch from Ishinomaki to Kyushu, and the fishermen's craft would be obsolete because no net is a thousand miles long and six inches wide."

"That is ridiculous," Hideo pointed out.

"Of course it is." Yukio chuckled. "Just think of the confused fish! For each of them, the journey across the reefs will be a lifetime. Some will live for years, some only for days, yet each life is a whole life . . . until their wristwatches tell them otherwise. Time, Hideo! Time is relative. A butterfly lives as long in a day as a tree in a hundred years."

"There must be a constant, Yukio."

"Perception is the constant, not time! Minutes are like snowflakes. Never in this world have there ever been two minutes exactly alike."

Ten months later, Hideo had recalled that conversation vividly.

Yukio had met him at the Ashmolean that evening, then had gone on alone. Hideo was too absorbed in a comparison of Euclidean logic and the alternate-path thinking of the Actualist school to stop for supper.

Outside, it was raining. Yukio had borrowed his friend's coat.

Moments after Yukio's departure, Great Tom had begun to toll. Hideo had granted himself a reprieve to rest his eyes, and was watching from the atrium window when Yukio set out across the quadrangle. As always—and particularly now, with Yukio wearing his coat—it had been as though Hideo were watching himself walk away.

But only a few dozen steps. Great Tom was still in its first thirty when the brilliant flash lanced out from somewhere above. In the dazzle, Yukio seemed to explode before his friend's eyes—to leap, dance, and fall.

Lightning, they said, is an instant death. Deep inside, Hideo had never been certain. It had *looked* like lightning, but somehow it hadn't *felt* like lightning. Whatever it was, though, Yukio was dead.

It was like losing a brother. Hideo had grieved. But somewhere in that time of grief, Hideo remembered butterflies and snowflakes . . . and the mullets with wristwatches. And he had mused over how much of life's experience might be compressed into the instant of a lightning bolt's strike.

From those fragmented thoughts had come inspiration. As though Yukio spoke to him from beyond, Hideo Ikebata had suddenly—startlingly—seen a reality that had always been just beyond his reach.

Time is not a constant! It is only a coordinate. It is not even a single phenomenon! Time is in one respect a perfectly synchronous sequence of moments, but in another respect time is the product of awareness and completely subject to its fits and starts of perception!

Now, two years almost to the day from Yukio's death, Hideo Ikebata's theory had borne fruit. Reams of calculation and exposition made up the work. He would defend his thesis before the dons, and in due course it would be published.

For his work's initial exposure, he had chosen the controversial title *Alternate Views on Where and When*. From his review committee, ripples of reaction were already spreading through the academic community.

The Euclideans despised it sight unseen, of course. Einsteinians puzzled over it, curious to see its details, and the rebellious Actualist crowd, quite predictably, loved it. *A Proposal Regarding Perception of Time* would be considered radical for decades to come. But it would stand, impervious to either adulation or attack. Theory to thesis to axiom, bichronism would become a law of science.

But that was for the future. For now, it was the Theory of Bichronism, as he called it—time viewed as two separate phenomena, coexisting within a single dimension. Sequential time, the master of clocks and calendars, he had relegated to axiomatic absolute, with its own name: Time2 or T2. Above it in the natural order of practical application stood T1—experienced duration, the time of the human experience.

"The time of our lives," Yukio might have quipped. "A new way of looking at snowflakes and butterflies."

Yuki and *chocho*. The snowflake and the butterfly. Metaphors to illustrate the truth of time. Bright banners to enlighten the tiresome path of exacting *seiri* discipline.

Carefully, meticulously, Hideo Ikebata, Rhodes scholar and a descendant of both proud samurai and determined Ikko from the ancient Ashikaga shogunate, subjected the intuitions of the dead artist to the disciplines of exact, mathematical science. From the matrix of Yukio's philosophy he coaxed mathematical equations and assembled them into a thesis. Clock time—the time of the mullets' wristwatches—he presented as a matrix continuum. But the time of human awareness—perceived duration—he explained and quantified as wave phenomena.

And the symmetry of the idea presented itself. Time as a duality. Bichronism! A departure from all previous paths.

Sometime, somewhere, technicians would tap the fundament of the Ikebata thesis and bring from it a technology that he could barely imagine. Yet Hideo knew it would occur.

Clouds hung low over shrouded St. Mary's now. A cold fog had rolled in, and the panes of his window began to frost. For a moment, Hideo saw furtive movement across the quadrangle—a small, darting form slipping from shadow to shadow, pausing in an alcove to look upward, directly at his window. It was no one he knew. Then the winds shifted and dense mist hid the view beyond. Yet through the mist, as precise as a slow, implacable metronome, the big bell tolled on.

"Arigato, Yukio-san," Hideo murmured again as Great Tom continued its count of 101 salutes. *"Arimasu, watashino tomodachi.* We have done a work, you and I. Honored Snowflake, I have identified your butterfly and displayed it for the world. The thesis is complete. Dr. Anselm says it is a work of genius. That is flattering, of course, but I would rather think that it is a work of art."

Even for England in September, it was an unusual turn of weather. The cold and the fog came abruptly, chilling and obscuring a gray evening in a matter of seconds.

In the shadows of a Tudor-era portico facing the quadrangle, 1KHAF4 pulled his cloak tighter around him and squinted. Big eyes that saw further into the infrared than most human eyes strained against the mist, trying to pick out details of the old building across the way. It took a moment's adjustment, then the lighted window above the girdling escutcheons swam into focus. Dimly, he could see again the outline of the young man standing there, peering outward.

"Ikebata," he muttered. "So my Delta *did* hit the wrong mark. You still live. Just as well, though. I will not miss, and your death will be my decoy."

Hollow-sounding footsteps echoed through the mist, and Khaf Four eased back, into the shadows. A group of young men, chatting among themselves, passed within a few feet of him, and he waited until they were gone before he moved. Then, stepping out of concealment, he opened his cloak and raised a weapon, searching again for the fog-obscured window sixty yards away.

The instrument he held would not have been readily recognizable, even as a weapon, in this era. The zen-gun, like Khaf Four himself, was a product of the future. Triple aiming systems—optical, laser, and radar—sheathed a slim muzzle that looked more like a series of capacitors than like a gun barrel, and behind the muzzle assembly was a thick, shielded bulge containing a powerful electromagnetic generator. Only the stubby shoulder stock, hand grips, and ringed trigger resembled those of a gun.

The zero-mass emission node, a responding capacitor invented early in the twenty-first century to replace the archaic shoot-and-sound technologies in geological exploration, was not initially conceived as a weapon. Not until the rise of the Federated Free Zones in 2012 did the technology emerge to transform an innocuous subterranean pulsor into a devastating instrument of destruction.

The zen-gun, dubbed *lightning rod* by early admirers, did not shoot bullets. Its projectile was pure electricity, concentrated in bolts of controllable force equal to the strongest natural lightning.

1KHAF4 raised the weapon now, but he could no longer see the lighted window across the courtyard. The cold fog was intensifying at an astonishing rate. Ordinary vision now was limited to a few feet, and even the "eyes" of the zen-gun's radar sight failed to penetrate the chilling mist.

Khaf Four lowered the instrument and growled, a hooded dwarf hidden in deep, misted shadow. "Come out, then, Ikebata," he hissed. "Come to me, out here where I can see you. I am waiting."

If anything would bring his enemies to him, he knew, it would be the assassination of Hideo Ikebata, the discoverer of bichronic time. Through long, helpless months of imprisonment, Khaf Four—Kaffer, the historian—had plotted timelines and probabilities, seeking the ultimate, intolerable anachronism.

He had found it. If Hideo Ikebata had died before publication of his thesis, the entire future history of temporal development would be lost. The Institute for Temporal Research, the Arthurian regime, the Universal Experience Bank, the Whispers themselves—everything that had contributed to major tides of the future from 1996 forward—would simply not happen.

Kaffer had sought the one unthinkable occurrence that the Whispers and all their indigenous timers could not overlook. And he had found it—the target, the time, and the place.

How they hated anachronism! To the World History Investigative Society—the Whispers—altering historic fact was an abhorrence. And to timers, too. Most of them, anyway. "Only the lowest life-forms foul their own nests," Adam had said. To most of them, the past was the nest of the present. Good or bad, they resisted changes in past events.

But Kaffer knew that all of them, Whispers and timers alike, had tampered with the past on occasion. Most of what he had done, to alter various probabilities, they had gone to great effort to undo.

If Hideo Ikebata died now, the first week of September 1996, they would *have* to intercede. Whispers or timers, someone would come, to reverse the incident. And Kaffer would be waiting.

The zen-gun was programmed to his comlink, programmed to the working TEF now in place in the second pyramid at Giza. Each discharge of the zen-gun would trigger a skip back in time, at random intervals ranging from a few seconds to just over a minute.

They could not let Ikebata die. They would have to come, to intervene, to undo the thing that he had done. And when they came for him—no matter how many, or for how long—he would be there ahead of them, waiting. It was for the best, he realized, that Delta Three had missed her target here in 1993—that she had assassinated the wrong man. As it turned out, Ikebata was the perfect Judas goat for his plan now.

Deep within his shriveled soul, Kaffer hoped that the first to interfere would be that hated timer, Adam. But first or later, it didn't matter. Only time travelers and timers could leap in to reverse an incident that had already occurred. Only those with four-dimensional mobility—either through mental manipulation of gravity and light or through the use of analogs for the same purpose—could hope to alter what he was about to do. And they would have no choice. They would have to come, or suffer the erasure of their entire history. Kaffer was ready for any or all of them.

1KHAF4 had once been a Pacifican, like the Whispers. He was of their race—small, bald, and big-eyed, a thirtieth-century being produced by genetic manipulation and cultural isolation, a product of his time. But he was no longer one of them. All his life, Kaffer had been different, and had known it. He had realized early in his life that he did not have the weaknesses of his peers, the limitations of conscience and empathy.

Kaffer had always known, and his peers had learned, that he was one of a kind. A wild gene had given him an intensity of intellect unbounded by moral or cultural concern. It was his destiny, he had known all his life, to be a god.

He had always been different, and now—after a foiled attempt to dominate all of history for his own amusement—Kaffer was truly unique. He had something now that he had never had before. Always cold, calculating, and ruthless, 1KHAF4 now had a driving passion to fire his efforts. That passion was hatred, and it suffused every element of his being.

Even in the dense fog, he knew when the light went out in the high window of the Ashmolean. Hidden by mist, he crossed the quadrangle and waited. Ten feet away, he could not see the door. But when it was opened, the warmth of its radiance was a faint glow in his wide-range vision. It closed again, but now he was not alone in the mist.

Ikebata, he thought grimly. *You are here*.

The man hesitated on the portico, puzzled by the intense, cold fog around him. Then, step by step, feeling his way, Hideo Ikebata set out for the Bull and Staff.

Behind him, Kaffer raised his zen-gun, sighting by radar. It was one of the little anomalies of dimensional manipulation that, to lure "heroes" to save the life of Hideo Ikebata, he must first kill Hideo Ikebata to get their attention. Only after Kaffer did the deed would they come, but their arrival would be within the moments before the event. And having killed Ikebata, Kaffer would instantly jump back to the time just prior, in order to be there waiting when the scholar's saviors arrived.

As he steadied his weapon, Kaffer sensed himself, somewhere nearby, waiting.

He zeroed the radar sight and fired. Brilliant blue glare, like lightning, flared in the mist and grew into the far greater, instant glare of raw, new light as the programmed TEF, through comlink trace, reached out from thousands of miles away to thrust him a few seconds upstream in time.

Now it began! He aligned the zen-gun, seeing in its sight

image not only Hideo Ikebata, just leaving the portico, but himself as well, a few feet away, pointing the weapon.

They would stop this, now. Before he—the other he—fired, someone else would appear here, to interfere. He tensed, waiting. But a second passed, then two, and nothing changed. He saw the lightning flare as "he" fired the zen-gun, and saw his "other" self disappear from his sight's image. But Ikebata was still there. Unharmed and unaware, the creator of time theory continued his cautious, mist-blinded walk, moving away.

With a curse, Kaffer zeroed his sight again, then gasped as the zen-gun burned his hands with intense, searing cold. He felt the flesh freezing on his fingertips and dropped the weapon. So cold it had become, so suddenly, that its node capacitor shattered as it hit the pavement. And in the mist, directly in front of Kaffer and staring at him eye to eye, stood a girl child.

"Ye're truly an ugly creature," she said, disgusted. "Evil ye be, evil as sin! But ye've tampered o'ermuch this time. Go away." With a dainty, slippered toe she kicked the wrecked zen-gun aside. Its broken capacitor seemed to explode, engulfing itself in a tiny, violent electrical storm, melting its metal and consuming its combustibles.

Thousands of miles away, the TEF in the pyramid reacted to its comlink's mindless programming. Again Kaffer felt himself thrust upstream by raw, primal light.

Weaponless and dazed, he stood in the foggy quadrangle, looking around. High in the old Ashmolean, a lighted window barely glowed in the deepening mist.

Footsteps sounded hollowly in the fog, and Kaffer scurried for the cover of the arcade. A group of young men, chatting among themselves, passed nearby—the same group he had seen from across the way. No one else was in sight. The apparition that had faced him—a half-grown girl of protomorphic stock—was gone, as though she had never been there.

Dazed, confused, and raging, Khaf Four keyed his link, overriding the program already there. Instant, intense darkness descended upon a frozen, motionless world, and inconceivable raw light grew to carry him away, back to his lair within an ancient Egyptian crypt.

At least, though, the lair was no longer a prison for him. With a TEF once again in place in L-270's nest, he could come and go as he pleased. The rage that suffused him was no longer a hopeless rage. He had the freedom now to concentrate it as he chose.

And he had already picked a target. That all-sequence message that L-270 had sent, back before he took it over, had been the key to the Whisper conduit. Somehow it had circumvented Arthur and made it downtime, and the loop L-316 had followed its trail back.

Without L-316 as an anchor, there would never have been a conduit. Without the conduit, Kaffer would have been unchallenged in this uptime world.

He didn't have the vectors for L-316's landing, but enough remained of L-270's logic banks to deduce them.

They thought they could foil his plans? They were mistaken. He would find L-316, and then all that had happened to him would be only a fantasy of memory. In real time, it would never have happened.

The dense fog of moments before seemed to be thinning as Hideo Ikebata stepped out into the arcade of the old Ashmolean. He could not recall ever seeing such a blinding mist, so suddenly developed. But now it was going away. Pulling his wool scarf snug within the upturned collar of his coat, he headed for the Bull and Staff. He would relax there for a time, before the warming hearth, and have his supper. Then he would seek his bed. Tomorrow, the rituals of critique and testing began—the first curtain rising on a stage where the Theory of Bichronism would one day change the world forever.

Molly Muldoon shuddered as she "slid the frost" to another time and place. The creature she had just encountered—that little, huge-eyed creature trying to change the primal sequence—had been full of hate.

Molly knew about Whispers. Zephyr had told her about them, about how he had been forced to rescue her from them—or them from her—when she was hardly more than a baby. Their meeting then—when her skills were still raw—could have been disastrous, he said. And she recalled the incident, though vaguely. It was after the death of her parents. There was the lady who clung to her in her panic, and then the Whispers, and then Zephyr.

As usual, Zephyr was abrupt in his comments. He always said that it was Molly who tore him from the peaceful pursuits of a gateway observer and made him a collector of strays. But then he would become thoughtful, and ask, "Which came first, child? The chicken or the egg? You were there to greet Ben Culver at the gate, but if it hadn't been for Culver, I'd never have found you—all that time before—to bring you there, would I?"

It was what happened, Zephyr had decided long ago, when dimensions cross. The resulting instability was a gate, but it was more than that. It was a chaos, as well. Convergence was that, she thought—a gate, a chaos held in check. And Zephyr was forever trying to bridge from there to this reality that was home to her. She had teased him, now and then, that his bridges were nothing more than the dross from frosting that others did.

But the teasing was kind, and done in fun. She knew the mind of the cranky Convergencer, and there were no evils in it.

Thinking of evils, her thoughts turned to Kaffer. In appearance, the disgusting K4 creature was like Whispers. But only in surface appearance. To her ESPer senses, Kaffer was an ugly, twisted, offensive thing—a monstrosity that left a bad taste in her mind. She was tempted to go back for a moment and freeze him where he stood. But it was not the thing to do. "Don't meddle with mainstream," Zephyr always warned her. "It isn't our concern. Only what distorts the prime sequence is of interest to us."

Still, she knew that there were those who *could* do something about the ugliness she had faced. Picking her vectors in the way an ordinary timer might, she materialized in a large, multiwindowed enclosure above a railroad yard. The momentary frost of her arrival fogged the windows of the place. Though she could hear voices just beyond an oaken door, she was alone in the big room. A few feet away stood a bizarre, complex montage of wires, coils, and frames that puzzled her for a moment, until she looked inside. Resting within the nest of components was a TEF.

With a nod of her pretty, twelve-year-old head, she looked around, found a little stack of stiff paper cards and a pencil. The cards were pronouncements for Anywhen, Inc.

On the back of one of them, Molly scribbled a message, and left it thrust into the coils of the TEF nest. The Whispers of this sequence, she felt, needed to know that 1KHAF4 was loose and doing mischief.

She thrust a few more cards into her own pocket and was summoning vectors when a sudden, deep mist swirled around her and a man appeared in it, vaguely seen. Molly eased into the shadows and watched as the misty figure turned, seeming confused.

The mist cleared, and she saw that he was tousle-haired and clad in pajamas. But he was turned away, and she couldn't see his face. Furtively, he crouched there a moment, then stepped toward an open crate and lifted out a conelike thing a little larger than a football.

He might have turned then, but the voices beyond the door caught his attention. Still holding the cone thing, he concentrated, and Molly felt a wave of empathy stronger than anything she had ever known. There was a suggestion of lightning, and he was gone, and the air where he had been was bitterly cold.

In the shadows, Molly blinked in awe. The power she had felt was like her own, but far more intense . . . and it had a taste of unawareness to it, as though the man had no idea what lurked within him.

And, abruptly, she knew who she had just seen. Ben Culver, a slightly earlier Ben Culver, had just visited here without knowing where he was, why he was here, or even how he did it. But he knew where he had come from, and now Molly knew, too.

On impulse, Molly wrote on another card, "When you see Ben, tell him Molly said hi."

The sliding frost, as always, was ready for her at the touch of an impulse, but first she "thought" a photogravitic shift, envisioning new vectors.

In a neat, quiet neighborhood in Pauls Valley, Oklahoma, Molly gazed at a hole in the ground—a hole in the middle of a residential lot, where once a house had been. Grinning, she shook her head. "An' all this, wi'out even knowin' how he does it," she mused.

Three blocks away, the little girl stopped at another house and left her second note there. Then she summoned the sliding frost and was gone, leaving behind only a cool breeze and a dispersing puff of mist.

No wake or ripple remained in the T2 matrix to tell of her passage this time. Molly was a timer, but as an ESPer she was more than that. Time travelers and timers could move at will in the fourth dimension, either way along the line from history to eventuality. But frosting, as Molly called it, was not time travel. Frosting was a leap from line to line, from coil to coil of the great spiral of universal existence.

Bridges and gates, the ill-fated explorers of the Lost Loop, L-270, had called the phenomenon when they first encountered it in the far-upstream morass of a forming universe. The descendants of migrating Whispers, downstream from the chaos of creation, would have names for it. *Timeline shift* and *alternate sequence* would be exact definitions for understood phenomena in some faraway reality.

Zephyr's own term for extradimensional shift was *making bridges*. But to Molly Muldoon, *frosting* seemed the better name. It fit so perfectly with her particular ESP talent—thermokinesis, the manipulation at will of thermal energy.

"When you see Ben, tell him Molly said hi," the little note in Nancy Culver's mailbox said. And all around the mailbox, and for several yards in either direction, the air was pleasantly cool even on a hot, sticky summer day. It was a whim. It was a nicety—the blending of uncanny supersensory powers with the bright, innocent prankishness of a twelve-year-old girl.

∞

Sequential time is not a single strand of events, but an intricate, woven bundle of possibilities, each progressing from past to future as a separate, parallel cause-effect continuum.

Every beginning is born in chaos, and every chaos is a beginning. Each strand of time is a wild strand. At every moment, everything that can happen does happen, creating infinite parallel offshoots of eventuality as alternate strands. Still, the laws of probability apply. Within any range of probability are varying degrees of likelihood, and historic progression is a resilient force. Natural selection weeds out the lesser likelihoods, giving certain consistencies to each progressive strand of cause and effect.

Eventuality, though eternally infinite, is not internally random.

With every passing moment, the world—in some of its versions—ends. Those strands simply disappear, and eventuality goes on without them.

Yet as wild alternates end, others begin. Each choice, each decision, each event or circumstance that might or might not occur creates separate, parallel possibilities, renewing the bundle of progression from past to future.

Contradictory timelines proceed separately and join the mainstream weave only when they are no longer contradictory. The weave of progressive eventuality is a dance of increasing and decreasing probability.

Three fundamental discoveries were logged

during Loop L-270's initial exploration of pre-Arthurian time:

1. The four prime dimensions of existence are interchangeable in certain respects and are mutually dependent for existence.

2. Eventualities may continue as separate strands for indefinite spans of time and still—at some point—rejoin their original sequence matrix as continuations of their expired and unseparated alternate strands, thus bypassing certain occurrences in normal time before rejoining their primary continuum.

3. The likelihood of gates and bridges between one probability strand, or timeline, and another—in the interval between separation and rejoining—is of a high enough order to suggest restudy of all known "paradox warp" phenomena.

—From the log of L-270, *UEB Archives,* 3006

∞

IX
Heat Exchanger

Dublin, Ireland
April 30, 1916

In a long-ago time this place had been Dubh Linn, which meant black pool. Now it was Baile Atha Cliath—the "town at the ford of the hurdles"—and the smoky morning sun rose above the Irish Sea just as it had done since the most ancient of times. To the supporters of Sinn Fein, the old city was the seething soul of Free Ireland. To the poets along the River Liffey, where everyone was sometimes a poet, it was the torn and bleeding heart of Eire.

In the souls of Irishmen, this city had many names and many meanings. But now, when the sea air reeked of bitter dreams still dreamed as the second decade of a new century unfolded, most of the half-million mortal souls abiding here called the place, simply, Dublin.

For almost a week, there had been fighting in the streets. Redmond's republic volunteers, led by Eoin MacNeill, had taken the Central Post Office and a dozen other buildings. But most of the combat had quieted now, for a brief nod. King's regulars had shelled the post office, and in the bombardment Patrick Pearse and his IRB contingent had surrendered.

Now the retaliations were in force, and in the still places could be heard the wails of those whose young men were gone. From the little bunker beneath the Metal Bridge, they could hear the volleys of rifle fire echoing across the Liffey.

The memories of the famines still lingered, and with them the bitter taste of freedoms sought but never gained. In the night's darkness many a freedom fighter had gone to ground, and now they held their breaths and bound the lips of the wounded so as not to make a sound when the squads marched past on the streets outside.

It was cold in the cable loft of Trinity Campanile, where two men and a child huddled among the bell ropes. Rory Muldoon shivered as he crouched at the outer wall, peering through the slit window. Below and beyond his peephole spread Library Square and the Kilkane, and just a glimpse of the Corinthian portico of the old chapel.

The bells of evening were silent now, and long shadows spread across the common. The setting sun only heightened the chill in the air. Rory's jaw muscles ached from being clenched against the cold, and beside him the stifled moans of Sean were like a soft metronome—flutters of sound that came with convulsive shudders.

"He's bleeding again, Uncle Rory," a child's voice whispered in the shadows. "The tremors have opened his wound."

Rory eased back from the slit and looked down. The child hovered beside the great hump of the iron vibror, the fixed bell known as Old Thunder. Between them his brother lay curled and trembling, great spasms of cold seeming to draw the life from him with each moan. Even in the gloom, the fresh blood was red on the soiled, caked bandage wrapped around his middle.

Why in God's holy name, Rory wondered for the dozenth time, had Sean been at Four Courts when the IRB rallied there? Sean was no fighter. He had always avoided the insurrectionists, preferring his little flat in Kildare, with his young wife and wee daughter and his dreams of a cottage farm in Glendalough, to the heady fury of political strife.

Glendalough. In memory he could still hear Sean's fine tenor voice from a few scant years ago. With his Kathleen at his side, Sean sang cheerily to the infant whose cradle they rocked:

"In County Wicklow lies a vale where ne'er an ill wind blew. The hills of green rise bright and clean 'round the Vale of Glendalough."

It was the day the brothers went their separate ways—Sean to his cobblery and his little flat and his dreams of better times,

Rory to follow the clarion call of nationalism, first with Balfour's Irish Volunteers, then with the "secret army," the Irish Republican Brotherhood.

Yet now, suddenly, the brothers were together again, and the bayonet meant for Rory had impaled Sean instead. Why had Sean even been there? And why in God's name had he brought the child with him?

There had been no time for questions. The regulars had been waiting for them, all along the Liffey. And now Sean lay dying, here in a cold hiding place, with his child at his side, and his brother still did not know why.

"It's the cold, darlin'," Rory muttered. "He's having the convulsions."

She crept closer, a pale little wisp of a girl, her eyes dark shadows in the gloom. "Will he die, Uncle Rory?"

"He'll not last till morning, I fear." Rory touched his brother's cheek with stained fingers, and looked away. "The bayonet has done him, and the chill will finish him. Pray for your father's sweet soul, girl. It's all we can do."

"Holy Mary, mother of God," the child whispered. "Blessed art thou among women and blessed is the fruit of thy womb, Jesus. Holy virgin, my daddy is a good man. Must he suffer so?"

"I'll have to get you safely home, somehow," Rory muttered. "Your mother . . ."

"Mam's dead, Uncle Rory." Molly's eyes upon him were deep, pleading pools of darkness in the gloom. "They shelled the post office, as she was passing by."

Rory stared at her for a moment, then turned away abruptly and pressed his face to the stone beside the slit, not wanting the child to see him now. The tears that had been just behind his eyes escaped now onto his cheeks. The poor babe, he thought. First her mother in the shelling, and now Sean . . . dying here before her eyes. That, then, was why Sean had brought the child to Four Courts. The streets had gone mad, and he had nowhere else to go. The bayonets of the regulars made no distinction between combatant and bystander.

And now Rory Muldoon hid here with a dying brother and an innocent child—and her not yet six years old. The old bitterness welled anew in him, fed by grief and outrage. Aye, he thought, this be the price of it. Let Redmond an' Kitchener an' the rest play at banging on tables, it is here that the splinters fall.

The bone-shaking chill seemed somehow less intense, as though the air around him were being warmed, and Sean's spasmodic moaning had eased. Rory wiped his eyes on a dirty sleeve and looked around. The loft *was* warmer now, and he felt soft heat on his face as from a cozy stove.

In surprise he sought the source, and found it. The great vibror was radiating heat, and as he looked at it he saw a deep, glowing redness in its iron. The bell was hot! As hot as if it had a coal fire in its belly. It glowed like a furnace.

To one side, Sean's girl sat huddled, bent over clasped hands, absorbed in a concentration so deep that Rory could feel it like a wave of force.

The entire loft had become as warm as a cottage hearth.

From somewhere outside, he heard shouts and the tramp of booted feet, and he turned again to the slit in the wall. At first he thought it had suddenly gone dark outside, then he realized that it was fog—a deepening, intensifying fog that blotted out the view of Library Square and its surroundings. Its wisps, coming in through the observation slit, were wet and cold on his brow—very cold. As cold as the interior of the tower was warm. In seconds the mist was a dark, blind cloud beyond the stones, and in its substance little ice particles twinkled in the faint glow from the big resonator bell beneath the high, silent chimes of the campanile.

Rory squinted into darkness, wiped his eyes, and peered again. The booted feet outside, below, were hesitant now, the ragged steps of men gone blind. And in the shouting voices were curses of surprise.

"Saints preserve us," Rory whispered.

At his feet, Sean stirred. "Kathleen." His faint voice was barely more than a dry wisp of sound. "Kathleen, wait for me, love. I'm almost there."

Rory thrust his rifle aside and crouched over his brother. "Sean, can you hear me? It's Rory."

The faint voice was silent for a moment, then Sean opened

dry, sunken eyes and looked up. "Rory . . . ," he whispered. "Is the child? . . ."

"Molly's here, brother. She's well."

"It's warm," Sean wheezed. "Is it warm now, Rory? Do you feel the heat?"

"I feel it. It is the bell. The big bell. It glows like a coal stove."

"Not the bell, Rory." Sean's voice was a feather wisp of sound from dry lips. "It's Molly. The child is . . . enchanted. What the old Scots call fey. Ah, the poor thing, some will hate her for being as she is."

Sean's breath was shallow and labored now, his face as white as chalk in the shadows. His gaze dimmed and drifted away. "Kathleen," he whispered. "It's all right. I've brought the child to Rory. I can rest with you, now."

Rory leaned close, but there was nothing more. A final, husk-dry breath and Sean Muldoon was gone. With gentle fingers, Rory closed his brother's eyes. At his side the child's hushed voice sang, in tiny angelic tones, "In County Wicklow lies a vale where ne'er an ill wind blew. Th' hills o' green rise bright an' clean 'round the Vale of Glendalough . . ."

Cold mist seeped in from outside, and the big bell's warming glow faded. Outside on the street, there were shouts again, and boots on paving stone. Directly beneath the loft, hinges creaked.

"They've found us," Rory rasped. He pulled a soiled blanket over his brother's dead face and stood, clutching his Enfield. "Hide behind the bell, Molly. I'll try to lead them away. God be with you, child." Without waiting for an answer, he dropped through the trap, screamed a battle cry, and charged through the crowd of regulars at the entrance.

His appearance was so sudden, his charge so startling, that he was through the squad and running before they could react. Fifty feet, a hundred . . . he ducked behind a statue of Shamus O'Neill and reappeared, weaving his way toward Kildare. And then the rifles opened fire behind him and he felt their sting. He managed a shot from the Enfield, then another, and saw a man fall. With the last of his strength he dived behind a budding hedgerow and levered the .303's bolt.

"For you, Sean," he whispered. "And for Ireland." They were already coming for him when he fired.

In the lower loft of the campanile, little Molly Muldoon felt terror for a moment as the gunshots rang out. Then it was replaced by a deep, lonely sadness as she crouched beside the body of her father.

There was nothing she could do for him, no way to make him live again, and the finality of that welled up in her big, dark eyes. Emotions that had been too long controlled, too long hidden, burst through the fragile barriers of a child's reserve. Da was gone, like Mam was gone . . . like Uncle Rory was gone now, too. Grief gave way to fearful loneliness, and that to anger, and the hard, bitter anger was far better than the loneliness.

Molly clutched at outrage as the only hope in a drowning world. She stiffened, concentrating. On the square outside the tower a tree burst into sudden flame, and then another. A cold so deep, so fierce that it cracked stones swirled around her, and still she held her concentration.

Without seeing it, she knew when first one and then another of the guns out there misfired. Here a rifle froze solid, along with the fingers of the hands holding it. There another rifle glowed fiery red, then exploded as the cartridges in its magazine detonated from heat. Molly heard the screams of men, and fed the awful torrent of raging thermals that swirled outward from the tower. Deep within her mind she sensed a pathway, open and inviting to her, requiring only a turn of will.

As clearly as symbols on a road map, the way to elsewhere and elsewhen lay before her, and she reached out for it . . . then stopped, startled, as an instant darkness beyond her control descended all around, dissolving into a flash of light too brilliant to tolerate but too quick to see.

A woman stood before her—a beautiful lady in leather clothing, a lady whose dark hair and kind eyes were somehow like Mam's. And the lady knelt before the child, reached for her, and pulled her close to her breast. "It's all right, baby," she crooned. "I understand. But come with me, now. I know where to go."

The child yielded to her, then stiffened, realizing that a stranger held her. In panic she struggled, her mind raging. The bell tower around them swirled, spun, and dissolved in a cold, blinding mist where lightning flared and danced. Molly threw herself into the pathway in her mind, taking the lady with her.

They knelt on a hilltop beneath a crimson sky and saw smoke and lava spewing upward in a sky-high column that grew into black, stinking clouds that rained stones . . .

Again the mist and the lightning, and they were in the middle of a wide, arc-lit street where great vehicles raced past on both sides. Lightning, mist, and swirling darkness, and it was noon of a cloudy day. All around them, howling men raced past—shaggy, long-haired men in leather jerkins who wielded short, deadly bows and waved stubby blades. A tide of shrieking barbarians swept around them, running toward a thin, double line of men with bright shields, brass-studded leather kilts, crimson cloaks, and bronze helmets.

The panic raged in the child's mind, then subsided as calm, gentle reassurance flooded into her from the otherness that held her. A battlefield of Romans and Celts became a peaceful scene—little boats on a wide river where people walked along stone paths above the banks . . .

One final spasm of what Amanda Santee could only guess was an enormous, wild psychic power, and they were in a place of wooded, brushy hills—primitive, untouched midland landscape where a furtive covey of smooth-faced men with long, black hair and copper-apple skin crouched at the edge of a thicket. Two or three of the men squatted over a pair of wide, parallel wheel tracks where grass was flattened along a stretch of broken brush. The rest of the men, most of whom carried stone-point spears, were gaping at a fantastic sight on a hill just ahead—a tilted, broken-backed, 1970s ranch-style house, which rested aslant there as though torn from its trenches somewhere and tossed here, foundation and all.

Cold fogs swirled again, with lightning in them, and suddenly they were in the campanile tower in Dublin, where they had started.

Molly collapsed into the lady's arms, sobbing.

"Wow, what a ride!" the lady murmured.

Amanda Santee had come as a timer comes, sure and direct, looking for the source of a thermal anomaly. She had found it, and now she held that frail little source close and fought to reassure it. "My name is Amanda," she said gently, stroking the child's hair. "I wonder who you are . . . and *what* you are. That—what *is* that—that thing you do, honey?"

"Frost," the child muttered, subsiding against her. "But I'm not supposed to tell anybody."

"Oh?" Amanda glanced past the girl's bowed head, at the dark, somber interior of the bell tower, the bloody corpse of the young man lying there. On impulse, she hugged the girl more closely and concentrated. All around them, existence darkened and slowed—energy to inertia, light to darkness, darkness to immense gravity to a huge, instantaneous burgeoning of raw, new light, washing everything ahead of it.

Amanda Santee willed the dimensions away and they jumped. Four thousand miles and eighty years, in the time it takes for a hummingbird's wings to beat once.

Molly gasped, looking over Amanda's shoulder at a wondrous place of bright light, vivid colors, and infinite virtuality—a place where little, bald people not much bigger than herself glanced around at her in wonder.

Amazed and frightened, the child stiffened, tried to thrust herself away from Amanda, and a nearby console of virtual displays scrolled dizzily.

Fogs rolled across the span between displays, and other fogs moved to meet them. Here and there, Whispers gasped and chattered as instruments and virtualities reeled crazily, trying to cope with realities that didn't match the logic of their master banks. The floor beneath them bucked and rolled, and waves of vertigo swept across the assemblage.

"The loop!" alarmed Whisper voices echoed. "Integrity distress! Override! Override!"

A strong, small hand clasped Amanda's elbow, and where no one had been, a frantic, pugnacious leprechaun of a man appeared, materializing out of nothingness. Hastily he pulled Amanda around, grasped the child's shoulder, and murmured, "Be still, wee one. No harm here awaits ye."

Alarms were going off all around them. Startled Whispers

croaked, "Topologic impossibility! Anachronism alarm! System integrity oh-point-six!"

With a quick, angry glance around, the stranger—a sturdy, bowlegged little man of gray whiskers and indeterminate years—shook his head. "A loop," he told himself. "A real, old-fashioned dimensional peculiarity, just as in the testaments." With an authoritative growl, he wrenched Molly from Amanda's arms. "Ye've no idea what you're dealing with here, woman," he said. "This juvenile has a wild talent that can disrupt every system in this loop, at the turn of a notion." At his touch, the frightened child became abruptly calm and stared around in bright-eyed curiosity. "That's right, wee one," the stranger crooned. "No fire an' ice now, for there be no enemies here. The little folk you see are but travelers, and will do us no harm."

Amanda straightened. "Who are you? What do you want?"

Aside, a Whisper stared at a console register. "How did he get here? There was no photogravitic event."

"You think I came through time?" Narrowed, wide-set eyes pinned the Whisper who had spoken, and leprechaun whiskers split in a grimace. "I'm an observer, not an antiquarian! I don't waste my energies on dimensions! But for your loop's own resonance, I'm standing exactly where I was standing just moments ago—and would be yet, if where I was then were a hair closer to where I am now."

The leader of the Whispers of L-383 stepped close and peered at the little man with huge, wise eyes. "Is that a riddle," Teal Fordeen inquired, "or a description of phenomena?"

"All that makes anything a riddle is not knowing the answer," the leprechaun growled. "For your information, I had no intention of being here, and wouldn't be but for the divergence you people almost suffered. It was the child's own doing that brought me." Then, to Amanda, "I'm called Zephyr, and I'll have to take this child, I suppose. Your eventuality is not yet ready for a shifter. This one needs a bit of duration, to conquer directions and learn some discretions. When she's ready, maybe ye can know her better."

With a frown, Amanda edged toward the creature holding

WHIS. He—he says what we set out to do has been done, unless we stop doing it before it's complete. And he says—he seems to be alluding to our temporal technology—he says, 'You ain't seen nothin' yet.' What is that, a vernacular expression?"

Amanda nodded. "It generally means exactly what it says."

Teal Fordeen was deep in thought. "What kind of dimensional transference moves from place to place but crosses no dimensions?"

"I don't know." Amanda shrugged. "But I think I've done it, with Molly. That girl has an awesome power! We even saw Ben Culver's house, resting on a hillside a thousand years ago. And I'd swear we saw a past or two that never happened."

"We'll have to isolate and analyze the root amendments he made," Deem said. "On the surface, it seems that our main bank now views the prime dimensions as existing within a universe not limited to them."

"The dimensions of psionics," Teal murmured. "Adam's hunch was right."

Again, the structure of L-383 seemed to swirl in iridescent patterns, and vertigo swept them like waves. Alarms chattered and flashed.

"Loop integrity critical!" a Whisper chirped. "We're losing stability!"

"Cause?" Teal snapped.

"It's the 'correction' that creature made!" Deem shouted. "Our main banks are assimilating it as root data. It's driving their logics insane!"

"Shield and block!" Teal ordered. "Cancel all input to main banks retroactive to nine minutes past! Divert console data to separate bloc and save for analysis!"

Whispers worked furiously at their consoles for long seconds, then the loop steadied itself.

"Report!" Teal ordered.

"Systems normal," Deem sighed. "With one exception. We've lost our 180-second temporal idle. We're resonating now at a six-minute interval."

"What was the data discrepancy?"

"We can't be sure, just yet." Deem frowned. "But apparently the new data demands a redefinition of infinity."

At one side, Amanda Santee stared around, wide-eyed. "What happened?"

"We almost lost the loop," Toocie Toonine breathed. "It seems the new base data that Zephyr fed in was inconsistent with present programming. L-383 was becoming schizophrenic."

"More like a large, unexpected dose of reality," Teal Fordeen mused. "A reality that our notion of temporal theory isn't ready to handle."

∞

Revelation is the towering peak that rises, clear and aloof, above the Valley of Mundane. From anywhere you stand, it can be seen, serene and lofty. It seems not remote, but only distant, and everyone with eyes knows that it's there. Its changeless omnipresence is a promise all accept—that just there, up there above confusion's drifting mists, dwells truth.

Always a few will scale the heights, dissatisfied adventurers not content with faith, but seeking answers. Scorning the comfort of acceptance, they take the slopes, to strain, sweat, bleed upon forbidding heights. Some fall, some fail, and some grow faint of heart, but now and then one will succeed. With his last breath, his final strength, he claws to the very top and glories in his conquest. Revelation is his!

But then he looks beyond, and now he sees the truth. What he has climbed is but a hurdle, with vistas of other peaks beyond, a stair of mounting peaks as far as can be seen, each offering that same promise. Here dwells TRUTH.

And each succeeding peak of revelation is higher than the one before.

∞

X

The Fog Hunters

The Appalachians
The Present

The Gulfstream 4 was over the Appalachians when the fog closed around it—a sudden, blinding fog of ice that came without warning, as the ambient air temperature plummeted from minus-eight Celsius to an impossible minus-twenty in no more than a heartbeat.

In the cockpit, pilot and copilot gasped in unison as every instrument on the panels went crazy. Altimeter, compasses, airspeed indicator—everything, even the clock, registered wild improbabilities as the pilot tried to hold straight and level with nothing to serve as point of reference.

The plane felt sluggish, the controls stiff, and there was a sensation of bucking, falling, diving dead-stick into the mountains below.

"Holy shit!" the pilot breathed, hauling back on his yoke as he increased fuel flow. It seemed to have no effect. The aircraft hung in spinning limbo, defying sense-deprived efforts to correct it. The instruments gyrated wildly, telling them nothing, but there was a ragged, sloppy feel to the airframe that the pilot recognized. Abruptly, the airfoils were icing over, losing their lift.

"Altitude?" the pilot demanded. "What was it, Howie? Two-two-five, right?"

"Check." The copilot stared at the useless panels, fumbling with switches. "That's what it was, anyway. Jack, the radios are dead. Everything! What is this, an ice storm? This high?"

"Must be. Hot wing! Do we have deice?"

"I can't tell. Nothing reads!"

"We're going downstairs," Jack snapped. "Tell them, back there."

The copilot thumbed a mike, then flipped switches and tried it again. "Passengers, fasten your safety belts, please! Passenger cabin, acknowledge!"

There was no response. "Maybe they heard me," he said.

Flying blind, with useless instruments, the pilot put the G-4 into a screaming, nose-down dive, praying that there was plenty of sky beneath them. Somewhere down there were the crests of mountains, but he could only guess how far they were. Ice crystals hissed like broken steam pipes, rushing past the Gulfstream's nose, and lightning flared around them.

As abruptly as it had begun, the blindness was gone, and in the clear air beyond the plane's forward shields, mountains were rushing upward to meet them.

Jack hauled the yoke back, applied power, and the Gulfstream slid into a gut-wrenching level a few thousand feet above the higher crests.

For a long moment they sat there, in silence, then the copilot said, "We have instruments again. Altitude seven-zero, airspeed three-eighty, course two-two-nine, skin temp coming up, two-seven . . . three-one . . . three-three . . . Good God, Jack, what *was* that?"

Jack didn't answer. Correcting trim, he began a slow climb at present course, then took a look around. "Where the hell are we?"

The terrain below was mountainous, but it wasn't the Appalachians. Nothing they could see was familiar, and there wasn't a town, highway, or even a farmed field in sight.

For a full minute they flew, over rolling, forest-clad peaks where no landmarks guided them. The radios were still dead, as though there were nothing out there to hear.

Here and there among the sloping lands were bald, rounded peaks like knobs of stone. Here and there they saw the glint of water—little streams, winding through pristine valleys. And here and there, where the forest broke into meadowlands, they saw animals. But there was no sign of human life, anywhere.

"This doesn't look like the Appalachians," Howie observed.

"It looks more like the Ozarks, except there aren't any farms or towns or roads."

"Well, keep looking!" The pilot scowled at his controls and flicked some levers. "And try that intercom again. Get Cozy on the interphone."

"I already tried." The copilot shrugged. "Nobody's responding back there, and they've got the bulkhead blocked."

"Hell!" Jack frowned. "Well, keep trying. Let them know we're still flying this bird, and ask Cozy what he wants to do. Our navigation systems are all dead air, and we need to refuel. We have maybe an hour's flying time, no more. We should be putting down at Winston-Salem, to fuel and inspect systems, and maybe find out what happened back there. But if Winston-Salem is down there, I sure as hell don't see it."

"I don't see anything down there," the copilot said, "except one hell of a lot of empty country."

"That's all you're going to see in this time," a deep voice commented, just behind them. Both pilots jerked upright, then swiveled and gawked. Filling the little space forward of the cockpit bulkhead, two men crouched, shoulder to shoulder. The speaker was a tall, dark-haired man in dark clothing. The other was an Indian.

"You're not going to find any airports," the first one added. "So let's get out of these mountains, then pick a spot to put this thing down."

In the luxurious passenger salon of the Gulfstream, Glome wiped blood from a split lip and crawled out of the tight space between two padded thrones. This was his first flight in the belly of a *krapp*, and though tumbled and shaken, he was not impressed. The thing roared and thundered, and obviously could reach the sky, but its flight was erratic. That sudden dive had been very clumsy. Any Viking flotman who ever set a sail could have trimmed to a smoother pitch than that.

Wading through the splattered gore of what was left of Cozy Maselli, Glome went to pry Healfdeane out of a little cabinet where the skald had hidden himself when the dragon began to dance.

A little panel on the forward bulkhead squawked at them in a foreign language, and they ignored it, just as they ignored the pounding at the little closed gate beneath it, where Glome had braced his bloody ax as a deadbolt. Obviously, there was someone on the other side of that portal, but it was no concern of theirs.

Beyond the little glass portals that lined both sides of the cabin, the sky was blue now, without a trace of the dark fog that had obscured them moments earlier. Tiny scenery crawled by, far below . . . farther than the drop from the highest crags of Kungsholm to the shores of Aldenfjord. Though they could not see the sun, the shadows below said it was behind them and that full morning had come.

"Skelselund," Glome announced, speaking with authority as he perused the tiny terrain below. "We must be above Skelselund. I know those hills. But I never knew there were so many of them."

Falls of the Arkansas
A.D. 1102

Like a great, hurtling bird the G-4 swept downward on full flaps, aligning on a mile-long stretch of sand where little runnels of water curled like snake tracks below a gigantic, motley dam of piled, tumbled logs and river debris.

Her tanks nearly empty, the Gulfstream had reached the end of her flight, and the dry riverbed was the only landing field they could find.

On a hillside overlooking the centuries-old logjam that divided a large, meandering lake from the dry bed below, the shaman Rainbird leaned on his banded staff and watched the great, shining thing circling high overhead in the midday sky. He had never actually seen anything like it before, but its presence did not surprise him. He had known that someone or *something* would arrive, to protect his people. He had listened to the smokes, and been assured.

Now a solemn crowd of nearly a hundred people gathered below the falls, waiting to greet the marvelous thing when it came down from the sky.

Rainbird knew—they all knew—that the wonderful thing circling above them was not a living creature. The people of the winding rivers were long-walk people. Neighbors to all nations and kin to none, they were far travelers and had seen many wonders. The shamans, keepers of craft and lore, were careful in their passage of wisdom from generation to generation.

Rainbird knew that the number of shamans preceding him was 843, and that the stories passed along to him—marked by the bands on his staff—were explicit and unembellished. Among many other wonders, the stories described flying baskets that once rode the winds over Atalan, the land of origin.

The big, shiny thing rushing around in the sky above the three valleys was, they all knew, some variation of a flying basket. It was a contrivance—a conveyance, carrying people on its stubby wings or, perhaps, in its sleek belly.

It *was* magic, of course, but Rainbird's people accepted that. In the world as they knew it, everything was magic.

The flying thing circled and descended, and the people below knew that it meant to land. From its configuration and its velocity, they surmised that its choice of landing place would be the dry bed below the falls. And like any flying thing, it would come down into the wind. So they gathered there, built a circle of little fires, and unpacked their trade goods while some of the women brewed capsin to welcome the new arrivals.

Rainbird himself had cautioned the people to extend every hospitality to whoever was coming to visit. It was always good business to be friendly, but this was a most special occasion. It was the arrival of the people's security from the threat of marauding hostiles.

With a scream of rushing wind, the big device flared like a striking hawk above the waters of the lake, flitted its shadow across the intervening tangle of the dam, and rushed to contact the sand below.

It was only then, just as the thing's balled talons smashed into the dry, crusted sand, that Rainbird noticed that there were arrivals among them already. Two tall, strange-looking men, both dressed in odd, fitted garments, stood near the capsin fire, watching the machine fall from the sky. The women there glanced up at them, and Honey Willow said something that Rainbird could not hear.

The two strangers smiled at the girl, and their responses were accompanied by gestures. The taller of the two, a man with very light-colored features, seemed to disappear for a moment, then reappeared a few feet away.

The darker-skinned one's hands made signs, and Honey Willow made signs, then she offered them cups of capsin and left them there, hurrying toward Rainbird.

"These are very strange people, Brother," she told him. "A moment ago, those two were inside that flying thing. But now they are here. The one with the talking hands said a 'plane crash' is more comfortable when viewed from a little distance."

In the G-4's cockpit, their faces white with strain, Jack and Howie ran one final check on the charts and settled the bird into a tail-down, full-flaps flare as the final waters of the lake rushed by below, and the hard sands of a dry riverbed spread before them.

At 115 miles per hour, the G-4 flared and settled, reaching for the sand. "Aw-w-w, *shit*!" Jack howled as the landing gear touched down, sinking into the crust as he fought to keep the plane's nose up.

Like a plunging fling-stone, sixty thousand pounds of luxury aircraft dug itself into the sand, ricocheted across a hummock, and plowed a furrow six hundred yards long—a huge, thundering, racing fount of sand and topsoil that rose around the monster, then descended like a blanketing cloud.

In the stillness of the cockpit, Jack and Howie stirred, peering out through a dirt-encrusted windshield. Carefully, tentatively, they moved a finger here, a hand there, then began breathing again.

"Jesus H. Christ," Howie muttered. "I think we're down, Jack. No wonder Pete Hanks calls this thing the Volvo of the Air. We're down! And I think we're still alive!"

Beside him, the pilot unstrapped himself carefully. "Probably not for very long, though," he said. "If Cozy's still alive back there in that cabin, he's going to kill us."

There was a series of clangs somewhere aft, then a grinding

thump, and the cockpit door slammed open. The pilots gaped at the apparition that filled it—a scowling, bearded giant of a man wrapped in fur garments and brandishing a huge ax. Blood streamed from a gash on his forehead, and one massive knee was skinned.

"Hvor krodt!" the giant roared. *"Krapp!"*

Behind the stunned Jack, Howie blinked, rubbed his eyes, and blinked again. "I don't think this is a happy passenger," he whispered.

One by one, the pilots were dragged bodily from the cockpit and hurled to the side, where a second barbarian—a cloak-hooded specter with a bloody sword—pointed at the port hatch. Howie glanced around at the destroyed interior of the once-posh cabin and felt sick. There was blood everywhere—blood and pieces of what had once been Constantine "Cozy" Maselli.

The cabin hatch was pitted with ax marks, bent, and almost jammed. But at the insistence of their passengers, Jack and Howie managed to open it. No ladder was necessary to debark. The C-4 lay belly deep in fresh-turned river sand. Its seventy-foot wings nestled like scarred sleds in the crater they had skimmed. Howie hesitated, then was flung out of the cabin, and Jack followed. The Vikings stepped out behind them, then stopped and stared in surprise. All along the low bluff on the north side of the stream were people—attentive, copper-skinned, raven-haired people who stood enraptured, like an appreciative audience watching a circus act. And among them, standing head and shoulders above most of them, were the two strange men who had been in the C-4's cockpit only moments before the crash.

The taller of these stepped forward, grinning. "Come on up!" he called. "You're among friends here!"

The two Norsemen didn't understand the words, but the meaning was clear. Healfdeane scanned the crowd solemnly, then slung his sword at his shoulder. With only a glance at the ruined aircraft that had brought them here, he stepped to Glome's side and peered up at the big Swede.

"I grow tired of your weird, Gladen Lodbrok," he growled.

"So much adventure confuses the mind. I feel no evil here, and I think we should rest for a time."

"That spooky one's the psychic," Billy Bluefoot told Adam, as sunset dwindled in a purple sky and the glow of fires reflected in the sheen of the wrecked G-4 in the riverbed. "His name is Healfdeane . . . at least, that's what he answers to."

"You actually *talked* with him?" Adam raised a curious brow. "In what language?"

"Hard to explain." Billy shrugged. "First time I ever talked to a telepath, as far as I know. But then, I didn't know I was one, either."

"You communicate, though. Semantically?"

"We use some words—" Billy frowned. "—but they're . . . well, when we talked, I guess I spoke some Nordic and he spoke some English, but it felt like making up words to match meanings. We can't exactly read each other's minds, like reading a book, but we communicate. He's a skald, among his people. That's something like a prophet or a fortune-teller, but with lore-keeping as a sideline."

"Does he know how they came to be here . . . in this time?"

"Oh, sure. He knows exactly what happened. Odin—that's the main god in Valhalla—got pissed because Harald Ericsson sailed his ship into a fog. It isn't quite that simple, but that's the sum line. It happened because of Glome's *weird*. Kind of like karma, or kismet, or destiny."

"Glome?" Adam gazed across the fires. "That's the other Norseman?"

"Yeah. The big one. He's a Swedish sailor. A *flotman*, to use Healfdeane's word. But it means sailor. They're both Vikings. I gather they were one of fourteen longships on their way to plunder a place called Northumbria, but they got lost in a fog bank and wound up in another world."

The girl Honey Willow came with cured hides and capsin and made them a soft place beside a cutbank. With a sardonic glance, Adam noticed that Billy Bluefoot seemed to have quite a way with the ladies.

"Another fog," Adam mused. "Well, Healfdeane's our lead to Ben Culver. I'm sure of it."

Billy gazed at him. "What is it with this Ben Culver business, Adam? Why is finding him so important?"

"I'm not sure," Adam admitted. "But it is. Because of him, we've discovered that there is more to dimensional transfer than just jumping around in times and places. There seems to be a lot more to it than anybody suspected. If a person can go . . . well, *beyond* dimensions, then there really are no limits to how much good—or bad—can come of it. The Whispers don't know what happens in these fog episodes, and I don't know, but obviously there's a power at work that has to be looked into. It's something beyond timing, beyond the ESP range. It's something awesome! And Ben Culver seems to be the key to it. So we have to find him."

Billy thought it over, then leaned back comfortably, accepting Honey Willow's adoring attention with a shrewd grin. "You want to wake the bear to see if it can be tamed." He chuckled.

"Don't take root, Billy," Adam said. "We've got work to do." They sat for a few minutes, watching the people around them and sipping capsin. It was a mild brew, but it reminded him of the Apache drink, tiswin. In the distance, across the river, a herd of woods buffalo had emerged from the trees to graze in the twilight.

The Tlogi—the friendly, copper-skinned people of the area—had cheerfully accepted the strangers among them, and were treating them like royalty. Billy watched with something like amusement as the hospitality of an ancient time progressed. More and more, the natives directed their attention to the Vikings—especially the big one. "So what do you want to do with him?" he asked casually.

"With Healfdeane?" Adam glanced at a nearby fire where dozens of people were gathered around the two Norsemen. The big one, Glome, had a girl under each arm and was swilling capsin from a big, dried gourd while Healfdeane, sitting on a bearskin, sang grand ballads that were no less captivating for the fact that nobody listening could understand a word of them. The two pilots were some distance away, trying to make sense out of what had happened to Cozy Maselli and his airplane. "Same as I did with you. We'll take him with us and go looking for another fog ESPer. One or another of you—or maybe all of you together—should have some answers for these anachronisms."

"Do you know where we are, then?"

"Where, but not when. I lost my bearings when we slipped to this time. This fog thing isn't like the temporal shifting that I do. But I know we're somewhere west of the Ozarks, and obviously in the past. Those baskets are Iroquoian, and the flint points on their arrows are Muskogee . . . but these people are a little different. They're red, but they aren't Mongolian. I don't think they're really the Native Americans we know. My guess is that these people—the Tlogi—are descended from an older culture—maybe some of those the archaeologists call Folsom people."

"Anasazi." Billy nodded. "The 'old ones.' "

"Yeah. Anasazi . . . Atapaigo . . . Folsom . . . Napi . . . Yunh'wisti . . . Toltec. The people before the people. They were around for thousands of years, and our legends mention them—the ones who were here before. Like the gypsies in Europe, nobody knows where they came from. They were just 'always here.' As you said, this party is a merchant tribe. The goods in their packs are from all over the continent, but I recognize some of the pieces. Mayan work, and maybe some Olmec. All pre-Columbian stuff. No Aztecan designs, though, so we're pre-Tenochtitlán. Maybe tenth century A.D. We'll shift downtime till we find a historical benchmark of some kind, then go from there."

"Fog-hunting." Billy grinned. "And we take the Viking with us? What if he doesn't want to go?"

Adam squatted beneath the cutbank, watching the stars come out overhead. "I thought I'd leave that part to you, Billy," he said casually. "You're the mind reader here."

"Thanks," Billy Bluefoot snorted. "A psychic Viking with a broadsword, and I'm supposed to *persuade* him of anything? What's in it for me?" His eyes turned again to the hovering Honey Willow, then to others of Rainbird's flock. "They *don't* look like us, do they?" he mused. "Coloration, maybe, but not their features. I've always wondered who they really were."

"Who?"

"The Anasazi. These could be some of my ancestors, you know, Adam. Down through the centuries, they mixed with the people around them, so now we all have a similar look. But Cherokee is still Cherokee, and we didn't come from Asia. Maybe the Cheyenne didn't, either, originally. Or the Delaware or Huron, for that matter. They've always been different, like the Cherokee. Our legends of origin say we came to this land from the east, from an island beyond the big water. It was called Atalan."

Adam looked at the man from the twenty-first century, trying to sense his thoughts the way Billy sensed other people's. "It might be interesting to find out," he suggested. "Is that what you want? To visit Atlantis?"

Billy Bluefoot nodded. "A bargain. I help you with your Viking, you owe me."

"Fair enough," Adam agreed. "*After* we get this Ben Culver thing sorted out, we'll do a little time traveling." If there's still a world here to travel in, he might have added.

"I accept time payments," Billy said.

Gladen Lodbrok lounged beside a friendly fire, cuddling copper girls with one hand while he ate a melon with the other. Never in his life had he felt more welcome than among these strange, friendly little people, and when Healfdeane came sidling up to him, suggesting that they leave this place, Gladen sneered at him. "I like this place," he said. "I don't want to leave." With a wave of his hand, he indicated the copper people. "I like these people."

"They only seek you out because they need you," Healfdeane said sourly.

With a gentle swat, the Swede cleared a pair of dark-eyed nymphs from his lap and stood, towering over the attendant throng around him. He swore a thunderous oath and pointed at a half-grown boy who was wandering around blindly, his head almost engulfed in Glome's horned helmet. "Bring that back to me!" the big Viking roared.

It was the first time that Healfdeane had ever seen anything like a smile on Glome's homely face, and the skald shook his head, muttering. He watched as the boy scampered to return

Gladen Lodbrok's helmet. In the background, behind the towering Swede, several children tried to lift Glome's big battleax, then gave it up and turned their attention to his shield.

"They have him entranced," Healfdeane muttered.

At his side, the leader of the copper people, Rainbird, made rapid hand signs and snapped orders in a musical language that meant nothing to the Vikings, yet seemed almost to carry meaning.

Instinctively, Healfdeane knew that there was no harm in these people—at least, no direct threat of any kind. They carried weapons—spears, slings, and fine bows—but not a point had been aimed at any of the strangers. Their attitudes toward the newcomers seemed to range from curiosity to outright affection. Yet their open welcome of the visitors, he sensed, had cunning purpose behind it.

On impulse, he turned, stooping slightly to confront Rainbird. For a long moment they stared into each other's eyes, almost nose to nose, and the skald opened his inner senses, the way he did when reading the smokes or when stating his demands to the god Odin.

Surprisingly, Rainbird did not recoil either from Healfdeane's startling visage or from the probing of his mind. Instead, the copper man matched the skald gaze for gaze and let him search for meanings.

And it was Healfdeane who backed away. Against an intelligence so bright and so straightforward, he had no defenses. But in that instant he knew, as though Odin had told him, who these people were and what they wanted.

With a sigh, he turned back to Gladen Lodbrok. "This is your weird, Glome," he said. "Your destiny. These people are yours for the taking, but they come with a price."

"They like me," Glome rumbled. "If I desire it, I can be king here."

"Yes, you can." Healfdeane nodded resignedly. "And that is your weird, Gladen Lodbrok. Listen to me! To these people, you are the strangest of all of us, and therefore a bearer of magic. They think you are a giant, come to guide them and protect them against their enemies."

"What enemies?" Glome's eyes narrowed. "How could such as these have enemies?"

"They have enemies," Healfdeane assured him. "They speak of them, though we do not understand. Fierce, warlike people roam these lands. These people call them Yaki and Pani. These people want you, Glome. If you desire to be their king, they will grant you that. They want you and your magic. That is why they coddle you so."

"Then I will do what they want." Glome shrugged. "Can you tell them that?"

"They already know it," the skald said. "Just as I do. It is your weird, Gladen Lodbrok. You will be a king . . . but you will never again find your home."

"The psychic will go with us, I think," Billy Bluefoot told Adam, indicating the skald who stood beside him. "He understands that he might get home if he will cooperate. The others aren't interested. The big one wants to stay and be a king, and those pilots over there refuse to leave their plane. They think they can make it fly, somehow, and they can't see past its price tag. They think they're rich."

"Do they understand that they're nearly a thousand years in the past?"

"I told them," Billy said. "They don't believe it, but I told them."

"Then that's all we can do." Adam shrugged. He glanced at Healfdeane. "Does he know that we're going to try a blending of powers? Is he ready for what may happen?"

Billy shrugged. "Who knows? I don't even know if I'm ready, because I don't know what's going to happen."

"You two are ESPers," Adam said. "I'm a timer. We're going to mix all that up together and see if it takes us where Culver went."

"Sniffing the bear," Billy muttered. "Chancy."

Adam nodded. "The bear we're looking for is a psychic fog." He stepped forward, hoping that Healfdeane was as cooperative as Billy seemed to think. He placed a hand on each of their shoulders. "Join hands," he said.

Billy took the skeptical skald's rock-hard hand in one of his own and grasped Adam's proferred hand with the other. With his free hand, Adam raised a little token before their eyes. It was only a brass pistol cartridge on a key chain—a souvenir of somewhen he had visited—but what it was didn't matter.

"For concentration," he said. "Just look at it. Let me do the rest."

The taste of psyche is eerie, like knowings that swirl in the air, just out of reach. Adam sensed the joining of the psi powers of the other two, like a wave of intuition. And with the discipline of the experienced timer, he joined, blended with, and directed the mix of minds.

In the instant of temporization, he felt himself losing control and tried to withdraw, but it was too late. It was like a time jump, but far more than a time jump. The awareness of dimensions wavered, unfolded, and something more than ordinary dimension burst forth. The awful power of the energies that transposed themselves then—absolute gravity to absolute, thrusting light—was beyond anyone's comprehension . . . had it lasted long enough to reach the senses. But it was only the barest fraction of an instant, and then the three of them were surrounded by milling, dusty cattle.

At sight of them, the nearest beasts panicked, turned, and ran, pursued by startled, wild-eyed riders. One of the horsemen spotted the three, hauled his mount to a skidding, hunkers-down halt, and reached for a handgun at his belt.

Healfdeane drew his sword, shrieked a battle cry, and charged, wrenching free of Adam's hold on his arm.

"Oh, Lord!" Billy yelled, and dived into the Viking's path. Healfdeane flipped over him, tumbled, and sprawled.

The rider was just coming up with his revolver when Adam caught his wrist, pivoted, and pulled him from his saddle.

"Herd cutters!" the man shouted. "Comancheros!" He spun around, looking for his gun, but the tall man who had jumped him was holding it.

"Sorry about that," Adam apologized. "No harm intended. We're just passing through. What year is this?"

"What?"

"The year," Adam pressed. "What year is this?"

"Why, it's . . . uh . . . I believe it's sixty-seven. Or maybe sixty-eight."

"Thank you." Adam nodded. Lowering the Colt Navy's hammer carefully onto an empty chamber, he threw the gun off into the brush. "It's yours," he said. "Go get it."

With a wary frown, the man backed away, then turned and ran.

"A trail drive," Adam muttered. "Well, we're going the right direction."

With a sigh, he rounded up his charges and took a firm grip on each of them. "Now what we did before," he muttered, "let's do it again."

Again sudden, heavy darkness descended, followed by a driving pulse of pure, unleashed light, hurling them ahead of it along the dimension of time.

On the third try, they materialized in a cold, dense fog. Currents of conflicting thermals swirled around them, heat and cold in an elliptical dance of little winds that sucked the moisture from the air and spun it into wild fogs. As the phenomenon dissipated, Adam knew that they were in no time or place that existed in his eventuality. Ahead of them was terrain—a simple, pastoral scene with odd little buildings in the distance. Behind them was a standing bank of fog, and off to the left another, taller fog that swirled, glowed, and towered high into the sky. Between the fogs, rolling hills and pretty vales were bathed in a soft, muted light that seemed to come from no particular source and cast no strong shadows. It was a peaceful scene, but there was an otherness about it that seemed unreal. Distances and spans blended to fool the eye. Nothing seemed quite straight or quite consistent, and the receding distances were foreshortened as though designed by a cunning artist to suggest more distance than was truly there. To Adam it was a dizzying, constricted panorama that teased the senses and made the stomach lurch.

It was like looking at the world through a distorting lens that turned randomly, extending and compacting the dimensions everywhere they looked.

For a giddy moment, Adam felt his senses reeling, then he recalled something he had learned from Teal Fordeen. "Gates and bridges," he muttered. "The random eventuality phenomenon."

Hauling the two startled travelers with him, he stepped through the distortions into something beyond his experience.

At his flank, Healfdeane murmured spells to invoke the attentions of barbarian deities, while Billy Bluefoot crouched, staring around him. "What did you do?" he hissed. "Where in hell are we?"

"Valholl!" Healfdeane decided. *"Hlidskjalf Wodenholm."*

Adam raised his head, nostrils flaring. He felt strangely confused, then realized that—for the first time since he was a child—he had no sense of dimensionality in this place. A mind used to dealing with what most people never experienced—the conscious awareness of four absolute, infinite, and tangible dimensions—is stunned when confronted with only three plus ordinary time. To Adam, it was like suddenly going blind. To make it worse, even the three physical dimensions he could see felt limited—as though they extended only a finite distance in all directions, then simply ended there.

"Weird!" Billy growled. "Look at the light. Where does it come from?"

Adam glanced upward. There should have been a sun in the sky, but there wasn't.

Behind them an irritated voice shrilled, "Poxes and leeches! Why me? Can't I even complete a simple observation bridge without being disrupted by strays and stragglers?"

They spun around. The little man behind them might have been a leprechaun, by his appearance. His clothing might have been Mardi Gras leftovers cut to size, and a jaunty tam sat aslant above bushy brows and bristling whiskers. "Shifters again!" he snorted. "Or are you the first? You might be, to just walk in without an escort. How did you do that? What is it all you people want?"

"Wulkenfolke!" Healfdeane hissed, reaching for his sword.

"Hold it!" Adam restrained the Norseman. To the leprechaun he said, "We're looking for Ben Culver."

"Well, you've come to the right place," the little man grumped. "Though I have to tell you, all this fog-chasing on your side is playing havoc with continuity on mine!"

"This is weird," Billy Bluefoot muttered. "This is really weird!"

∞

History is tenacious. If nothing else, the great experiment of the World History Investigative Society proved that. On the grand scale, the sheer resilience of the timeline's accomplished sequence of events far outweighs the little chaoses and chance anachronisms that inevitably result from time travel. Paradoxes blend, anachronisms cancel one another out, and the mainstream of history proceeds unscathed.

By its nature, time travel is intrusive. People who weren't there when, now were, and paradoxical coincidence occurs. Maybe an event or two are added to the fabric. Maybe a detail here and there is changed, but history is far less vulnerable to minor manipulation than early theories suggested.

Once initiated, each sequence of temporal events in history's weave proceeds, despite minor snags and bulges, to its infinite conclusion. The past upon which the future is built remains essentially intact.

The real threat to history is intentional, destructive, malicious anachronism that attacks not just the threads but the weave itself. Temporal vandalism can occur, and the premeditated sabotage of an entire history is theoretically possible.

This became the ultimate goal of the monster Kaffer, following his escape from Khafre's tomb, and he chose his point of attack with great care. The moment of greatest weakness in a historic matrix is the moment of its birth.

The history of technological time travel—as a fact beyond theory—began the moment Loop L-316 sacrificed itself to create the Whispers' up-time conduit. Having failed to modify or manipulate the history of time travel, Kaffer set out to eradicate it, and that moment in time was his target.

∞

XI

Time Trials

Osawatomie 1887

"Locked down?" Faron Briscoe frowned, squinting at the Whisper barely visible within the coils of Leapfrog Waystop's TEF nest. "What exactly does that mean, 'locked down'?"

"It means," Artee Six explained, "that Anywhen, Inc., has a pair of tourists at large in past time and can't get them back because they have somehow circumvented the retrieval impulses. And since their location is in our proximity, the Hawthorns want us to find them and get them back on the program."

"Well, where are they?"

"They seem to be inside a steel water tank, about four miles from here on the Marais des Cygnes. As you know, ferrous steel can divert a photogravitic event, if it's anchored to the terrain."

"Yeah, like you can't transport a railroad track in time." Briscoe nodded. "But the only water tank over there is that steel-plate reservoir at Bleck's Crossing. That's where the tornado went through two days ago. There's nothing left there, except that tank. What are they doing there?"

"Apparently," Artee Six suggested, "they crawled in to get out of the wind. They were on a whirlwind tour. Maybe they got tired of it."

"So what does Waystop I want me to do?"

"Go out there and persuade those two to come out of that tank, I guess." The Whisper ducked back inside the nest, where he was inspecting circuits. "They can't be retrieved until they come out."

"Lord," Briscoe muttered. "That is exactly why I've avoided Lucas Hawthorn's little venture. I don't relish dealing with tourists." With a sigh, he pulled on his high boots and picked up his coat and hat. "Well, it's a nice day for a drive, I suppose. What are the names of the misplaced travelers?"

"Westin and Smith." Artee Six's voice came from inside the flowing nest of copper coils. "They're one of Edwin Limmer's projects. Political people, he said. They wanted to analyze the operations of Anywhen, Inc., so he involved them in a time-and-motion study." There was a pause, then skittering noises inside the coils. "Wait a moment, though. What's this?"

The little Whisper emerged from the top of the nest, holding a rectangle of white paper. "Someone has been here, Faron. There's a communication here, to WHIS. Do you know anyone named Molly?"

"About a dozen. Which one?"

"This one's name is Molly Muldoon. She says Khaf Four is loose!"

"Who?"

"Kaffer. The renegade who took L-270. He's the one who tried to destroy Waystop I."

"But he's sealed up in a pyramid, isn't he?"

"Not according to this." Artee rubbed his bald head, his big eyes narrowing. "I'd better get this to Teal Fordeen," he decided. "Will you activate the TEF for me, Faron?"

Briscoe stared at the little person. "Now? You mean, this is ready to operate? But we haven't tested it, yet."

"Then consider this the test." The Whisper scampered past him, to stand impatiently on a section of floor covered with sheet steel. "You have L-383's coordinates, Faron. Just tap them in and activate the generator."

"Well, if you're sure . . ." Briscoe stepped to the console and entered coordinates. "Good luck, Artee." He flipped the switch.

"Thank—" For the barest instant, darkness and impossible heaviness descended upon the beam field over the steel floor, then a flicker of light—light that would have fried everything around it had it lasted a perceptible time—and Artee was gone.

The steel plates glowed with polished brightness, every speck of dust and rust gone from their surface.

"I guess it works." Faron shrugged. He put on his coat, secured the penthouse, and descended to the roundhouse below. Outside, he waved at a hostler. "Bring the surrey around for me, Mike," he called. "And ask Agnes to pack a picnic lunch, please. I'm going for a ride."

The water tank was the size of a sod cabin—a seam-welded steel-plate egg standing on sturdy I-beam anchors atop a little hill above the valley of the Marais des Cygnes River. Its pump house was shattered, its filler pipe gone, and its spout was somewhere in the next county, but the tornado had left the tank itself intact except for some loose seams.

It—and the rails—were about the only recognizable artifacts remaining. The materials of a barn, a work shed, and a dozen buildings were scattered all over the landscape, and a ragged line of ruined telegraph poles leaned drunkenly toward the northeast. But the water tank was still there, squat and ugly, just above the littered rails.

Somehow the strayed time travelers had managed to find a loose plate, crawl into the tank, and then beat the plate back into place behind them. It took Faron Briscoe nearly an hour to pry the hole open, and when he did, the stench from inside was overpowering.

The two men in the shadows inside were both nearly naked, filthy, and half-starved, but only when Briscoe threatened to shoot them did they give up and crawl out.

At gunpoint, he herded the wild-eyed pair down to the river and made them bathe. When they were presentable, he issued them blankets, coffee, and roast beef sandwiches.

For a time, the famished NERCs seemed bent upon foundering themselves, but finally the feasting slowed. When he had their attention again, Briscoe asked, "Which of you is Smith and which is Westin?"

The nearest one squinted at him, cocked his head, and shouted, "What?"

"I'm W-We-uh-Westin," the other said. "He's S-Sm-Sm . . . uh, he's Smi-Sm-Smi-i-i-whoever."

"Quit your damn mumbling!" the first one shouted. "Speak up! What's he want to know?"

"He . . . he . . . uh . . . he w-w-wa—"

"Spit it out, man!" Smith opened his mouth wide and wobbled his lower jaw, trying to clear his ears. "Damn wind deafened me! Who is this guy?"

"I'm Faron Briscoe," Briscoe introduced himself. Then, more loudly for Smith's benefit, "Briscoe! *Briscoe!* I'm Faron Briscoe! I've come to help you back to Waystop I!"

"What?"

"W-wh-what's Wayst-way-uh-W-Waystop-uh-Wu—"

"Waystop I!" Briscoe repeated, shouting it for Smith's benefit. "Anywhen, Inc! Where you started!"

Westin stared at him, his mouth opening and closing. "Those pe-p-pee-*people*! They t-t-t—"

"They tried to kill us!" Smith shouted. "Put us in a room and turned on turbines or something! The wind! The damn wind—"

"—t-t-t-tried to k-ki-k-k-kill us!" Westin agreed.

"Oh, nonsense." Briscoe grinned. "They only sent you back in time, to see some tornadoes."

"What?"

Westin leaned close to his partner. "He s-s-says they s-sen-se . . . uh . . . sent us ba-b-b-ba-back in time!"

"Back in time?" Smith bellowed. "In time for what?"

"I've seen this before," Briscoe muttered. "Damn fool must've yawned into the wind. Anybody knows not to yawn when you're caught in a dust devil, much less a tornado. It clears the sinuses and blocks the ears. He'll be deaf as a post for a while."

"What?" Smith demanded.

Westin shook his head and shouted, "He s-s-s-says . . . says you're d-d-de-uh-d-de—"

"Deaf?" Smith shouted. "That's easy for you to say! I'm the one who can't hear!"

"Oh, s-sh-sh-sh-sh—"

"Shut up!" Briscoe finished it for him. "If you fellows are feeling better, let's get you into town."

Herding and prodding them, Faron got the pair loaded aboard his surrey and took the back path south, back to the roundhouse.

Number Nine was on the turntable—a tall, stately engine slowly reversing its direction to begin a new journey. As Briscoe herded his fugitives toward the stair, the big engine vented steam. Westin shrieked, jumped a foot off the ground, and lost his blanket. Nearby trainmen turned, staring as the naked man streaked up the stairs to the loft.

"These fellows are time travelers," Briscoe explained to the workmen. "They're from the future."

Nearby, a chief oiler nodded sympathetically. He had seen lunatics before. The asylum for the less than rational was only a few miles away, and there were escapes now and then, from the fields. Usually they were harmless. "I come from Halley's comet, myself, Mr. Briscoe," he said. "Glad you caught them before the poor souls got theirselves hurt." He turned back to his work, chuckling.

"What?" Smith demanded.

Faron Briscoe picked up Westin's blanket, drew his Colt Dragoon, and pointed. "Upstairs!" he ordered.

At the top of the stairs, entering the penthouse loft, they met the gibbering Westin coming the other way. "A cre-cre-crea-c—a *whatsit*!" he stammered, pointing back toward the heavy oak door, which stood partly open now. The bald, big-eyed head of Artee Six peered from it.

"I see you found them," the Whisper said.

Faron Briscoe put an armlock on Smith and regained Westin's attention by cocking his drawn Dragoon. Getting the pair across the loft and into the chamber designated as Leapfrog Waystop took all of Briscoe's skill, but he managed it and slammed the door closed. The two gaped at the Whisper, then almost went ballistic again when they looked past him and noticed the steel flooring, I-beam tower, and TEF nest of a temporal velocitor.

"Wh-wh-wh—" Westin demanded.

"Oh, shut up and wrap this blanket around you," Briscoe ordered. "You're indecent."

"What?" Smith croaked hoarsely. "You can't treat us like this! Do you know who we are?"

"Yeah, you're a couple of blame nuisances."

"What?"

"He s-s-s—uh, he s-said w-we-w-we're nu-nu-nu-nu—"

"Oh, shut up, Westin! I heard him!"

"Tourists!" Briscoe growled. "What's up, Artee? I didn't expect you so soon."

"Big problems," the Whisper said, his huge eyes narrowing with concern. "Teal Fordeen has called a conference at Waystop I. Apparently the news about Kaffer isn't the only critical situation. Deem Eleveno says some new findings have cast doubt on the entire universal matrix theory. They think there's been a breach in eventuality itself, and people are jumping around from one timeline to another."

"I didn't know that was possible." Briscoe scowled.

Artee shrugged. "It isn't. But, then, neither was time travel, by pretemporal standards. What do you want to do with these two?"

"Just what was requested. Let's send them back."

Artee Six turned to the TEF controls. "Back where they started? Waystop I? What's our T2 vector?"

"Concurrent duration." Briscoe shrugged. "What is that, two or three days after they left? Doesn't matter, I guess. We'll send them. After that, they're Anywhen's problem." He nudged the NERCs with his Dragoon and prodded them toward the steel-floored field. "Hope you gentlemen have had a nice time in the past," he drawled. "Bye-bye, now."

He stepped back, studied the conduit-use readings, and frowned. "Am I reading this right, RT? Is there this much uptime traffic?"

Artee nodded. "It's the migration. Waystop I is accelerating thousands of persons per hour, and Peedy Cue is completing the transfers to shunt most of them on to Leapfrog Waystop. That's what we're seeing now. When we get the signal bell installed, we'll have a fail-safe against commingling of transfers."

"Thousands per hour?" Briscoe raised a sardonic brow. "What are they doing, abandoning the future?"

"The traffic uptime has increased tenfold in the past few days." Artee shrugged. "Teal doesn't know why. The early teams found some interesting phenomena in the ancient past, and now it looks like everybody wants to see. Teal's waiting for word from UEB on the increased traffic."

"Can they handle it all? It's like a flood!"

"They're shunting traffic over to Leapfrog as fast as possible. The volume isn't a problem, but L-383 is trying to clear Waystop for standby. They've developed some stability problems. So we're getting a lot of the flow. Zeem Sixten is still corroborating my calculations—he's a stickler for time trials and not sure yet about our tests. But Peedy is in charge of the shunting, and he's going ahead with it."

"Can we handle it?"

"We already know our system is operational," Artee sniffed. "I used it myself, remember?"

On the field floor, the two NERCs were becoming panicky. They had noticed the sheet-steel floor beneath them, and the big, ominous TEF installation. They would have bolted already, except for the persuasive authority of Faron's unwavering Colt Dragoon. At any moment, though, they were apt to lose the last of their composure. "Yeah, I remember." Faron nodded. "Let's go, then. I'll watch for a gap; you send."

He concentrated on the flow indicators and found a blip. At his signal, Artee Six activated the TEF.

On and above the steel floor, there was that instant of slowing, darkening descent from light to gravity, followed by the characteristic split instant of overpowering light. It was only an instant, but in that instant Faron Briscoe imagined that Smith and Westin were not alone there in the transfer field—that the NERCs were surrounded by close-packed, surprised little people.

The send was complete, the transfer field was empty, and the steel floor gleamed brightly as it did after each TEF activation. Nothing was ever missed in a time transfer. When the temporal effect focalizer flooded its field with the phenomenon of electromagnetic energy translated into elemental photogravitics, everything above the steel departed, riding ahead of the flicker of new light that transcended time. People, objects, *everything* went, including every tiny particle of dust, rust, and soot accumulated on the floor.

Faron Briscoe stared at the empty field, still holding his gun. Then he turned to read the little screen where both the intended and the actual transfer vectors were displayed.

"Oops," he said.

Waystop I
The Present

"We believe your brother has opened a can of worms, Miss Culver." Teal Fordeen perched on a countertop in Maude Hawthorn's kitchen. "Emergency reorientation has been required, to maintain the integrity of Closed Loop L-383, and we are still asynchronous to a factor of point-nine."

Nancy Culver stared at the little being, then at the several other Whispers with him, in confusion. "I don't understand," she admitted. "What did Ben do now?"

Deem Sixten, who was helping himself to sweets from Maude's refrigerator, turned and frowned at the girl. "Among other things, your brother has aided and abetted a monster, created at least twenty major anachronisms, subverted the entire technological basis of photogravitational temporization, and very nearly destroyed a working chronoloop," he snapped. "Not to mention the filching of a temporal effect focalizer from Leapfrog Waystop—which is now in the hands of the aforesaid monster."

"That is an exaggeration, Deem," Teal Fordeen hushed him. "It was all inadvertent. Unfortunately, the chain of events resulting from Ben's sleeptiming *has* become a can of worms. The worms were always there, of course, but they have become a factor largely because of your brother's somnambulistic excursions."

"I'd hardly call it 'worms' when two thousand years' accumulation of temporal theory and technology becomes abruptly obsolete," Deem Sixten argued.

It was more than a conference, this gathering at a pleasant house resting on a sedate acreage in the extraurban area of Eastwood, Kansas. The home of Lucas and Maude Hawthorn was, at the moment, the site of an intense briefing on situations involving time, history, and the questionable finiteness of the universe.

Maude had two percolators going, and an efficient relay from freezer to microwave oven to maintain a fresh supply of brownies and blackberry cobbler, and the kitchen was packed with various kinds of people.

"So what do you want to do?" Edwin Limmer asked.

"We need a fixed base, at least temporarily," Teal Fordeen said. "An enclosed, static location large enough to house about half of L-383's research and analysis capacity, as well as duplicate processors and data banks. And we need it in a location as near as possible to this base."

"That's a tall order." Lucas Hawthorn frowned. "That's . . . what? Maybe a hundred and fifty thousand square feet of interior? There are some buildings that size in Wichita. Warehouses, transit barns, and like that. The only thing right around here that's that big might be Willy World. That's a retail store," he added, for the benefit of the Whispers. "A big chain discount house over on Pawnee."

Limmer considered it, gazing at Lucas. "Well, how about Willy World? Maybe we could use it for a while?"

"Oh, sure! I can see it now. 'Welcome, Willmark shoppers! Today's Red Tag Special is hard to find because it's hidden behind virtual-reality displays operated by short, bald people from the future. Please remain behind the ropes, and avoid people who don't look like you. They may be preoccupied with reorienting the dimensions of existence.' "

"I don't mean while the store is open." Limmer grinned. "But I suppose we could close it for a time. That's simple enough. The Limmer Foundation has certain clout. I can just go back to the latest major-projects meeting of the Williams Enterprises executive board, and run in a remodeling-renovation schedule targeting the Eastwood store. I'm sure Williams Enterprises will be interested in a test-marketing venture suggested by the Limmer Foundation. Public reaction to double-deck aisles, or something of the sort."

"You don't need to bother," Maude suggested. "The store's already closing. Don't you ever read the paper, Lucas? They've been having shut-down sales for a week."

"I gather the store is what we need." Teal Fordeen nodded. "Since you've already arranged it."

The telephone rang, and Maude went to the hall to answer it. She was back in a moment. "It's Pete," she told Lucas. "He's got a crew ready to go to work on the Willmark building contract, but he doesn't have any work orders."

Lucas shrugged. "Tell him hang tight, and I'll call back." To Limmer, he said, "Looks like we already did it, so let's go do it."

"Two sends," Limmer decided. "I'll go to Atlanta three months ago and get the program going with Willmark. Lucas, you'll have to set up the job contract from your office."

Lucas thumbed through Maude's day-to-do calendar. "I'll be there two months ago," he said. "I was out of the office most of that month, so I won't be running into myself there."

Nancy Culver stared at one and then another of them, glass-eyed. "What?"

"Don't worry, dear," Maude assured her. "It gets confusing, but it's only a matter of time. The Whispers need the Willmark building, you see, so Lucas and Mr. Limmer arranged that it be closed for remodeling. And Lucas has the construction contract, so the Whispers can use the inside while Hawthorn Constructors renovates the outside."

"But . . . but first they said they'd arrange all that, and now it's already arranged, but they haven't done it yet."

"They have to do it, so it will have been done when it was done," Maude explained. "If they don't do it, it will never have been done to start with."

"Oh." As it soaked in, her blue eyes shone with the mercenary innocence of a real estate speculator touched by angels. "Oh!" she repeated, mostly to herself. Visions of high-dollar commissions danced in her eyes. "Wow! Retroactive commercial development . . . my God in heaven! I thought that only happened in Arkansas!"

"Forget it, dear," Maude murmured. "Anachronisms aren't commodities."

All through the conversation, the little bell in the TEF chamber had been pinging at intervals. The time conduit was busy today. Each ping signaled a party of Whispers on their way uptime, into the past. But now a double ping sounded, and Mandy Santee came in from the control booth, which had once been a closet.

"We're clear for a little while," she announced. "What traffic do we have out?"

"Two tour groups," Maude said. "Party of ten watching the Cherokee Strip land run, and the Snyder family attending

Hildy's grandparents' wedding. Oh, and Faron Briscoe has those two federal gentlemen who got lost on the whirlwind tour. Apparently they've had as much fun as they can stand."

"The NERCs?" Amanda frowned. "But he already sent them down to us. Eight minutes ago."

"Well, they aren't here. You don't suppose they could have, ah . . ."

"Oops," Lucas and Mandy said simultaneously.

Ed Limmer peered into the TEF chamber as another transfer bell sounded. The instant of light there left the impression of dozens of little, bald Pacificans, all tightly packed into the acceleration mode, all heading upstream past antiquity to times unknown.

"Actually, it could be worse," Limmer said. "I traveled with Whispers, myself, you know. They're far better company than those two witch-hunting jerks have been keeping."

Residential privacy was the touchstone when those adjoining sections now called Eastwood were first subdivided for development. And, so far as humanly possible, privacy had remained the watchword of the area. Unlike various other groups, varieties, and persuasions within the extraurban population of Kansas, busybodies had not yet provided themselves with either a categorical lobby or special privileges under the law.

Thus Eastwood had maintained a generally agreed accord discouraging certain undesirables. By mutual consent of the developers, the brokers, and the established residents, a degree of selectivity had been achieved. It wasn't redlining, so much as an accepted ethic that had become ingrained in the community. By and large, known snoops and busybodies—those whose abiding interest was surveillance of their neighbors—often found themselves better suited to other locales than to Eastwood.

If there had been an unspoken motto for the area, it would have been "Let's all mind our own damn business."

Human curiosity being what it is, that ethic had been severely tested ever since Lucas and Maude Hawthorn went into the time-travel business. It was difficult to ignore things like the theft of a horse by an armed nineteenth-century Cossack, or an eighteen-wheeler overturned in a flower bed miles from the nearest highway, or occasional glimpses of small, bald, big-eyed creatures who didn't appear quite human. The occasional presence of an Australian aborigine on a garden tractor might have been overlooked, like the occasional landings of odd-looking experimental aircraft in the back pasture. Even the Hawthorns' peculiar penchant for abrupt household remodelings, and the comings and goings of groups of people dressed in period costume aroused only mild gossip. But the occasion of a great, dark UFO-like cloud hovering above the Hawthorn house and unleashing lightning had left a lasting impression.

Some school bus and mail routes had been quietly modified since that episode.

Still, this was Kansas, and this was Eastwood, and the transit of a convoy of Hawthorn Constructors trucks carrying indescribable equipment and little bald people from the Hawthorn house to the Willmark building tended to be stoically disregarded by those who noticed it at all.

Within hours, L-383's analytical facilities were safely ensconced in Willy World, and research had begun on the cause of the loop's instability.

"This is something beyond our technology," Teal Fordeen told Ed Limmer. "Something beyond—or outside of—the four fundamental dimensions has distorted the timeline in ways we don't yet understand. The evidences are widespread. Some, if not all, of the meteorological anomalies we have been tracking are obviously related to this phenomenon. It is as though the dimensional framework 'slips' a bit, exposing what we can only assume is an alternate timeline—another reality, so to speak—and each time it happens, there is a telltale climatic anomaly at the point of occurrence. Cold fog within an electrical field, like a storm in a bottle."

"Can you find the source?" Limmer asked the solemn Whisper.

"We hope so. If we know the source, we'll know the cause. Right now, our technicians are tracing the phenomenon along the time dimension. It seems to have a limited span, both future and past."

"How limited?" Limmer asked.

"Uncertain downtime." Teal gestured vaguely. "Five hundred years or so. We'll require more study. But uptime, the point of beginning is precise. Even to the date and hour. It is in the year 1951."

"And it's a dimensional warp? Like the T1 conduit warps the time dimension?"

"Not exactly," Teal said. "The conduit only appears to warp reality, by giving selective direction to an existing dimension—time. This phenomenon is more like an entire multidimensional reality being spliced with another reality. It's a total overlay. Each is what the other might have been, but isn't. The time conduit is a one-dimensional distortion, Edwin. This thing—this 1951 phenomenon—is a distortion of *all* the dimensions."

"What could distort an entire reality?" Limmer puzzled.

"That's what we must determine." The Whisper tapped impatient fingers. "We do have a point of departure, though. The point of beginning of this 'parallel world' is exactly the time and place at which the anchor loop, L-316, sacrificed itself to bring the time conduit through the Arthurian Anachronism."

Limmer stared at the little Whisper, his mind racing. No one ever knew what became of the crew of L-316. Their loop had been sacrificed, as planned—its temporal energies realigned to create a conduit following an unknown path. But the Whispers aboard the loop, and all their equipment, should have been there to be picked up by the first survey team through the conduit. The exact vectors were known—February 9, 1951, local dawn, just eighteen miles from the subterranean singularity that would one day be called Deep Hole.

But they were not there. They weren't anywhere. L-383 itself had thoroughly scouted the area—vast plains and wheat fields, low sagebrush hills and a wide valley, a sprawling, arid winterscape dotted by isolated farmsteads, and here and there a few little towns. The nearest settlement of any kind was the little grain-elevator village of Kismet, Kansas.

There was no sign of L-316's survivors, and no trace had ever been found.

"Is it possible that L-316 caused a distortion in sequences?" Limmer asked.

"Anything is possible." Teal Fordeen shrugged. "But we've reviewed procedure on that, and don't see how it could have been done . . . not without two simultaneous time warps, and L-316 didn't have the equipment for that. But we'll find the answers, one way or another. A more immediate concern is the renegade 1KHAF4."

"Kaffer?"

Teal nodded. "We know he has the means to escape from his prison. According to a note Leapfrog Waystop found—from someone named Molly—the criminal is already at large. Kaffer is dangerous, Edwin. There's no way to describe just how dangerous he is, and the only person we know who might find him—Adam—has disappeared. We've tried to contact him, but he doesn't respond."

"What do you think Kaffer will do, Teal?"

"I wish I knew," the Whisper said.

∞

From a seed, a sprout ascends into sunlight. Above ground it falters, then divides into two tendrils. Twin branches become twin stalks, each rising to become a sapling with branches of its own. Parallel and separate they grow, then by chance meet, meld, and graft each to the other. Through the seasons and the years they become a single trunk, fused in bark and sapwood. Then as the seasons pass, the forces of chance come again. The double bole becomes two boles, growing apart.

Is this one tree or two? Each now stands separate and independent from the other. Each has full access to the root system. Each is capable of being an entire tree.

But the roots of one are the roots of the other, and somewhere between the ground and the lower branches the two trunks are one.

The double tree is a paradox. Each tree has present and future independence, and each has past separation. Yet in their seed and their roots they are the same, and for the length of that portion that is fused they are—then and now—the same tree.

In that interface, has one tree rejoined or have two trees melded? Is each bole increased by the other, or is each tree in fact the other tree under slightly different circumstances?

The paradox of the double tree is a prime metaphor in temporal research. From the common root through the separate stalks to the convergence of the splice, the tree is a topographic circle. Yet the flow of its being is not around and around, but upward—from root to splice to separation above, and onward from there. The circle, therefore, is an illusion. What seems a closed loop is actually a segment of something else, suggesting further metaphors . . . like half of the figure eight.

Or like the beginning of infinity.

∞

XII
A Splice of Life

Southwest Kansas
February 1951

Logic told him how the Whispers had come into pre-Arthurian time. He had been aboard L-270 when it smashed through the anachronism, and when it sent its broadcast message back to the future. He could extrapolate the rest. Somehow that signal had reached the future, by random eventuality curve. Its path—through the uncharted morass of probability—had become the time conduit for the Whispers.

For that to have occurred, a time loop had to have been launched back along that beam, then uncoiled into a conduit from a secure anchor point on the uptime side.

The point of complete vulnerability of the Whispers, then, was that point of anchorage, at the moment the anchor loop ceased to be a loop.

With unerring reason, the being known as 1KHAF4—or Kaffer—planned his strategy. It was a tedious business, pinpointing the exact dimensional coordinates—the precise where and when of the anchor loop's emergence into pre-Arthurian time. But Kaffer was patient. There was only one way that the Whispers could have bridged the anachronism, and Kaffer homed in on probabilities. Master historian and temporal mathematician, he narrowed the field, dimension by dimension.

With mathematical precision he isolated the coordinates on a global matrix—latitude, longitude, surface elevation, and exact T2 parameters. Then he tuned his restored temporal effect focalizer to those vectors minus one hour, and gathered the materials he would require.

A power takeoff and a sunburst power pack were among the materials he had salvaged from the fragments of old L-270 within his reach inside the Pyramid of Khafre. Copper filament from a water regenerator, a reversible electromagnetic generator, a set of optics from the fore viewfields of the old loop, bits and pieces of the remaining inventory of what had once been—and always would be—the most powerful contratemporal singularity ever devised, Time Loop L-270.

The loop itself no longer existed. With its dimensional stability compromised, it had become a nonevent. Most of its remains were now simply debris, buried within the stone of the second of Egypt's Great Pyramids, the Horizon of Khafre.

The being called Kaffer assembled his salvage and selected armaments, and gathered them on the steel pad beneath his TEF, along with various tools and one complete, uncompromised thrust-nav system. The unit loop had been a highly specialized configuration, designed for chronogational integrity and topologically resistant to flux. A living example of the net-zero law of quantum physics, it carried the retrosynchronic power—in its t-nav node—to smash through the time-bending morass of a monumental anachronism.

That power was Kaffer's now—the power to thrust past distorted temporal currents, to reorient chaos into a temporal recession.

The thrust-nav system would have the power to redirect a simple "uncoiling" of a torus loop—the relaxation of a closed warp into a linear succession of moments, a self-contained segment of time conduit along which retrosynchronous traffic could flow.

When all was ready, Kaffer gathered his implements within the TEF field and joined them there. With a cruel smile of impending victory, he triggered the focalizer—triggered the electromagnetic analogy that called into play the massive, universal forces of pure gravity and pure light to produce the phenomenon of temporal transference—and stepped forward into the cold, clear air of a winter morning in the great plains of North America.

The true mark of his genius now was the fact that he had cross-connected his timefield generator to do something never done before, outside a loop. When the generator fired, when the temporal effect focalizer translated an electromagnetic reversal into its analogous photogravitic event and hurled Kaffer and his tools back to a set location on the ninth day of February, 1951, the TEF went with him.

Sagebrush horizons miles apart delineated the course of a wide, grassland valley where shallow, icy streams laced the sandy bed of what had been called "the world's greatest invisible river." The Cimarron flowed beneath deep sands and only rarely poured forth the mighty torrents that had earned its reputation as a killer stream. Usually it was a placid, arid thread of surface water only hinting at the vast river beneath the sands.

Within sight were a single, abandoned farmstead marked by its little grove of winter-gray elms, and miles and miles of low, grass-and-sagebrush hills, bordered by vast, tilled fields now pale and desolate with winter. The only other signs of humanity were the silhouette of a grain elevator far away across the low hills, and a distant, bleak stretch of highway.

Here, at this point on this day in 1951, an event was about to take place for the first and last time in history—the materialization and unraveling of a full-torus time loop. Through sheer logical deduction, Kaffer knew what must happen here.

It would be a torus-configuration loop, and in order to provide an anchor in time it would have to stabilize momentarily—to cease all T-dimension external motion. It would become visible, and for a moment vulnerable, and it would cease to be a loop. The doughnut would unroll. Within microseconds, it would become a chronosynchronous conduit—a tunnel through time—linking the infinite past to the infinite future. What had once been a loop would be the anchor for all future Whisper expeditions. If that did not occur, all that followed would never happen.

If the anchor loop did not anchor, then the only future presence ever to have penetrated upstream past the Arthurian Anachronism would be L-270. And the only future being in this past world would be L-270's sole survivor.

Kaffer allowed himself an hour to prepare his ambush.

Convergence

"They say it's a splice," Ben Culver explained, gesturing vaguely around, indicating the entire "place" called Convergence. The group, which to Cindy Bruce looked like mixed refugees from a costume party and a circus, consisted at the moment of four more or less ordinary people—if a futuristic Native American could be counted as ordinary—plus one cloaked Viking and a small flock of "little people" whose appearance and attire suggested a blend of Gaelic folklore, Bavarian revelry, and Japanese silks. They strolled across a pleasant knoll, from which pastoral terrain extended into the distance to the right and the left and disappeared in foggy horizons not far away ahead and behind.

The nearer of the fog banks, the one ahead of them, seemed a towering, standing wall of cloud, ascending into the flawless sky. It glowed with a strong, inner light that grew brighter as they neared it.

Cindy stayed close to Ben Culver, shooting suspicious glances at Adam, Billy Bluefoot, and especially at the somber, hooded figure of the Viking skald Healfdeane. In the hours—if there were hours here—since she, Norma Jean, and Ben had been introduced to the new arrivals, Cindy had come to the conclusion that the whole world had gone hopelessly insane . . . again. Improbabilities heaped upon improbabilities left her with a feeling that the nearest thing to a normal person around here was the odd man whose slanted, broken house had somehow started all this.

She had lost Norma Jean as an ally in rejection. The little girl hardly blinked an eye at the improbabilities, and seemed right at home here with her new friend. Right now she and Molly were a few hundred yards to the right, riding together on the back of a prancing pony.

"These people—" Culver indicated the little folk. "—are Convergence Colony. They're from the other timeline that spliced with ours here. The bright fog bank ahead is a mystery of some kind. Some 'shadow people' who showed up here when all this began lit it up and disappeared into it. These people think we can see something in it that they can't."

"Because we're timers?" Adam peered at the approaching fog. "Or because of psychic senses? I don't have any mental direction in this place. The dimensions are all out of kilter, like a surrealist painting. The perspectives are wrong. How about you?"

"It makes me dizzy," Ben admitted. "Disoriented. But Jaeff wants us to look at whatever's there in the fog."

"You are time movers," one of the little people said. He looked like a bewhiskered pixie with a slouch hat. "You see more than ordinary people see, and you move in directions we can't even find. Powers brought you here. Even if your senses are confused, you must still have them."

Ben glanced down at the little man, then looked at Adam again. "That's what they've been telling me," he said. "I think they're sincere. They're pretty much like us, in a lot of ways. They even think we might all have some common ancestry, though some of their other ancestors sure aren't ours."

"Zephyr believes that," the pixie said. "We don't know."

"Large eyes," Billy Bluefoot mused to himself, gazing around at the little people. "Big eyes and small stature. Interesting. But they do have hair."

"There are maybe fifteen or twenty of them here," Culver continued. "Or more. It's hard to tell. I'd practically swear that their native language is Esperanto. It sounds like the Esperanto I studied in college, but not exactly. Most of them speak ordinary American English, too. They're sort of a committee, keeping an eye on the paradox. Convergence, I mean. They've been trying to explain it to us, since we got here."

Adam squinted, turning full circle to gaze at the hazed horizons. "It could be a vortex," he mused. "Two parallel timestreams coming together, in tandem. Blended dimensions—the stress on stasis must be enormous."

Ben Culver nodded. "Exactly what they told us. I guess you know about this dimensionality thing, then. They say I know it because I'm a timer. The cold fog around the periphery is atmospheres. They meet somehow and create a thermal inversion, that just sort of goes round and round. These people use free kites to measure it. There is some kind of boundary between here and the regular world—or worlds—but even if it could be seen, the fogs hide it."

Adam looked back at the misted horizon, miles away but still giving the vale a constricted, caged feeling. He couldn't seem to shake the slight sense of vertigo that this place gave him. It was as though there were less here than met the eye. His highly developed dimensional awareness kept searching for more—for a complete picture—and found nothing. "That probably explains the cold fogs we've been tracking," he said. "Weather anomalies—spin-off vortices dancing around in time and space. What caused all this?"

"We don't know," the nearest little person said candidly.

"They don't know," Culver echoed. "They don't know what started it, any more than they know how we got caught up in it—myself, and Molly, and maybe others." He tilted his head at Adam. "You three are the first ones to come across from our side uninvited, I guess, though they tell me that we—Cindy and Norma Jean and I—were the first to find the interface . . ."

One of the little people—a short, wide-shouldered individual with plump, whiskered cheeks that made him look like a wise chipmunk—interrupted him. "In ordinary sequence, you three and these three are all firsts," he said. "But that gets into the linear succession question. The point is—" He glanced at Billy and Healfdeane, then squinted up at Adam. "—you three in tandem not only located, but also penetrated the interface without someone from over here to lead you. That's why we want you to see the funnel."

"Funnel?"

"Isn't that the right word?" The small person turned to another of his kind. "*Pensi,* Teejay," he said. *"Stanca il Angla est mesto sur tero?"*

"Strecita mesto." Teejay spread his hands uncertainly. "Funnel? Bright cloud? Standing fog? *Ka bonlengo,* Jaeff. *Bonpensega. Stanca kaj mallumo, farigis lumo.*"

"The shining cloud," Jaeff said to Adam. "Inside it is a howling core. It's as good a description as any. We call it *staniu*. Molly named it the funnel. We've tried to explore inside it, but we can't get there. Maybe you can see what we can't."

"I'm willing to take a look," Ben Culver said. Then, to

Adam, "These people think I'm a magician of some kind, and Molly, too. And they know the three of you combined your visions to bridge across the interface, into Convergence. They're pretty impressed with that."

Jaeff nodded. "If you did it once, you can do it again. You manipulate time and space dimensions, Adam. The two with you are sensitive to past and future. The visible *stanca* is a simple thermal engine. A permanent weather. But there's something inside that keeps it going.

"Time and direction are all tangled up in there. All the dimensions are. We don't know where or when the shadow folk—according to Zephyr, you call them Whispers—went. But if we knew more about what the funnel is, we'd understand this whole convergence phenomenon better. Maybe you people can take us inside. Maybe what started all this is still there."

"A tangle of time," Adam muttered. "And this—this has all been in existence since 1951?"

"We found the phenomenon the day it appeared," Jaeff said. His cheek whiskers tilted in a grin. "By your calendar that was the fortieth day of the year 1951. Zephyr claims he found it first, but that's just the way he is. If it's unclear, unexplained, or unexplored, he considers it his. He's been obsessed with this paradox since the day it appeared."

Beside him a sturdy little female called Gambit frowned. "Zephyr's a loose kite," she chirped, pronouncing it "Z-4." "He's one reason the rest of us started a colony here, in this betwixt place. There's no telling what Zephyr might do if we weren't here to mind him. He even suggested reviving temporal technology to explore downstream along this interface."

Adam's eyes narrowed. "You have time travel?"

"Have it? No. We had it, though. Our early ancestors did. The light-gravity spectrum, all that. The technology was discarded ages ago. It's dangerous, and redundant. What's the point? We've already been upstream. We came from there. And one tomorrow at a time is all anybody can really handle."

"But your ancestors had time technology?" Adam pressed. "Chronolog capability? *Whisper* technology? Analogous spectrum reversal? How about autotemporal talents?"

"Like you and Ben?" Jaeff shrugged. "No, we have no

natural timers. Never have been any among us. Genetics, maybe. In our reality the skill never surfaced. It's just as well. This interface doesn't confuse our senses, the way it does yours, because we accept limited dimensions. Through your eyes, though, and his—" He pointed at Culver, then indicated the little girls on the pony nearby. "—and maybe theirs, you can see the interplay of the four dimensions. That's how you do it, you know—the time-warping thing. Telekinesis based on an inherent, vivid dimensional awareness. No one in our reality has ever achieved it . . . or wanted to, as far as I know."

"You could measure the interface," Adam suggested. "You're curious about its duration. With time travel you could jump ahead and look."

"We probably could, but we don't need to. We know it's still here for at least another five hundred years. We can read that from the kites, even from our own side of Convergence. What we don't know about is the *staniu*."

"Five hundred years?" Adam paused, his hooded eyes thoughtful. "That goes way past the Arthurian Anachronism. Maybe even past the rift. Five hundred years spans all known future history of our kind of people, according to the Whispers! After that, there's no record of us in their future. And Whisper history just begins about that time!"

"Anachronism?" Jaeff blinked. "Rift?"

"The time storm." Adam raised a brow at the little man. "At the year 2050. And there's a transpolar planetary rift at about 2410. The Whispers don't have that exactly, because there are no concurrent records of it."

Jaeff paused, the other Convergence people gathering around him. "We don't have anything like that in our future," he said. "Surely the kites would show us something like that if it was there."

"What's this 'kites' business?" Billy asked, of no one in particular.

Beside him the little female, Gambit, pointed to a speck of color high up, moving with the winds, its track paralleling the outer bank of fogs. "Free kites," she said. "We release them on schedule, and they drift away along the splice of Convergence. Time is slower there. They fade out and disappear, into the past. And we retrieve kites sent by ourselves in the future, coming the other way. So far we have kites from as far away as five centuries in the future."

"This place is like a river," Billy Bluefoot mused, his dark eyes distant like one who sees what most people don't. "Strong current in the middle, eddies and slow water along the sides."

"Eine flodenfjord," Healfdeane elaborated solemnly.

Billy nodded. "Exactly. With the wind blowing upstream and the water flowing down. Some people live on one bank and some on the other. This is an island in the stream. The winds of time blow one way, the waters of existence flow the other."

"That's it!" Jaeff beamed. "A paradox, you see. Eons of ordinary existence, and we didn't even know there was a river until the gate appeared and we saw the island."

Healfdeane seemed to have no trouble following all this, and Adam realized that the two psychics were thinking in tandem. The words meant nothing to the Viking, but in the way of the skald he perceived their meanings as Billy saw them, and assimilated. *"Valholl,"* he growled now. *"Die lukket ubrist."*

"Gates and bridges," Adam mused. "So this thing you call the interface is like a splice—a graft where two separate timelines meet—and Convergence is an island between them?"

Jaeff nodded. "That's one way to look at it."

"Then the bridges that Zephyr envisions are like conduits from the island to either shore?"

"Exactly." The little man grinned a chipmunk grin. "From each shore, there is a potential link to here, accessible only by routes not distorted by dimensional warp. Psychic routes. The 'path of the psyche,' you might say. Easy to see, but hard to find."

"You people got here without psychics," Billy Bluefoot pointed out.

"We found a way." Jaeff shrugged. "We decided we'd best maintain a presence here until the interface is past. We found that by pooling our dreams, it could be done. Everybody has at least a little ESP. It took twenty-three of us in *synpensitia* . . . ah, let's call it *concentration* . . . to bridge to here the first time. Now Zephyr thinks he can do it alone."

"I gather he hasn't succeeded?" Adam pressed.

"He complains of interference," Gambit said. "Personally, I

think he's his own interference. He thinks he's making bridges, but each time he only links with someone on the other side who has the skill to link. He always finds his route in fogs, and they're always somebody else's fogs. Ben made a lot of fogs. Then Molly, then you three in tandem. Zephyr's bridges are your bridges, not his."

They were very near the standing fog now, and the procession stopped. "What do we do?" Adam asked. "Just walk in?"

"How would we know?" Gambit demanded. "We've never made it to the middle. We try, but we keep coming out again where we went in."

Molly and Norma Jean scampered through the hesitant crowd. "It's easy," Molly said. "You just have to believe your mind, and not your eyes. I'll show you."

Gambit stared at the girl. "You've been into the funnel, Molly? Why didn't you show us?"

"You never asked." Molly shrugged. She took Adam's hand. "When you're confused," she suggested, "just think someplace else. You can pick and choose."

37-09-59 × 100-35-32
February 9, 1951

Joe Greer cupped his hands to blow into them, trying to warm frozen fingers. By bleak dawn light he gazed out across the Cimarron valley, wondering for the thousandth time what inner perversity had ever prompted him to set out with a thousand-dollar camera and a five-hundred-dollar car to chronicle the saga of Great Plains agriculture.

A month ago, sitting in the cozy warmth of the Jack of Diamonds, listening to the clatter of the Chicago El, with his belly full of prime rib roast and Cutty Sark, it had seemed a grand opportunity—a chance to carve himself a unique niche in photojournalism, to do the definitive work on contemporary Mid-Americana: DUST BOWL TO CORNUCOPIA . . . FORTY YEARS OF HIGH PLAINS PROGRESS. Fame, recognition, publication rights, and five grand in grants from the ASCS. And a first-rights advance from the *Great Plains Journal* for his wintertime folio.

Somehow, the inspiration of that evening in Chicago had become very elusive in the weeks following. Why did the nation's breadbasket have to be so monotonously dreary? And so damn windy and cold? Why were little-town motels so austere, nightlife so lacking, and farmland cafés just food and no entertainment? Why did the wind always whine? And why were eye-appeal landscapes so hard to find in winter-wheat country?

With a frosty sigh, Joe gazed across the empty miles beyond his chosen quarter section of drab, gray wheat field and tried to find a counterpoint there somewhere—some little feature that his lens could capture to give life to a totally dull photograph.

The valley sloped away, lazy little hills like descending layers of drab grass, sagebrush, and occasional yucca—or "soapweed," as the locals called it. Far away, it bottomed out in a meandering flat dotted with little groves of barren, defeated-looking trees, and just a hint among them of the wide, sandy bed of the frozen trickle that was called Cimarron River.

He scanned the distance with his spotting scope. At first the only movement visible anywhere was the rippling of drab, gray grass in the erratic wind. Then he saw a covey of quail racing low across the landscape, and peered back along their path. There was someone down there, partly hidden by a little crest—someone doing something with various mechanical-looking things.

"Some other damn fool out in the cold," Joe muttered to himself.

Beyond the river, the scene reversed itself, climbing slowly away to the line of distant, featureless fields miles away on the other side.

Midway up that far slope was the remains of an abandoned farmstead—a sagging roof over broken windows and a shiny new windmill. There was really nothing else to see. Nothing alive, nothing of interest, not even a jackrabbit.

This shot would be a bust, where the grand panorama was concerned. Even the magic of his lenses couldn't draw blood from a turnip, or graphic interest from this scene. He sighed again, got out the Voigtlander, and snapped it onto the tripod.

The field before him was one of the ASCS "musts," and therefore worth forty dollars plus prints. So he'd snap a roll and settle for that.

With the big lens in place, he peered through his viewfinder, adjusting angles, framing his shot, and fine-touching his focus. He snapped a couple of frames at 1/100, hoping the dawn light across the ice rime might add an element of mystique, then settled down to serious work at 1/25. Sometimes, with the right fine-grain film and enough exposure to bring out hidden colors, the darkroom was where the magic happened.

He was on his tenth frame when his eyes widened, hugging the viewfinder. Something was happening, there in his prism. He gasped, and frozen fingers triggered the shutter and advance spasmodically, as though by instinct. Something entirely new, entirely different, and entirely unexplainable had filled his view for that one moment. He had a confused impression of bright lights, busy people, flowing movement, and sudden chaos, all centered on a huge, quivering, domelike shape that virtually covered the floor of the valley and then erupted in a rush of unbelievable brilliance. But only for an instant.

Shaken, he fumbled for his spotting scope and played it across the vista ahead.

Nothing. The scene was as it had been—barren, desolate, cold plains riven by a wide, shallow valley where the frigid sagebrush was the only dark contrast in a world of bleak browns and grays. Even the lone figure down by the river was gone, along with all those mechanical things.

Joe packed his gear, got the Chevy going, and wheeled onto a bumpy little two-track road that headed down into the valley. In the distance, he saw frightened cattle running blindly as though in terror. At a zag in the road, a pair of coyotes and several panicked jackrabbits thumped past. It looked for a moment like the rabbits were chasing the coyotes. Then they overtook them, ran among them, and went on. When he had gone about a mile, he ran out of road.

Here, right around here, was where the thing had been. But now there was nothing—no big, eye-confusing *thing*, no busy little people, no scorched earth or debris. Only the sharp smell of ozone in the wind verified that he had actually seen something here.

In confusion, Joe picked up his Voigtlander and stared at it. "What the hell have I got in here?" he muttered. Backing the Chevy around, he headed back to the main road. In Hugoton he could find a darkroom.

Willy World Store #641
The Present

Everything the UEB files contained, regarding the fateful uptime mission of L-316, had been transferred by E-mit to the banks of L-383, and now resided in universal access mode in the impulses of the gas-crystal vats in the Willmart megacenter on Pawnee Street. Above and around a dozen temporarily placed webframe generators, occupying all of what had been the Housewares and Floor Coverings sections, in the back of the big, warehouselike building, tall visions rose and spread. Massive, exquisite displays of color, form, and contour, the virtual-reality holograms grew, screening and eliminating every distracting detail beyond them.

As the flawless displays came alive, Teal Fordeen stepped out from the control island to face the ranked Whispers and their indigenous guests—an unusually quiet, awed gallery of faces peering upward at the holograms dancing above them.

"We have traced the original path of Time Loop L-316," the leader of the Whispers said solemnly. "With the upload of Universal Experience Bank data, and the new parameters provided by the being known as Zephyr, we have achieved a moment-by-moment record of that crucial event." He turned slightly and pointed upward, indicating the dozen separate virtual realities displayed above. "From UEB's own records, we have the initial formation of L-316—a torus time loop similar in conformation to our own L-383—at Pacifica Base in the year 3005. From extrapolation of E-mit downtime data we have its emergence in real time at the anchor point on the ninth day of February, 1951.

"And now, using the new dimensional parameters dictated

by Zephyr's 'corrections,' we have an exact, charted log of the T1 path of L-316 through T2 time—and thus the path of the time conduit itself. The blind section of our route past the Arthurian Anachronism is no longer blind. You see it before you here, presented in visual imagery, topographic interpretation, mathematical equation, four-dimensional extrapolative chronography, and universe-oriented cartotempography. The route is displayed here in every fashion we possess, and the discrepancies in presentation are obvious.

"Time Loop L-316 went—and we who have followed its conduit have all gone—where our best science maintains that it is impossible to go."

Complete, stunned silence filled the gathering area as he strode from one display to the next, highlighting corresponding features of various holograms. "The time conduit is a continuity," he said. "An invariable integrity from point of beginning to antiquity, with its pivot at point of anchor. And yet nine hundred and ninety-seven one-thousandths of its route from beginning to anchor does not exist by any previously known standard in our universe. Only the few moments from touchdown to loop conversion can be quadrangulated entirely within the four known dimensions. The ensuing five hundred forty-nine years and eleven days downtime are chartable, but only partially. Throughout that span, as we ourselves have observed, the conduit is never entirely bounded by T2 time."

He paused, sighed, and scanned his audience, his eyes touching each of them. "We have always wondered," he said, "why there are no people of the pre-Arthurian races in our time of origin. We have puzzled over the remarkable differences between our era—which originates between the years 2450 and 2600—and the mainstream thrust of the history we entered upstream from the Anachronism.

"This graphic delineation of our journey has given us the precise parameters of the puzzle, and presented us with the answer. From the year 2499 onward, there is no common reference in any of this universe's prime dimensions between our time conduit and the history through which it passes.

"In effect, between 1951 and 2499 our timeline flows entirely out of one history and into another, and it was from that other history that our journey back through time began."

In the entire room, only a single, quiet voice broke the silence.

"Well, I'll be damned," Edwin Limmer drawled. "So that's how it happened! Now the question is, why?"

A hundred hairless, huge-eyed Whisper faces turned toward the man who was—so far as anyone knew—the only living anomaly. Beside him, Nancy Culver felt a surge of sheer awe. She had come to this place looking for her brother. Instead, she had found marvels and mysteries beyond her wildest imaginings—people who traveled in time, people who visited the past and the future as casually as one might visit a neighbor . . . and people from another time, who were unlike any people she had ever known. Now she gazed at the huge, indescribable visions standing in thin air above the ranked machines of the Whispers, and at the intent, alien visages of the Whispers themselves, and felt she had never seen anything so stunningly beautiful.

"Why did it happen?" Limmer elaborated. "And *when* did it happen? I mean, obviously it was always this way in normal, T2 time, but this relates to L-383's present instability, doesn't it? You know it took more than a dose of advanced theory to threaten the loop's integrity, Teal. Something has happened in current duration to cause that. And it has to do with the L-316 anchorage a half century ago. T1 is out of sync here, isn't it? What's going on?"

Teal Fordeen smiled a tired, fond Whisper smile at the man from both future and past who had shared so much of the Pacificans' great adventure. "As usual, Edwin, your knowledge of our culture is augmented by the intuitions of your own. That is exactly the question we face now. And here is a clue."

At a touch of Whisper fingers on a console, one of the virtual fields dissolved and regenerated itself, this time in two flat dimensions. The image was an old, silver-iodide-process photograph, enlarged and enhanced so that every minute detail was vivid and clear. "This image has been preserved in UEB deep storage almost since the beginning of the World History Investigative Society," Teal said. "It is a photograph held originally in the archives of the Institute for Temporal Research.

"This picture was made by someone named J. Greer, on February 9, 1951. Obviously no one at that time had any idea of what it is. This may be the only existing photographic record of a grounded time loop in visible stasis. It is Loop L-316, at its moment of transition from loop to conduit. And here—" A small section of the displayed foreground became highlighted. "—is what may have occurred at that moment. See, outside the perimeter of the loop, these arrays are obviously not contemporary technology. This one, right here, is unquestionably a device for generating a TEF field. The focalizer is clearly visible.

"And this person beside it, despite his bizarre attire, is a Pacifican. Microelectronic enhancement verifies his identity. This is a photograph of 1KHAF4."

"Kaffer," Limmer growled. "So he *is* loose again. When was this, Teal? The alteration, I mean. When, in durational time?"

"Apparently it hasn't happened yet, but the probability effects are increasing." Teal shrugged sadly. "Any time now, I'd say."

Near the rear of the assembly, the timer Amanda Santee stepped from shadows. "I'm going," she stated thinly. "He has to be stopped. Give me vectors, please, Deem." Across the heads of the ranked Whispers, she caught Limmer's eye. "Damn it, *where is Adam*?"

∞

It was the best of times, it was the worst of times.

—Charles Dickens

∞

A closed fist isn't a tool, it's an attitude. You can't grasp anything with your fist closed.

—Molly Muldoon

∞

XIII

Chronogenesis

Convergence

The fog rolled and billowed like cold, wet smoke. At times they could see several steps ahead, then a moment later the visibility would be no more than an arm's length. Here the stony ground was bare and damp. Nothing grew but lichens on the rocks.

Still, it was bright with a glow that seemed to come from ahead, but maybe came from all around. There was no sense of direction, no path to follow, no point of reference anywhere—nothing but the elusive light and the blinding fog.

Molly Muldoon led the way, still clinging to Adam's hand. Through the girl's touch, he found that he could see through her eyes, sense through her senses. The sheer power of her presence in his mind was awesome. It was like the taste of telepathy he had felt, in contact with Billy Bluefoot and the savage Healfdeane, but more delicate—more open and innocent and as a result much stronger.

As they picked their way forward through the shrouding mist, the timer relaxed his logic and let his intuition guide him into the intricacies of psionic communication. He found there the texture of his own talent for dimensional manipulation, but without the hard, restrictive binding of a single skill. Instead, he discovered that the manipulation of environment by the mind was a complex tapestry of skills, without subject limitations.

"A person doesn't have to be like a closed fist," Molly chattered, squeezing his hand with childish reassurance as she read his thoughts. "Just open your fingers and there's nothing you can't grasp."

Three hundred yards, by Adam's guess, into the fog, he seemed to have lost all contact with physical reality. Vertigo came and went, and he was dizzy. Another two hundred yards and his senses reeled. It seemed as though they were walking horizontally along a vertical wall, where up was to one side and down to the other . . . or they were upside down, defying gravity as they walked a dark ceiling in a shining place. Then after a moment they were facing straight down, with the path they had paced all above them.

Adam crouched as waves of logical confusion assailed him. He felt the need to cling to the shifting surface that was the only solid thing in this world, but Molly tugged at him. "Trust your senses, not your mind," she urged. "It's not how you think it ought to be that matters, it's how it truly is."

She practically had to shout it, Adam noticed. The light was intensifying and with it grew sound—a sound that was like all the sounds he had ever heard, and none of them. It was a constant, rising wail that made his ears ring and his skin crawl. He knew he was hearing only part of it—that part that was within the audible range.

Behind and around them, others clustered close, wide-eyed and terrified. Cindy Bruce held Norma Jean close and clung to Ben Culver, whose eyes were nearly closed as though he was walking in his sleep. "The child is right," Ben gasped, opening his eyes and then closing them again, quickly. "It's an optical illusion or something. I keep thinking I'm going backward, but I know I'm not."

Around the seven humans, a cluster of terrified little people clung to them and to one another. The procession into the fog had started as a parade. Now it was a tangle of tightly pressed bodies with a lot of arms and legs.

"This is amazing," Adam muttered. "My sense of direction is as screwed up as my sense of dimension, but if I close my mind to it, this is just a fog and nothing more."

Behind him, Cindy shrieked. She gripped Norma Jean with all her strength and leapt onto Ben's back, wrapping her legs around his middle, her free arm around his neck.

Ben was nearly bowled over by the sudden assault. He stumbled, scattering Convergencers around him. "Shut your eyes!" he gargled, trying to wrench the woman's choking arm from his throat.

Cindy closed her eyes as tight as they would close, then slowly relaxed her grip and got her feet on the ground. "I thought I was flying off into space," she said.

Under her arm, Norma Jean caught her breath and hissed, "Mommy, don't be such a wimp!"

The light now was so bright in the radiant mist that it hurt their eyes, and most of the party closed them. It seemed to help a little. Ben Culver and Billy Bluefoot both had grips on Adam's belt, now. Healfdeane had one hand full of Billy's coat and the other full of drawn sword. Cindy and Norma Jean clung to Ben as though their lives depended upon it.

"The blind leading the blind," Molly muttered, her voice lost in the rising cacophony of sound that was the song of the light.

Gusts and bursts of strong wind whipped at them, coming from random directions, then settled into a rising gale that pummeled them as they staggered through it.

The cascade of sound had begun to warble now—a confusing, across-the-scale resonance of harmonics that was angel choirs and the drums of hell, all mixed up together. And through it came the eerie, haunting wails of rising wind. "Hear the banshees?" Molly shouted. "We're at the funnel!"

They clung and listened, and Norma Jean peered around through slitted eyes. "Where are the little people?" she wondered.

The others looked around, too. There was no sign of Jaeff, Gambit, Teejay, and the rest. The entire flock of Convergencers had disappeared.

"They went back." Molly grinned. "Stubborn, they are. Stubborn and logical. They always follow the straight path. And it always takes them back to where they started. That's why Zephyr keeps trying to build bridges."

The banshee wails howled and buffeted them, and windborne fog pushed at them like a cold, driving wall. But as they went on, it diminished, and abruptly it died to a low, gusting breeze and a deep rumble of thunder. Adam opened his eyes and blinked. Ahead of them, just at their feet, was a nothingness that seemed to go on forever. An abyss, he thought. Infinity and eternity. The mother of all abysses.

The eye of the vortex of Convergence.

Molly faltered now, and Adam sensed her uncertainty. Abruptly the sure, melodic aegis of her ESPer mind lost its harmony, and the senses she projected were full of confusion. She had led them this far, by meticulous, uncluttered intuition. But now, faced with a reality beyond comprehension, that intuition became shreds of doubt.

Holding her small hand in his, Adam felt the full impact of her uncertainty. This formidable creature, this bright, evolving intelligence that was so far beyond the ordinary human psyche from which it had evolved, was still only a little girl—only a frightened child facing the visage of chaos.

But another, stronger psyche took over then. "I see it," Ben said, as much in projected thought as in words. "This is the key. The *staniu* . . . the funnel is the heart of an occurrence. Everything about it is in it. My God," he breathed aloud, "I understand!"

Adam turned to him, marshaling his thoughts. Without speaking, using only the intuitive, commanding concentration he had learned from Billy and Healfdeane, he let his strength leap from mind to mind. Then show us, Ben, his thoughts said. Make us see it, too.

The response was a silent flood of discovery, bits of puzzles coming together and displaying themselves to be seen.

The shadow people of Convergence lore were Whispers—the survivors of the anchor loop, L-316. In a temporal vortex they had activated photogravitic reversal, and this light was their legacy. This *staniu* was the foundation of Convergence. It was what Convergence was all about.

"The funnel." Molly pointed. "It's your turn, now, Adam. See if you can think us somewhere else."

The timer stared into nothingness, and more pieces of puzzles fell into place. The multiple minds of psionic melding had expanded his awareness. He felt as though he had been blind, and deaf, and lame, but now he was whole. Here on the verge of eternity his evolved senses returned to him, and he knew the dimensions as never before. He saw them now complete, and he was awed. There was more to the matrix of direction and dimension—so much more, that he had never even imagined.

For the first time—for the first time in his life—Adam knew exactly where he was, in a universe whose blends and balances for the first time he truly could see.

And more than that! Deep within, he knew the answer to the riddles that had for so long haunted Teal Fordeen. Intuition released from old constraints presented new perspectives. With certainty, Adam knew why the Whispers—with all their focus on world history—had never found themselves in it.

It was always a question of perspective, he thought wryly. Only when viewed from limited dimensions is the universe bound by dimensionality. To view the infinite as finite is like framing part of a picture. Seen face-to-face, infinity is not a vast ball with a central point, and eternity is nothing like a straight line.

The universe is universal in all respects, not just a few. Its fundament—its center, its pivot, its core, its essence—does not have to be anywhere, because it is everywhere. The only trick is to know when one has found it.

The view from the gate is not limited.

It's beautiful, isn't it, Ben Culver's thoughts radiated. Maybe with practice, I can see it the way you do. But it is your turn now. You know the way of vectors, the tricks of travel. It's your turn.

Adam sensed the concurrence of those around him. He did not need to ask Molly what vectors she preferred. Nor did he need the approval of the Cherokee, the Viking, or the sleepwalker. In his mind he knew their minds, and it was his choice. Around him he could "feel" the reality of the funnel and read its credentials. It was a shunt . . . a conduit . . . a vortex continuum that had a point of origin, and he chose that point to target the mental process of photogravitic reversal that was second nature to him.

There was no slowing, no heaviness building to darkness and instant light. This time he was only a navigator. The funnel itself was the photogravitic engine—the primal exchange of the universe: pure gravity and pure light, each reproducing the other.

To the mind of a timer, coordinates were more than a set of intersecting vectors, more than an equation of numbers in quadrangulation. To the timer, destination is a time and place, sensed as intimately as though he were already there. Adam concentrated on the origin of the funnel, and the rest went with him into transference.

37-09-59 × 100-35-32
T2 minus 2' 12.44"

Seething, long-held hatred guided Kaffer as he placed his TEF in its makeshift nest and refined the calibrations to Nordstrom and Sol. He hated timers. He hated a world that had for this long refused to bow to his domination. And most of all, he hated Whispers. In a mind uncluttered by empathy, hatred had become a seething rage.

The icy wind of this drab dawn in this wild, hostile place only fueled his hatred. Always it came back to this place—the endless plains of this region of the earth, beneath which lurked a restless singularity. Everything had begun here—the origin of time travel, the old Institute for Temporal Research that would one day center here where gravity was fluid, the rise and fall of Camelot, probably even the early experiments from which his race of Pacificans had evolved. From the Pacificans had come—or would come—the Whispers, and the conduit to the past. And here was—or would be—its anchor in real time. All of what occurred in that future past began right here!

But not when he was finished. Once and for all now, he would end it. Everything that would happen here, when he was done, would never have happened at all.

Never since L-270 had Kaffer doubted his destiny. The Arthurian Anachronism, dividing all of history into two neat sections, was made to order for him. It was his ambition and thus his destiny to seize that history before Arthur and thus to control what came after.

He was here to rule the world. The great, primitive cultures of the protomorphic world were destined to kneel at his command, and future history was to be his to dictate. All the power and the comforts of reigning perpetuity were to be his, by whatever means were required to make it so.

Yet at every turn he had been thwarted—by Whispers, by meddling timers, by the very people he despised. And always, *always* the source of his annoyance tracked back to the inception of the Whisper conduit. Always it came back to these barren plains, to this place on this day of this year.

And here he would put an end to it.

At dawn, T2 minus 2 minutes and 12.44 seconds, he aligned his TEF field, and just moments later he felt the crackling, shifting "itch" in the air that signaled the winding down of a massive resonance. Across the icy sand flats, birds burst from sparse cover. A covey of quail raced past, winging away. Along the bottoms, jackrabbits bounded from shelter to shelter, and a pair of coyotes broke from cover to race away, up the slope.

In the air, above the sighing wind, a sound grew that was more than sound—an immense, deep rhythm too low to hear but powerful enough to be felt. It was the sound of a temporal singularity, slowing from drive mode to static equilibrium. The anchor loop had arrived, following the trace of a random message from the scout loop L-270.

T2 minus 86.03"

A faint shifting of air currents in the cold wind, and the loop materialized. In normal mode, shifting back and forth across a durational parameter from immediate past to immediate future, a loop was invisible externally. Its shell was not substance, but only a configuration. It was a flow of atmospheric gases held in concert by mutual temporality. At static resonance its presence in any given moment was too brief to perceive.

But, slowing toward immobility, it became visible. At a nine-second resonance interval it was a huge, ghostly shape of fluttering light and shadow, a thing of pulsing hues settling to the surface of the earth. At a four-second interval the contour of its featureless surface was clearly discernible.

The loop was huge—far larger than Kaffer had expected. A

thirty-six-minute durational loop, he estimated—more than half an hour of closed time compacted into one massive moment. To the eye it was a hazy mountain of fluttering mist—a quarter-mile-wide doughnut of contained energies lying on the sloping prairie. Its near perimeter was no more than fifty yards from where he stood, and in the pulsing glow of its exuded light he could see the shadows of equipment within, and the little, moving shadows of its crew.

T2 minus 17.09"

Counting down, Kaffer aimed and steadied his TEF field, letting the nest's resonance coordinate itself to that of its target. At the instant of stasis, the loop would be completely vulnerable. In order to exist, a time loop must be in constant relative motion along at least one axis of a four-dimensional parabola. But three of its dimensions were static now, resting on the prairie. At T-zero the loop would be no longer viable as a temporal anomaly. For a moment, it would cease to exist, before transferring its energies into T2 to form a conduit. Before or after that moment of stasis, there was no way to reckon the effect of a separate TEF field at right angles to the loop's own field. But just *then*, at the instant of conversion, the two fields should blank each other out.

The great loop would simply cease to exist, and the impetus of conversion would become a mass-energy reversal. Every tangible thing within the loop would be consumed in the split second of conversion.

The sustaining resonance whined down to a massive flutter, then to a shiver, then to a mounting, receding whine, and Kaffer touched the set stud on his TEF control. Sensors came alive, reading the resonance of the loop, harmonizing and synchronizing the TEF.

There had always been the possibility—even the probability—that someone would try to interfere at the last moment, and Kaffer was ready. The entire TEF assembly was ringed by sensors, the perimeter crisscrossed by capacitors with ready zen charges.

T2 minus 9.96"

The countdown was only heartbeats from zero when the timer came. Kaffer was mildly surprised, and a little disappointed. He had really expected Adam. Twice before, the man Adam had interfered. But it was not Adam who came now. It was a female.

She was dark-haired, graceful, and probably pretty, among her kind. She materialized directly in front of Kaffer and went immediately for the TEF assembly. The sensors tripped and the zero-mass emission nodes fired, creating a deadly fence of pure electrical discharge. A single beam tore at her right arm, shredding fabric and flesh . . .

Kaffer felt the wrench of time manipulation. The female timer was at the barrier, springing toward the TEF. Sensors tripped and the zen nodes fired, but she was out of reach, diving below the fence of electrical energy. "Timer," Kaffer growled, and triggered his second defense. Thermal charges in a tight ring blasted upward, smashing into the woman as she—

"Timer," Kaffer growled, realizing that she had jumped back a moment in time, to dodge the zen nodes. He triggered his second defense, and thermal charges blasted upward, but she threw herself to one side. Just in that instant, in the space of a blink, the woman had timed twice, each a feint to dodge the set defenses.

Amanda Santee's green eyes blazed at the little monster before her as she dodged the thermal charges and rolled aside. For a moment, the brilliance of the charges blinded her, and she tripped and fell. Struggling upward, her injured arm collapsed under her just as someone materialized beside her. They collided, fell in a tangle, and Amanda found herself clutching a squirming, struggling little girl as a woman rolled away and came to a crouch.

T2 minus 6.18"

For an instant, Amanda had a glimpse of wide-set eyes and honey-blond hair in the dawn light. In her arms, the child pushed away from her and shouted, "Momma!" The blond woman whirled around, stood upright, and just beyond her Amanda saw Kaffer raise a handheld weapon. Frantically, she dived toward the woman, reaching out to touch her, to time her out of harm's way. But it was too late.

L-383
The Present

Only a maintenance crew remained aboard Time Loop L-383 as the probability gradient of the loop declined. All nonessential personnel had been transferred to the fixed-base analysis facility located in the closed commercial building provided by Ed Limmer and Lucas Hawthorn. If there were to be a technological solution to the probability crisis, it would be found there.

Meanwhile, Teal Fordeen and his top technicians struggled to keep L-383 alive. Maintaining open comlink channels with Willy World, L-383 broke out of its hover mode and conducted a search for temporary sanctuary. In theory, T2, or fixed time, was never precisely constant in the vicinity of any planetary mass, and the Whispers had already learned that variations in gravity, light activity, and durational time were common occurrences at various places and times on Earth. Just possibly, Deem Eleveno's technologists felt, there might be a time and place where L-383 could ride out a probability dip.

At Teal's direction, the loop emerged from harmonic idle and went in search of such a place.

By quadrants and vectors they surveyed a quarter of the Earth's surface, in a hundred-year-plus time range. Emerging at ten-year intervals, L-383 scanned the range from 1890 to 2010, approaching dangerously near to the time storm, the Arthurian Anachronism of 2050.

In moments of emergence, powerful sensors and scanners aboard the loop recorded and analyzed wars, plagues, droughts, and population shifts. Voracious banks received and dutifully filed whole patterns of history, as reflected in day-to-day life and development of most of North America. They saw the emergence of transcontinental transportation, the development of aeronautics, the Johnstown flood, and the New Madrid Fault quakes. They witnessed the great cattle drives and the placement of orbiting satellites. They saw the emergence of homestead farming and the spread of the great grain belts from the Ozarks to the Rockies. They saw covered wagons and supersonic jets, the rise of skyscrapers and the sprawl of urbania.

In duly processed bits and splashes, the banks recorded the temporal checkerboard of a century, and sensors searched for a hole in time, somewhere.

They saw time move with blinding speed, and they saw days and minutes that seemed to have no end. But nowhere, nowhen did they find a haven for a deteriorating time loop. Finally L-383 returned to its accustomed hover above the central plains, in the vicinity of what would be Deep Hole, some two hundred miles west of Waystop I.

Here, in the area where time technology would be born, at the very epicenter of the Arthurian Anachronism that would occur in fifty years, seemed to be the place of greatest comfort for a deteriorating time anomaly.

As a torus loop, L-383's greatest strength was also its weakest point. Unlike the ball loop L-270, which had scouted upstream time, L-383's topology was that of a doughnut. Its relationship to the Whisper conduit was that of a coil to a rope. It was separate in configuration, but still part and parcel of the conduit. Should the conduit cease to exist, L-383 would also cease to exist. And now existing was the problem.

"The probability of our existence is at twenty-three percent now," Toocie Toonine reported soberly. "That is down seven points since last reading, and still dropping."

Teal Fordeen closed his big, tired eyes and rested his face in delicate hands. "What word from analysis?" he asked.

"Positive confirmation that the source of our instability is the event of Anchor Loop L-316's conversion," Toocie said. "The probability that the conduit will never have been formed has risen to seventy-seven percent."

"Can we confront Kaffer directly?"

Toocie shook her bald head sadly. "KT-Pi ran a direct intervention scenario, with zero-null results. The presence of L-383 at the L-316 event would entail a certainty of massive anachronism at emergence."

"Could that be worse than what we're faced with now?" Peedy Cue demanded. "Either way, we cease to exist, don't we?"

"An intervention anachronism would ripple all the way downtime to our own era," Toocie explained. "Then it wouldn't be just Whispers wiped out. It could be the entire Pacifican race."

"Then what *do* we do about it?"

"Nothing," Teal said. "Aside from keeping L-383 viable as long as we can, there's nothing we can do but wait. Wait, and trust that our friends of this era might somehow stop Kaffer before he destroys the conduit."

Peedy blinked large, frightened eyes. "But what can they do? Edwin Limmer is the only protomorph we know with any real grasp of Whisper technology. The rest—the Hawthorns, Faron Briscoe, even George Wilson—they're just indigenees. They're no match for Kaffer."

"I'm thinking of Amanda," Teal muttered. "She . . . all the timers, they have resources we don't have. Powers that even Kaffer doesn't have. Some of them, I believe, have abilities that even *they* don't know they have. Do you know, she told me once that she had a hunch—an intuition—that the answer to everything was as simple as the sign for infinity. I wish I had thought about that more."

"I don't understand," Peedy said.

"Neither do I. And maybe she didn't, either. But it was intuition. I should have trusted her more, because now that's all we can do. Amanda has gone to intercede. Maybe she can. And then, of course, Adam is out there somewhere. We wait, Peedy. We hold our idle here, we maintain viability as long as we can, and we wait."

At a dedicated console, a team led by Cuel Denyne had synchronized the probability readings against T1 duration approaching the 1951 metamorphosis—the sacrifice of L-316 to create the conduit. The synchronization was exact. By degrees of probability and by seconds of duration, it was a countdown to oblivion.

In the final seconds, the crew of L-383 gathered around

that single display, watching the numbers scroll down: probability-11, termination minus 5.5 seconds . . . p-8, t minus 4″ . . . p-6, t minus 3″ . . .

Big, sad eyes roved around at the receding virtuals that screened the nothingness of the temporal loop that had been home to all of them for nearly fifty years by T1 duration—a nothingness now headed for oblivion. As project notarian, Zeepi Arr had brought up the mission log. It was his responsibility, as Elzy Pyar's successor, to maintain a chronicle of the mission of L-383, and he didn't want to leave it incomplete. Even if no one would ever read it, he wanted it done right.

He scanned the final entries, then let his screen scroll back to those unanswered questions that Teal Fordeen had posed—so long ago, it seemed:

> Why, with all its historic research and its resources, did WHIS never suspect that there were timers in the past—individuals among the predecessor races who could do by act of will what WHIS must do through elaborate technology?
>
> What became of those predecessors? Where did they go during the Locked Centuries of Pacifican origin?
>
> Why has WHIS, with the ultimate breakthrough in practical time travel, encountered no one except ourselves traversing the conduits of time?
>
> *Why have we not met others from our own future, making use of our discoveries?*

Almost as an afterthought, Zeepi added a riddle of his own to the dimming screen: "Why, from the millions of our own people now streaming back through time in search of the earliest beginnings of it all, have none returned? Where did *they* all go, and what did they find?"

The countdown neared zero. Probability-3, t minus 1.5″ . . . p-1, t minus 0.5″ . . .

L-383 faded, became insubstantial. For all its vitality and all its essential reality, the great loop was still only a temporal distortion, a manipulation of dimensions dependent each instant upon the instants before. Now it darkened and faltered. Then in a blaze of unimaginable brilliance it was no longer there.

∞

Forever is one of the varieties of eternity. Always, there is another.

∞

XIV
The Many Paths of Time

37-09-59 × 100-35-32
T2 minus 6.18″

Like seeds sprayed from a rotor, the seven from Convergence had been separated and scattered in the instant of vortex.

Cindy Bruce came out of the funnel clinging to Norma Jean and sprawled on cold grass on a dawn-lit slope. She raised herself to her knees and was knocked sprawling by someone tumbling toward her. They fell, rolled, and Norma Jean twisted away. Coming to a crouch, Cindy gasped at the sight of her daughter in the arms of a dark-haired woman on the ground before her.

Norma Jean looked up, gaped in terror, and shouted, and Cindy leapt to her feet.

Since the day she set out for Independence—a lifetime ago, it seemed—the whole world around Cindy had gone crazy. Cold fogs and disappearing roads and broken houses and bears—that had been only the beginning of it. There had been Ben Culver, and for a moment the illusion of sanity in an insane universe, but then it had only gotten worse. Jumping from place to place, from time to time, monsters in pyramids and a hypnotic cone, leprechauns and imps and a place where even the landscape was distorted . . . then the falling through a black vortex, and now this . . .

Somewhere along the way, she had lost all sense of reality. Nothing made any sense, and she had just about stopped expecting it to. But now, at this moment, something basic snapped into place. Here before her, a kneeling woman with an injured arm crouched on hostile ground, gripping Norma Jean as though in bondage. The sight of her daughter held by a stranger, the sound of Norma Jean's cry, pushed everything else aside. Cindy growled, tensed, and made claws of her fingers. On the frozen ground before her the strange woman gasped and lunged, reaching for her . . .

T2 minus 4.88"

Dazzled by his own thermal charges, Kaffer crouched and came up with a handheld zen-gun, his blinking eyes searching. The timer had dodged the thermals, the way she had dodged the zen nodes. She was still out there, just past his perimeter, and still coming to interfere with his plan.

In vague dawn light, his eyes still registering the glare of the thermal charges, he saw a silhouette arising, only a few feet away. It was a woman—a trim shadow in the glare-shrouded dawn. It was her! He pointed the zen-gun and squeezed the stud. There was a confusion of silhouettes there, like several people where there should have been only one. But as he activated the zero–mass emission node weapon, shadowy figures merged, separated, and one of them charged forward, directly at him.

The shadow was almost on him, reaching past the TEF assembly, as the gun unleashed its lightning. Searing light and crackling energy bathed the advancing figure, which abruptly seemed taller, heavier than before. Bigger and somehow far different, even to dazzled eyes. In the blaze of electrical charge, the silhouette jerked upright as though impaled on the bolt of energy. From head to knees, the figure burst into flame, but still it came toward Kaffer, one staggering step, its charred hand reaching out . . .

Kaffer backed away a step and held the zen-gun steady. Like torrents from a hose, the searing static charges shot out, burning and consuming fabric and flesh. The specter staggered again, then fell—a charred, smoking corpse, one hand outthrust as though reaching for the TEF.

Kaffer peered at the fallen assailant, and the bile of frustration arose in his throat. The corpse was a man, not a woman.

The female timer was still around, somewhere. How many of them *were* there?

T2 minus 3.03"

In its humming nest, the temporal effect focalizer began to glow as its resonance matched the rhythm of the anchor loop's drive field, ticking down toward stasis. Kaffer turned toward it, and a monstrous shadow towered over him. His zen-gun was knocked aside, and his big, dazzled eyes saw the sweep of a long, iron blade.

"Wulkenfolket!" the shadow roared. The blade swept high and descended. The last sounds that 1KHAF4—the being called Kaffer—ever heard were the terrible thud of a sharpened edge cleaving flesh and bone, and the thump of hard ground against his head . . . a head severed from its body. Big, glazing eyes stared out from a not-quite-human face at a dimming, topsy-turvy world, then blinked once and died.

T2 minus 0.00"

The declining harmony wound down and ended. Stasis occurred and the final slow pulse of time shift was as near to perfect synchronization as it would be. And in that instant twin temporal effect focalizers—one within the nearby haze of a collapsing time loop and the other separate, its timefield at right angles to the first—unleashed the raw power of the universe's two primal forces, gravity and light.

The synchronization of the two generators was almost perfect. It might have been perfect, except for the infinitesimal resistance of psionic resonance implanted in the shell of the TEF salvaged from the remains of the old scout time loop, L-270—extrasensory homing coordinates placed there by one of the finest minds ever to evolve from the construct race of Pacifica.

From the cold wash where he tumbled, Adam saw and understood the ensuing seconds on the prairie beyond, but it was too far away to reach, and the moments of sensory adjustment after the vertigo of the funnel vortex defied his timing skill. He heaved himself up from the draw and ran, knowing that he was too late. Kaffer was there, and Kaffer was ready.

In the dawn light he saw Amanda charge the renegade Whisper's TEF installation, and saw her disappear and re-appear twice in the blink of an eye, dodging the traps Kaffer had set.

He heard pounding footsteps just behind him, but didn't look around. In the confusion ahead he saw Molly Muldoon appear suddenly. She was there—and then instantly gone—and he saw Cindy Bruce getting to her feet. She was a silhouette against the dawn sky, rising into view as Kaffer raised his zen device. Adam wanted to shout a warning, but there was no time. Then, abruptly, Billy Bluefoot was there, and Adam saw him take the charge from Kaffer's weapon.

Like a torch, Billy took the full blast of a zen weapon and burst into flame. He took one blind step, reaching out . . . then fell. And behind Kaffer a tall, ragged shadow arose. It was the Viking skald, Healfdeane—huge, dark, and ominous, big bare arms under cloaked fur wraps wielding a fifteen-pound blade that was as light as a toothpick in his strong hands.

Great, instant darkness fell and huge, instant new light flared, and on the sloping prairie above the Cimarron there was only a stunned, motley group of people, staring now down-slope, where the enormous, thinning shadow of a massive time loop had rested moments before. There was nothing down there now—nothing for the eyes to see, nothing even for the enhanced senses of the ESPers among them to detect.

The loop and all it contained were gone, as though nothing had ever been there at all.

Adam arrived at the scene as Amanda Santee got to her feet, still holding the child Norma Jean with her good hand. Adam slowed, and Ben Culver rushed past him to engulf Cindy in trembling arms.

Norma Jean broke free of Amanda's grasp and ran to the two of them. Cindy knelt to wrap the child in her arms, while Ben placed himself between them and the grisly remains almost at their feet, and edged them away. Adam looked around bleakly, then took Amanda's injured arm in gentle fingers, raised it, and frowned. "You might have a scar, here, Scarlett," he decided.

Mandy looked up at him, startled. Adam's voice was the same gentle voice it had always been, but something had changed. His words seemed to blanket her, to wrap themselves around her like caring thoughts. She *felt* what he said, even as her ears heard it. "What . . . ," she began, then hesitated as a reassurance that had no words swept over her.

I've been some strange places and seen some strange things, his unspoken thoughts whispered in her mind. We're more than we thought we were, Amanda. We're just beginning to learn.

Mandy let her eyes rove over the scene before her. They stopped at the smoking, charred corpse beside the TEF uprights. "Who . . . who was that?" she whispered.

"An Indian," Adam said bleakly. His flooding mind-flow seemed to recede from her, as though by will, and his words were words again. "Just a wandering Cherokee. His name's Billy Bluefoot. He doesn't . . . didn't have any use for scags. The big barbarian with the sword, that's Healfdeane. He's a Viking. He . . . well, it's a long story."

Together they stood, gazing around them. Kaffer's severed head lay against a TEF brace, sightless eyes staring upward into the coils. The little, decapitated body was several feet away, sprawled across the blackened remains of Billy Bluefoot.

Healfdeane squatted there beside them, his hood-shadowed head bowed. With a muttered oath he lifted the headless body of the renegade Pacifican, flung it aside, muttered a few words over Billy, then turned away and began calmly cleaning his sword on Kaffer's stained garments.

"So that . . . that little monster . . . was Kaffer." Amanda shuddered. "I tried to stop him, Adam. When we learned he had escaped . . . then when Teal and the other Whispers found that old photograph, we knew he had come here, where L-316 anchored the conduit. He—" She stared at the severed head of Kaffer. "How could such a being exist, Adam? Didn't he care about *anything*? He came to abort the Whispers' anchor event, to have time all to himself. To wipe out the history of his *own people*! I thought I could . . ."

Adam was barely listening. His gaze was intent upon the

standing TEF nest, and in his dark eyes a wonder grew. "Look," he said.

Amanda looked, and gasped. The TEF rig stood dark and cold now, inert and passive. Its tower braces, its field generator and vectoring mechanisms, were bizarre pieces of outlandish hardware girdled around the coils of the central nest.

But the nest was empty. Where there should have been a translucent TEF cone—the projecting tip of the temporal effect focalizer—there was nothing. The TEF was gone.

"Did I . . . did we fail?" Mandy murmured. "Did the anchor fail? Is everything the Whispers accomplished—their whole journey into the past, L-383—is that all gone, Adam? Did none of that ever happen?"

"We're here," Adam said thoughtfully. "We're here, and we remember. Would we remember so much of something that never happened?" He shaded his eyes against the first glow of sunlight, looking out across the slope and the river valley beyond. There was no sign that a durational loop had ever been there, and no sign of the conduit it should have become. But then, the conduit was never visible from normal time, anywhere or anywhen. It was a tunnel through time, with only one external dimension. All of its spatial dimensions were internal, concomitants of its temporal base and unrelated to spatial dimension outside the conduit's own reality.

"We can find out, I suppose," he said. "Whispers or not, we're still timers, you and I. If a future presence still exists this side of the Anachronism, we can find it."

"What about all this? And them?" Her gaze fixed on Ben Culver, kneeling nearby with Cindy and Norma Jean. "That . . . that's the sleepwalker?"

Adam nodded. "That's him. He's a natural timer, like we thought. But he's more than that, too. He's . . . I think he's what we are going to become, when we learn to spread our wings."

"If there are any left to spread. So what do we do now?"

"Let's look for Whispers," Adam decided. "Let's find them, then I'll come back and attend to this."

They vectored on L-383, Amanda choosing the route, using the range of coordinates that had been the loop's harmonic "hover" for so long. Hands clasped together, they willed transference and materialized nearly a half century downtime, on a summer-hot gravel road at the edge of a wheat field. "It isn't here," Amanda said. "It's gone."

"Or we missed it," Adam mused. "Let's try again. Use homing, Mandy. Don't try to vector. You jumped from there, now jump back to where you were, but now."

Again the instant of intense, heavy darkness and of pure, blossoming new light.

A small presence jostled Amanda, and a shrill Whisper voice said, "Oops! Didn't see you."

Adam grinned. They were standing in the crowded interior of the big, shrouded building that had been Willy World Store #641, and all around them busy Whispers scampered here and there, feeding and harvesting the data banks beneath arrays of big, holographic virtualities. Across an expanse of shrouded counters and aisles, a deep voice shouted, "Hey! Where in hell have you two been?"

Lucas Hawthorn hurried toward them, trailed by a wave of curious, excited Whispers.

"I forgot," Amanda said sheepishly. "I didn't jump from L-383. I jumped from here."

"If you're looking for L-383," Lucas said, coming around a countertop, "then join the crowd. A few minutes ago, they broke off contact, and we can't find them!"

"Can't find them?" Adam frowned. "You mean the loop's gone?"

"I'm sure it isn't gone," a reedy voice pronounced. Deem Eleveno's eyes looked almost frantic. "It just . . . well, it isn't where it was, and we haven't traced it yet."

"Where's Teal?"

"He's wherever L-383 is." Lucas scattered Whispers ahead of him as he hurried up to them. "What happened, Mandy? What about Kaffer? And what happened to your arm?"

"She has a zen-burn, Lucas." Adam peered around, studying some of the big holographic virtuals above the Whisper analytic consoles. "Is that the conduit reading?" He pointed. "Is the conduit open?"

"Of course it's open," Deem snapped. "It has always been open, since it was formed."

"Then Kaffer failed," the timer told Mandy. "You got there in time." He looked more closely at the scrolling readings on one of the virtuals. Nearby, a tall hologram revolved slowly that was like nothing Adam had ever seen—infinite-seeming traceries, random and dizzying in their number, yet forming a pattern of sorts, as they flowed inward into the graphic's center and bundled there, intertwining like the center of a massive, infinite figure eight.

"Infinity," Amanda muttered beside him, following his gaze. "It looks like infinity . . . or like the roots and branches of a tree."

But there wasn't time to study the display now. Adam turned back to the scrolling visual where the Whispers were clustered. Dimensional graphics—closely spaced intersecting lines that traced contours and extents—portrayed a glowing tube with more dimensions than the eye could decipher. What caught his attention was a bulge—or bump—at one section of the curving display. "What's that?" He pointed. "An anomaly?"

Deem nodded. "It just showed up. It's a discontinuity of some kind, in the curvature of the conduit. We haven't identified it yet, but it doesn't seem to be doing any harm. It's at the L-316 coordinates."

"It looks like a tire patch, on the graphics," Lucas noted. "What about Kaffer?"

"He's dead," Amanda said tiredly. "He had a TEF set up to sabotage the L-316 conversion. I tried to stop him. We tried. He's dead, but the TEF fired. I don't know what happened then."

"Tire patch?" Deem was squinting at the holotopograph. "A primitive simile, but apt. It does resemble a patch, doesn't it."

Lucas exchanged glances with Amanda and grinned. Sometimes, it seemed, the very single-mindedness of Whispers was their greatest obstacle. "Take care of her, Lucas," he rasped. "I'm going back there. By the way," he told Deem, "I found the sleepwalker . . . Ben Culver. You might want to let his sister know that he's still alive."

* * *

"You won't be permanently scarred," Em Ten assured Amanda as she applied a film of re-gen to the timer's injured arm. The little Whisper had come with Amanda to the Hawthorn house, by what was for both of them an unusual mode of transportation—Lucas Hawthorn's Explorer. Now they rested in the comfortable living room while Maude Hawthorn matched wits with a vagrant goat, which had taken refuge in the back bedroom.

The goat was a refugee from fifteenth-century Spain, a stowaway on the return trip of the Wentworth party's excursion to the court of Ferdinand and Isabella. In all, the excursion had been a success. Cristóbal Colón, who would later be called Christopher Columbus, had set sail from Palos bound for the new world; the Wentworths had returned to Waystop I bedecked in Castilian trinkets and Florentine finery, and the stowaway goat was being busily banished from the house.

From the living room, they heard sounds of scuffling, then the slam of the sunporch door. A moment later, Maude emerged from the kitchen, wiping her hands on a dishcloth. "That beast is out there now eating my petunias," she snapped. "We need better control on retrievals." She crossed to the conversation corner and stooped to look at her sister's arm. The injured area was muted now, covered by the thin, translucent film of the Whisper remedy. "How's the burn?"

"She'll be fine," Em said. "A few hours of fibril regeneration, and there won't be any dysfunction or even a little scar."

"I'm okay now," Amanda insisted. "I want to help Adam." She pushed Em aside and stood, then swayed dizzily and collapsed into the chair.

The little Whisper clicked her tongue. "I told you," she said. "What do you think re-gen is, a bandage? For the next few hours, most of your vitality is being drawn to that arm. Regeneration requires a lot of energy, you know. It isn't a magic poultice, it's a re-gen pad."

Maude frowned at her sister. "In other words, stay put! Is there anything you'd like?"

"Yeah." Amanda sighed. "I'd like to know what happened to L-383, and I'd like to know where and when Adam is."

37-09-59 × 100-35-32
7:41 ACS, February 9, 1951

There wasn't much surface water in the Cimarron, and what there was was crusted with icy rime, but Healfdeane found it adequate for his purposes. He had made two trips from the valley slope down to the river sand, each time carrying at least three hundred pounds of load, then used his sword to gather dry logs from a driftwood pile.

Now a huge pyre burned high on the river sands—a boat-shaped pyre twenty feet long, with the corpse of Billy Bluefoot in its center and the headless remains of Kaffer at his feet. Every trace of Kaffer's implements and assemblies were also there, thrown unceremoniously into the bonfire.

It was the last thing a Viking—the original scag—could do to honor a man who had shared his thoughts and become his friend.

The only remaining artifact from Kaffer's attempt to rule the world was Kaffer's head, which sat now atop a weathered fence post, where the dead eyes could gaze toward the fire.

Ben Culver stood on the low bank above the sands, with Cindy and Norma Jean huddled close by him, and understood the solemn nature of the occasion. The funeral pyre burned high, and would burn for an hour before collapsing inward upon its ashes. Everything within it that could burn, would burn. All the rest—ashes, hardware, and implements—would sink into the endless sands as surely and finally as a burned-out longship might sink into the sea.

They were there when Adam materialized on the slope, and he walked down to where they stood.

"He cremated them," Ben explained, indicating the blaze below. "I guess that's the best thing that could be done. Ought to do something about that head, though."

"Your sister is looking for you," Adam told him. "Can you get yourselves back to base time, to the Hawthorn house?"

"I guess so." Ben nodded. "I'm getting the hang of this jump business. I can probably go anywhere I want—and anywhen—just like you."

"You can," Adam agreed. "Only keep it to four dimensions.

Try to avoid that other thing until we all know a little more about it. To take these two with you, keep hold of them and pull them along. I'll give you coordinates. Can you handle vectors?"

"Give them to Norma Jean." Ben grinned. "She's our navigator. I'd like to know, though . . . what happened here?" He turned again to the funeral pyre in the riverbed, where Healfdeane stood lonely guard over the dying flames. "What was all this about?"

"I don't know all of it, yet," Adam admitted. "I'm trying to find out."

"What about him?" Cindy pointed toward the river. Healfdeane was on his knees now, still facing the pyre. He held his sword high, hilt up to the rising smoke. Bits of his funeral chant drifted up to them on the wind. *"Tre gange galdrede Odin . . . Forste gang var det ild . . . anden gang is . . ."*

"It's ironic," Adam muttered. "Billy Bluefoot hated scags, and now a scag is ushering him into Valhalla." He looked away. "I'll take care of him," he said. He knelt beside Norma Jean and muttered coordinates to her, holding her hand as he did. Twice he reviewed the vectors, picturing the time-place destination in his mind as he repeated the numbers. In his mind, in some area beyond the narrow confines of rational logic, he knew that she had them. "Go now," he told them. "I'll see you again when I can."

Albemarle Sound, North Carolina
The Present

Of all surface vessels, in all times, the Nordic longship is arguably the most elusive. And as a fully accoutered twelfth-century warship sailing in twentieth-century waters, *Erethlyn* had an additional advantage. Of all the thousands of people who happened to witness the dragonship on its voyage down the Atlantic coast, only a few dozen were gullible enough to truly believe what they had seen, and those few dozen were not believed by anyone who mattered.

At a tidal cut below Knotts Island—a breach left in the wake of a hurricane—*Erethlyn* slipped into Currituck Sound and put in for provisions at the tiny village of Quarles. Legends were born at Quarles that day.

Traversing the North Waterway at night, *Erethlyn* rounded Powells Point and made west up Albemarle Sound past Edenton before running aground in the Chowan backwaters. It was there that Adam and Healfdeane found them, and made it clear to Harald Ericsson that they could return home if they wished.

The conference lasted all night, enlivened by a case of good Scotch and several kegs of beer from the ruined but compensated bait camp at Quarles. At first, most of the older Vikings were in favor of going home. But gradually, Invar Crovansson and the younger raiders won them over. If they went back to Vestfold, they argued, there was nothing to look forward to but further expeditions financed by Olaf Magnusson, who always stole most of the profits. Here, though, was a new and wondrous land, where opportunities abounded.

In the end, it was the women who made the decision. At dawn, Fancy DeLite and Honey Bunn came to Adam and indicated the blissful tangle of Norsemen now sleeping peacefully all around *Erethlyn.* They had debated the matter until they were too drunk to stand up. "The boys have decided to stay here." Honey grinned. "Maybe we'll build us a town or something."

Healfdeane was dour and thoughtful, but after a time he agreed. *"Jeg har solgt,"* he decided. *"Der er ikke mere at finde ud af i Vestfold."* In his mind it was clear, and Adam understood. There was nothing worthwhile for the skald, or for any of them, where they had come from. He would stay. *"I tager af sted i morgen tidlig?"* Healfdeane asked, rising to extend a big hand.

Adam clasped forearms with the Viking. "I leave this morning." He nodded. "*Haer finde var Odin, rath* Healfdeane."

"*Var Odin,* Adam," Healfdeane growled, then turned away. When a man said he was going, he was gone. Farewells were a useless waste of words.

"Take care of them, ladies," Adam urged the former party girls. "They'll need some civilizing to survive, but this world hasn't seen the likes of them in far too long a time."

"You can say that again," Fancy agreed, her eyes sparkling.

In normal time and space, a time conduit isn't exactly anywhere. Having only one external dimension—the dimension of time—it is neither visible nor findable by ordinary means from any point in a three-dimensional world.

But since his visit to Convergence, Adam's perceptions had expanded. He understood—had always understood—the principle that any dimension must be intercepted by a vector at right angles to it in the plane of the vector and the dimension. Now he understood a truth beyond that: *every* dimension, in any composite of dimensions, is intercepted by a vector that is at right angles to all of them simultaneously.

Using this rule as his guide, Adam applied his dimensional awareness to the unique, inherent skill of the timer and went in search of a Whispers' conduit.

I haven't seen a tire patch in years, he told himself sardonically as immense, instantaneous gravity darkened the morning around him, replaced instantly by an immense wave of new light.

∞

Crest, surge, and blend are properties of flow—the act of substances, sequences, or patterns moving in a continuing stream. With respect to dynamics and interactions, any flow event may be described and analyzed in terms analogous to any other flow event, whether the subject be the water of a stream, the currents of the air, the blood within a vein, the progress of a thought, or the order of occurrence of an event.

Being continuous, the phenomenon of flow—even if unlimited as to duration or volume—requires the restriction of containment.

—ROBERT HEALY, USACE

∞

Like, man, everybody's got to be someplace!

—HAROLD (MOONFLOWER) GORMAN
SAN DIEGO "HAPPENING," 1973

∞

XV
Quality Time

The Time Conduit
Sector Prime
Anchor Point Zero

To be inside a time conduit—a self-contained retrosynchronic durational flow phenomenon—is to be, like the conduit itself, never exactly anywhere but always somewhen.

Externally, a conduit has only one dimension and is thus not subject to physical location. Internally, though, the phenomenon contains and *is* the full spectrum of dimensions. The principle behind this seeming paradox—limited infinity—is the simple law of recurring continuity: the shortest straight line is the one that meets itself at beginning and end and is thus perpetual and endless.

But like many of the laws of actualism, a T1 conduit in practice is far easier to understand than to perceive. Even for those practiced in the application of tunnel dimensionality, the reality of a conduit seen from inside is beyond visual comprehension, and can cause symptoms ranging from vertigo to violent indigestion.

For this reason, the cross-time conduit established by the World History Investigative Society was veiled internally, its indescribable peripheries hidden by sensor readings and virtual displays to serve as observation ports for those within.

Adam had seen the inside of a time loop many times, but this was his first experience of the conduit and he found it breathtaking—a wide, serene tunnel extending to eternity in either direction and lined with beautiful visual displays of everything imaginable and some things beyond.

As far as he could see, he was alone in the tunnel, but he

knew he was not. The surging, flowing motion that he sensed around him was, he knew, thousands and tens of thousands of semiaccelerated Whispers on their way uptime. At this juncture in the conduit, he was somewhere between the prime accelerator of Waystop I—the Hawthorns' waystop—and the Leapfrog accelerator operated by Faron Briscoe upstream at 1887. Further upstream, further into the past than Leapfrog, these vaguely sensed transients would not be perceptible at all as they sped along on their way to the beginning of time.

Adam didn't know what to look for, but it didn't take long to find it. In one "wall" of the conduit, for a span of several hundred yards, the screening virtuals were dead. Here the transit stood unscreened, allowing a dizzying, inconceivable glimpse of the busy nothingness that was the linear skin of the conduit, exposed.

He was unable to look at it for more than just a glance. Nothing in human evolution had ever prepared the human mind—even the mind of a timer—for dimensions that bent inward upon themselves. But the sheer alienness of the span told him what it was. There was a hole here—a wormhole through four or more dimensions, held in check only by a countermingling of reverse dimensions along its length.

"I thought so," he muttered. Then, with the delicate subliminal force of a mind attuned to dimensionality, he concentrated on uncertain vectors and timed himself forward the equivalent of three hundred feet and thirty seconds.

The place where he found himself was a silent howling of universal forces barely in leash—a garish, nightmarish tumble of shapes and surfaces where busy, panicky little people hurried here and there doing incomprehensible things. It was difficult to recognize that this shambles of substances and energies had once been—and in fact still was—an exquisite toraform time loop.

Adam made his way through the throngs and tangles to a semiorganized area of intense activity and approached one of the little people. "Hello, Teal," he said. "Can I give you a hand with this mess?"

L-383

T2: February 9, 1951

"Have any of you ever seen a garden hose?" Adam asked, looking from one to another of the dozens of Whispers gathered around him. Then he shrugged. "No, I don't suppose you have. It's a resilient, bendable tube, of indeterminate length, used for transporting water to the posies. It might be a simile for a temporal conduit. Put a coil in that hose and elevate one end, and the coil will travel downward along the hose. The hose isn't the coil, but the coil *is* the hose, and it goes where it's drawn without interrupting the flow of the hose."

"Interesting," Teal Fordeen agreed. "An amusing simile for the relationship of a torus loop and its conduit, but hardy accurate as an analogy. In a temporal phenomenon, the loop can occupy spatial coordinates quite separate from the conduit. L-383 is more than just a loop in a tube. Normally, we move independently from the conduit."

"But what ails the conduit ails the loop," Adam pointed out. "Why is that, Teal?"

Peedy Cue raised his hand for attention. "L-383 is a torus," he offered. "It has no . . . no *continuity* of its own. It isn't structured as a singularity, as a ball loop might be. A torus loop is a toraform appendage."

Beside him, Cuel Denyne scowled. "You should confine yourself to mammalia, Peedy. That explanation is pathetically oversimplified."

Despite himself, Adam grinned. Whispers were always Whispers, he thought. Even in a state of calamitous emergency, when they hadn't the vaguest idea where they were or what to do about it, still they would take time out to debate semantics. "It's an adequate answer to my question," he told Peedy. "So as a toraform appendage, the loop is responsive to the condition of the conduit?"

Teal Fordeen nodded. "That is correct. But, Adam, our present problem is that we don't know what has happened. The loop has lost its configuration, and we have lost control. None of our navigational devices function. We have no comlink, and L-383 is deteriorating rapidly."

"We don't even know where we are," Peedy added.

"I do," Adam assured them. "L-383 isn't a toraform loop anymore. It's a tire patch, and it's impeding the progress of an ongoing dimensional transition that occurred at this juncture at the time you call Anchor T-zero. The transition was . . . is instantaneous and is the cornerstone of two complete histories. But right at this moment it is simply a work in progress, because L-383 is in the way."

In silence, Whispers exchanged puzzled glances, then turned back to Adam.

"Kaffer failed to stop the anchoring of the conduit by L-316," the timer said. "He tried, but he failed. In the attempt, though, something else happened. I suppose overlapping TEF fields caused it, somehow, but instead of canceling the history of the conduit, he simply shot a hole in the tube. It caused a blowout, and the blowout is trying to happen but it can't because L-383 has covered the hole in time-space where it occurred. L-383 is acting as a bandage. A tire patch. It has to be removed."

Again there was a long silence. Dozens of Whisper faces stared at the timer, their eyes reflecting confusion and dread.

"Has to be . . . *removed*?" Teal almost choked on the words. "But why, Adam? Do you know what you're saying?"

Adam leaned against an overturned console, sighing. "I know how it sounds," he admitted. "Based on what I've told you, it sounds as though I'm asking you to commit suicide and take your conduit with you. It would sound like that to me, too, if I were you."

"That's exactly how it sounds, Adam," Toocie Toonine said softly.

Teal Fordeen tilted his bald head, gazing at the protomorph timer with huge, unreadable eyes. "Is it something you can explain, Adam?"

"I don't have time, Teal. This configuration is deteriorating rapidly, even if your instruments don't show you that—"

"They do," Cuel Denyne admitted. "We have less than an hour of duration remaining to us, unless we can revive our loop. But we don't know what is eroding us."

"Your sensors can't tell you that," Adam said. "Your entire

technology is based on the concept of a neat, self-sustaining four-dimensional universe. The sensors don't know—*you* don't know—that there is anything beyond that."

"But you do?"

"I do. There is more to the continuum than the four prime dimensions. I know what it looks like, and a little of how it works." He shrugged, trying to find words for something indescribable. "I don't understand it, but I've seen it." He stood upright, spreading his hands. "I think I can help you, if you'll let me."

"Help us to do what?" Teal pressed. "Save the conduit?"

"There's nothing any of us can do about the conduit. I don't know what will happen to it when the blowout comes, but I know it will still exist. I know, because I know what it's really for."

"It's for uptime exploration," Cuel snapped.

Adam shook his head slowly. "No, it isn't. I know that's why WHIS created it, but that isn't all it does . . . did. It will do far more than that. But what I can help you with, I think, is to save L-383. I can be your guidance, when you pull free of the conduit. Teal, can a torus once formed be regenerated? Can a change in configuration be undone?"

"Topologically, yes, of course." Teal stared at him, puzzled. "As long as the integrity of the whole isn't destroyed, it can be reshaped from any configuration."

"Can you do that?"

Teal hesitated, then glanced at Cuel.

Cuel nodded. "We have configuration control. But how do we know that what he says is true?"

"How do we know otherwise?" Teal mused. "Our sensors tell us nothing."

"Apparently I'm the only eyes you have," Adam said. "I guess you'll just have to trust me."

"What if we don't?" Cuel snapped. "You aren't one of us. You're an indigenee . . . a protomorph!"

"If you don't," Adam sighed again, "then what is happening will happen anyway, when the patch blows. But you won't see it. None of you will. And I'll have lost some friends."

The silence this time was long and thoughtful. Adam lowered his head, feeling the grief he knew would come when they rejected his offer. These brave little people—they would try to salvage their loop, in their way, and they would fail. They didn't have the mind sight to see what he had seen, there at the funnel in Convergence—what he had seen again in the suggestion of a hologram in a converted retail mart. The patch would blow, and they would all be gone.

"Infinity isn't a figure eight," the timer said desperately. "It's . . . it's like a tree. Infinite roots at one end, infinite branches at the other, and in the middle a trunk, which is the mainstream timeline you call T2. Only it isn't just a single continuity. The trunk is interwoven bundles of fibers, as infinite as the roots and the branches. It's *all* mainline time, *now*! And it's as many histories as all the eventualities there ever have been.

"You've wondered where your people came from. Well, out there in the future, you were isolated from the rest of the world when a new branch took off. Maybe the transpolar rift caused it, but the world of your future isn't the world of ours. Different eventualities, different realities. But when you followed that blind path upstream to create your conduit, you wound up prebranch, going backward in a world where you never existed and never will, except in the past.

"Somewhere in antiquity your migration found a gate, between realities, and went through it. There's another history in another matrix of dimensions, where the people are the descendents of both my ancestors and your migrants, and these two histories have grafted here in 1951 where L-316 anchored the conduit. The crew of that loop saw what had happened, and somehow vented that splice so that it will heal itself. They used Kaffer's sabotage to power the healing. They created a buffer and called it Convergence. But now the flow is blocked.

"If L-383 isn't shifted from that splice, neither your future nor ours can ever happen. Please, you have to try." The enormity of what he was explaining hit him as hard as it hit those around him, and he heard his voice go hoarse and choked.

Little fingers touched his fingers, and a little hand crept into his. "I trust Adam," Toocie Toonine said. "I think we should do as he says."

Teal looked up at the tall timer. Big, speculative eyes

scanned him as though reading his soul. "Very well," Teal said. "Stations, please, everyone. We'll let Adam guide us as we pull free of the conduit. Stand by for reconfiguration as soon as we are free. Adam, can you use a fixed console?"

The timer nodded. "I can try."

"Then stand by to launch," Teal said. "We'll use Adam's eyes to vector."

Willy World
The Present

"T-zero is unstable," Deem Eleveno explained, standing on tiptoe to point out configuration anomalies in a tall holograph representing a sector of the time conduit. "Lucas referred to this discontinuity as a tire patch, and we believe Adam has gone in search of it."

Beside the little Whisper, and surrounded by several others, Edwin Limmer rubbed his chin thoughtfully, gazing at the display. "It does look like a patch," he agreed. "Is it doing any harm?"

"Not the patch," Deem said. "That's deteriorating, apparently, and we don't even know what it is. But the integrity of the conduit just beneath it is questionable. These interrupted radial graphics—" He stretched high, pointing. "—these are stresses in the time-space continuum of the conduit. A serious instability."

"I see." Limmer nodded. He stood for a moment in silence, thinking. "It's at T-zero?"

"Precisely. Anchor T-zero, the exact coordinates of L-316's conversion."

"And L-383 is still missing?"

"Without a trace."

"What kind of conduit control can you exercise from here?"

Deem looked startled. "Conduit control? Well, actually very little. We have the accelerators at Waystop I and Leapfrog, but that's only flow control, not control of the conduit itself. We can flow that, too, of course, but that only shifts the nature of the singularity. It doesn't change it."

"Can you transplant sections?"

Deem stared at him blankly.

"I mean," Limmer explained, "can you move portions of the conduit from one place to another, or replace one with another?"

"That's ridiculous," Deem snapped. "The conduit doesn't have 'portions.' It's a continuity."

"We could balance the stress at that point with a similar stress at another," KT-Pi offered. "We did that on a shunt once, and it worked."

"This isn't a shunt!" Deem scolded. "This is our conduit!"

"And that instability has something to do with L-383's disappearance," Limmer stated. "Obviously Adam suspected a connection, and went to do something about it. Can you contact him? Can you contact *anyone*?"

"We have distress messages out on all bands," KT-Pi said. "From here we're very limited, though. We can't even contact UEB. We don't know if we're reaching anybody."

Deem's eyes had narrowed. "This is a Whisper problem," he pointed out. "Adam is an indigenee!"

"So am I," Limmer reminded the Whisper. "Which means my specialty, like his, is creative thinking. Adding two and two and coming up with a dozen." He looked down at KT-Pi. "What happens if you counterbalance a stress?"

She blinked. "Well, in that shunt, it was pretty exciting. Three of us were blown entirely out into main time. Jaydee and I landed in 1836, and Aren Three wound up in 1821. But the shunt held, and aside from those two gaps there was no further damage."

"That was just a shunt," Deem repeated. "What would Teal say if we took chances like that with the conduit?"

"Teal isn't here," Limmer reminded him. "Do you have any better ideas?"

"We need to do *something*," another Whisper noted. "That instability is doubling every three minutes, and accelerating."

"Where would you put the other stress point?" Limmer asked Deem. "If you were to consider it, of course."

Deem rubbed his nose. "Probably downstream, as far as possible," he said. "Somewhere past the anachronism. Far enough past not to be affected by it, but not far enough to interfere with UEB history. Maybe four or five hundred years . . . I guess."

Limmer turned away, a trace of a smile on his face. "Think it over," he said. "It's your conduit, not mine. I had my ride."

"Somewhen around 2400," KT-Pi murmured, peering at temporal displays. "That would put it in the Locked Centuries. There's nothing to see along there, anyway."

Limmer paused, and looked back. "What was it like, Katie? When you were blown out of the shunt, what was it like?"

"It was just an abrupt transition from plus T1 to plus T2." The little Whisper shrugged. "Sort of like falling into a funnel."

L-383

"We can't move, Teal," Cuel Denyne said sadly. "The TEF field is compromised here. I'm afraid we're stuck."

"You've tried everything?" the Whisper leader asked.

"Everything. Electromagnetic conversion falls short of the boost required to pull us free. The fail-safes kick in ahead of analogous reversal, which means that if the drive TEF *were* to fire, it would simply melt down its components. It's unlikely this would free us. And even if it did, we'd have nothing left for reconfiguration. I'm afraid the loop is finished."

All around Adam, Whispers threw stricken glances at one another. "Well—" Teal Fordeen sagged. "—it was worth a try."

Adam shook his head. "You're giving up?"

"There's nothing more we can do," Teal said.

"That's no reason to just give up!" The timer crouched, peering around like a feral beast—like the primitive he was. "Show me something solid, Toocie. Something I can grab, that's framed into the whole structure of your components!"

Toocie Toonine turned full around, then pointed. "I suppose the TEF standards, Adam. The field drives the entire loop . . . when it's working."

Adam strode across jumbled spaces and tangles to where a TEF cone rested in a huge, elaborate nest. He glanced at the rig, up and down, then gripped a stanchion and tugged at it. Nothing moved. "This?" he called. "Is this part of the bracing?"

"It's the main brace," Teal called back, from the consoles. "What are you—"

Gripping the brace with all his strength, Adam closed his eyes and concentrated on dimensions and coordinates. Sweat beaded on his brow, and muscles rippled in his back with the intensity of his concentration. Carefully, maintaining a state of almost hypnotic awareness, he willed the mental act of transference.

All around him, a heaviness grew—gravity multiplying upon itself in that instant until the very light seemed drawn from the scene and darkness descended. In the smallest part of an instant the world around the timer became a miniature black hole, then reversed itself, flowing forth a massive flash of new light.

The "tire patch" shuddered violently as forces almost equal to the forces of stasis battered its inertia. But then the light evened, and Adam sagged. I can't do this, he realized. I don't have the strength.

He lowered his head in defeat, and felt a hand close over his own. A hand! Not a little Whisper hand, but a full-sized, protomorphic hand like his own. He gasped, looked up, and blinked at the grinning face of Ben Culver.

"Looks like you could use a little help, hoss," Culver said.

There were others behind him, then, and all around. In amazement, Adam saw Molly Muldoon clamber around a tangle of fallen hardware and shake her head in disgust. Just beyond the stanchion, others appeared. There was a lean, blond man in World War I British garb, a lady wearing a Victorian dress with frilly lace and pearls and an outlandish hat the size of a washtub, a sturdy, athletic youngster with thick glasses . . .

Adam looked from one to another and knew who they were. He even knew the names of some of them—Anya Karasova, Victor Kreske, Sundara Raj, Octavio diCapro—a dozen faces Adam remembered from various wheres and whens. Some were people he had rescued from the Delta killings, people he had aided in their development of skills, people he had known, and who had known him. And there were some he did not know, except as what they were.

Timers! They were all *timers*!

He stared at Ben Culver. "You? You did this?"

"Me and Molly." The sleepwalker grinned. "What's the good of ESP if you can't use it to holler for help?"

Amanda was beside them then, weak and shaky from the slowly disappearing re-gen on her arm but still able to time. Her good hand grasped the stanchion, just below Adam's. Other hands closed around and over them. "Let's see if we can move this thing," Mandy said.

Molly Muldoon crowded in and stood among them, touching them all, and her clear, ESPer thoughts cascaded among them like sundrops in a flower garden. The scintillation of her psychic presence seemed to serve as a catalyst for other, far deeper ESP resonances that Adam realized came from the awakened mind of Ben Culver. To the skills of the timers, the keen dimensional awareness they shared, was added now a deep, growing undertone of psychic reverberation that went beyond dimensions. Adam gasped at the sheer force of the sensed awareness, and others around him blinked and winced in awe. Somehow Molly Muldoon's wild talent had reached the core of Ben Culver's evolving mind and turned the switch. The sleepwalker was awake now. Culver the shifter had come of age.

Let's try it now, Culver said, and there were neither words nor sound in the command. Its meaning flowed among them in waves of psychic resonance.

Again the concentration, this time in massive concert . . . again the darkening of enormous gravities, and the instant flood tide of brilliant new light, and all around the knot of indigenees, Whispers scampered and chattered. Abruptly the resistance of inertia was gone. L-383 floated free, a flattened doughnut of effervescence in bright sunlight, quickly expanding, fading, and disappearing as huge harmonics went into play and the resonance of multidimensional stability surged and grew.

Eastwood, Kansas
The Present

For once in her life, Maude Hawthorn seemed speechless. Abruptly her house was full of people—people of all shapes and sizes, Whispers and "ordinary" people alike, bustling about, chattering excitedly, seeming to fill the place.

"We had the key and didn't know it," a Whisper exclaimed. "Deem Eleveno's probability equations . . ."

"We'll have to start from scratch, mathematically," someone else was explaining. "Parallel universes, quintangle vectors, cross-dimensional analysis . . ."

"Eternity and infinity," a voice expounded somewhere else in the crowd. "I always thought there was more to them than . . ."

"With infinity equations it's always the same," somebody griped. "All or nothing . . ."

With Adam's help, Maude and Em Ten shooed various people out of the best chair in the living room and put Mandy in it.

"Don't have a canary fit!" Mandy fussed. "Another hour or two and I'll be as good as new."

"You need to rest," Em Ten urged.

"I need to rest," Mandy echoed.

Crammed into a corner by the gun rack, Teal Fordeen told Lucas Hawthorn, "L-383 is fully functional again. We'll be ready to vacate the Willsmart premises when you send trucks."

"Willmart," Lucas corrected.

"What?"

"Willmart. Not *smart*, just mart. It's Willy World."

"Whatever."

"Okay, so is somebody going to explain what's been going on?"

"I'm sure we can clear it all up," the Whisper said, "if we can get all these people settled down."

Near the east bay window, voices were raised in what had become almost a shouting match as various individuals exchanged views on the ramifications of intersequence transfer.

"Do you mean to suggest," Deem Eleveno demanded, "that

Ben Culver's materialization in a Great Plains village was what triggered the later gravitational anomalies in the Deep Hole area? That is patently ridiculous!"

"I'm only pointing out a possibility," another Whisper insisted. "You yourself said the evidences of planetary wobble seem to match the shifter episodes."

"I wonder," Peedy Cue interrupted them, "what effect gravity variations might have had on mammalian development. Don't females indigenous to western Kansas seem to have—"

"I find that suggestion a bit insulting," Nancy Culver snapped, glaring at the Whisper. "Oklahoma is just as—"

"I'll make coffee," Maude decided. She glanced at Lucas. "Do something," she ordered.

Lucas shrugged, then drew himself up tall and took a deep breath. "Attention!" he roared. In the startled silence that followed, he grinned sheepishly at his wife. "How's that?" he asked.

In the busy kitchen, Ed Limmer ran a finger down the Anywhen, Inc., day list. Most of the tourists had been accounted for. All but two. "What about those NERCs?" he asked. "What were their names? Smith and Wesson?"

"Westin," Maude said. "Smith and Westin. We found them, not far upstream, but they refused to come back. They're happy where they are. They're hoping to work for a senator named McCarthy. I guess they're happier back then. I just hope they don't make too many anachronisms."

"They already did," a passing Whisper said. "That agency they worked for—the NERC—it doesn't exist. It never did."

Ed Limmer turned away. "Those boys should fit right in," he muttered. "Can I help with that tray?"

From the log of L-383:

The paradox and the puzzle: how often, in this adventure of all adventures, have I enjoyed the heated debates of Elzy Pyar and Zeem Sixten over precise meanings of these two concepts. A puzzle is a reality that defies understanding. A paradox is something that cannot be, but is. It is sad that Elzy could not be present to experience the perspective that brought our own riddles into context.

L-383 owes its existence to those strange, pre-Arthurian people we have labeled as timers. So, for that matter, do all of us involved in the great Whisper adventure. And so, we know now, do an entire world of people whose existence we never suspected until Adam told us about Convergence . . . and about ourselves.

We came into this age from the future, just as we always believed. But not from *this world*'s future. The future we came from was our own, in a separate eventuality that apparently began in this world's era 2300–2400 plus, when our race, the Pacificans, was literally created through genetic experimentation.

It is likely that the probabilities branched apart—becoming two separate lines of eventuality—during the cataclysmic time of the transpolar rift, in this world's year of 2410. In our own history, we record our earliest *known* origins in the period 2450–2600, and we were always—in our time—the only people on Earth.

So how did we come to be in this alternate world? In the year 3004, when the UEB received the last and only downtime message from the scout loop L-270, the message came by random eventuality curve. Its route from the past to the future was unchartable, but when the anchor loop L-316 launched in 3005 it set its course by following—or backtracking—the course of that single message, moment by moment back through a history that could not be seen—the so-called Locked Centuries.

And at some point—Adam estimates at about 2400—that fragile trail led L-316 across a dimensional warp and into this world's reality. Adam believes the warp was—or will be—the dimensional fallout from the reseparation of two timelimes at the downtime end of the Convergence buffer.

The rest is recorded data: L-270's trailblazing penetration of the time storm; L-316's sacrifice to create the time conduit; the journey and tragic demise of the original scout loop, L-270; the opening of the conduit for exploration uptime to antiquity; the creation of the accelerators Waystop I and Leapfrog; and the recent (in durational terms) eruption of a rift between this and another, separate eventuality that had grafted but not spliced.

The rift is not chaotic. The two histories are buffered by that "dimensional island" that Adam calls Convergence. Beyond it, but held separate by it, is that other timeline. It is this world, but with another history—a history in which some of the ancient ancestors of the people there are *us*! Our migration to the past found the gate between these two realities, and we *became* the alternate people, intermingling with the earliest of the protomorphs who were common ancestors to both realities.

The UEB is closing its base at 3015. Most of the World History Investigative Society and a majority of the Pacifican race has migrated uptime now, and within a year's duration there will be only a few remaining in that overlapped timeline that we once thought was the entire universe. The Sundome installation will be moved upstream to a far earlier time in this world, to expedite analyses of the alternate history findings that have forced a reevaluation of everything we thought we knew.

We probably will not attempt to enter the alternate probability, even though there is now a gateway between the two at 1951—a gate that opened when L-383 released its pressure on the conduit anomaly caused by the renegade Kaffer. We *are* the history of that other eventuality, and to interfere with it in any way, most feel, would be to again jeopardize our own existence.

The timers, however, have plans of their own for the buffer area known as Convergence. Adam and several others have proposed that Convergence become a sanctuary for timers—a place where they might gather, free of threat even from one another, while their evolving minds mature and they become whatever they are destined to become.

Psychics and timers, shifters and what Molly Muldoon calls frosters—every indication is that these people may be the progenitors of a new kind of human, possibly even a new race. Whatever they are, it may be a strange and wonderful sort of people that occupies their particular branch of the infinity tree.

As to Kaffer, the only true criminal ever to spring from our Pacifican race: Adam brought us a gift, after L-383 was restored. He brought us Kaffer's head. It is his suggestion that possibly our scientists, with the tools and techniques at our disposal, can determine by analytical dissection what makes an otherwise normal, intelligent being become a psychopath.

Adam believes that there might be no greater tribute to humanity in all its varieties than to finally discover what makes some of us, with our enormous capacity for good, turn bad.

Not all of us will go from here and now to the new UEB base in antiquity. The conduit will remain open, and the phenomenon called L-383 will continue its function as a staging area for whatever missions may be assigned by UEB. A few of us may stay around, just to see what happens next.

As Peedy Cue phrased it, "You haven't seen anything until you've seen it all."

—TEAL FORDEEN, FINAL SUBMISSION

EPILOGUE

Svenskholm

Valley of the Ferns
A.D. 1105

Above a hidden valley, carved deep between rolling, forested hillsides, the tribe made camp before sunset, and Glome himself led scouts forward to explore. These were new lands to the tribe, and there might be enemies. Towering over the young men who followed him, Glome raised his head to taste the messages of the wind. It was a south wind, barely strong enough in its gusts to move the lower leaves of the elm trees, but its scent spoke to him. There was water ahead, and a pleasant, cool-green smell like moss on stone. It was a scent he recalled from a long time ago, in another place—the scent of hidden glades where summer ferns drooped over deep, cold pools. It reminded him of times and things long since lost, and the memories were pleasant.

Even the trace of woodsmoke in the air was a pleasant trace, though it told him there were people nearby, and in wild lands all strangers must be regarded as enemies.

Glome's beard had grown long and bushy in the seasons since the voyage that had brought him to strange and magical shores. He was now more sun-weathered than then, and his manner had changed in some ways. Though still a formidable warrior, Glome now had more bounce to his step and more sparkle to his gaze than in those old times that he thought of as his other life.

Not since that incredible ride in the belly of a metal dragon had Glome seen sailing ships, or even a sea. But what he had found was a degree of happiness among the small, brown people who were now his people.

Of the infants, crawlers, and toddlers among them now, several were of his own blood. Four of them had blue eyes, and one or two of them even had flaxen traces in their hair. Their mothers displayed them proudly, often pointing at Glome as they chattered over women's work, and their glances were full of fondness.

He had long since discarded his horned helmet and his studded shield, finding such things awkward and useless in this land where no enemies carried swords and where the stone-tipped arrows were diverted as easily by a light shield of bison bullhide as by iron.

They told him—those who were now his people—that he had become legendary among the scattered tribes. He knew that this was so, because often during the warm seasons people of other tongues and other customs approached his camps, wanting to trade and to share a fire. And some of them stayed and became his people, too, because he was Glome.

For two seasons they had made their homes along the sandy river, until the *fletermaksin* that he called Krapp sank out of sight beneath the shifting sands and the two white men who worshiped it wandered away to join one of the migrant tribes.

But in the third season, game had been scarce, and wild people had come from the west to make war. Glome had enjoyed the fighting, but as more and more of the barbarians came, he grew tired of it. And so the people had begun a trek to a new place, that Glome felt he would recognize when he found it.

They had seen many places since then, and now had come to this place, and in the evening light Glome and his warriors crept to the edge of a high cliff and looked down into a deep, walled valley, and abruptly Glome felt homesick. The valley was like another place—a slice of another world, set down in this one. Down there, water rippled over little waterfalls, songbirds flitted among the trees, and the stone and earth of the rich floor were shrouded in a hundred shades of green.

It was a secret place, a hidden place, and it was like another place that Glome remembered. From the ledge, this valley looked and smelled like the Vale of Snowflowers in the mountains above Vest Fjord. It reminded the Swede of home.

The smoke came from a few little cooking fires scattered across the valley, and at two campsites they could see people—small, brown-skinned people who cleaned rabbit skins and wove grass baskets in the evening light. Wanderers, passing the time.

"Come away," Glome told his warriors. "Tonight we camp beyond the hill. Tomorrow we will return. Tomorrow, we will taste the water down there, and turn the soil, and explore the cliffs around. If it is good, we will stay."

He slept that night with his best wives and some of his children crowded around him, and he dreamed of Vestfjord in Hartzel where he had been a child before he learned to be a man.

And when he awoke, Gladen Lodbrok, whose name now was Glome, knew that he had found his weird. Here in this place, with that secluded valley as its stronghold, he would make his home. They would erect huts here, and later good pole lodges, and here the children would grow.

The vision went with him into the valley the next day, and all things there were in accord with it.

In time, as the seasons passed and silver crept into the dark gold of his beard, Glome would come to think of this as Vestfjord Vale, the Vale of Snowflowers, and in the evenings he would occupy himself with the preserving of the marvels he had seen. He would carve runestones to proclaim the goodness of the Earth and his thoughts about it.

"Go warily in foreign times," his runes would warn. "Go with sword in hand, for there be dragons."

Foremost among the runestones, though, would stand one that he had already carved. It was his claim, for himself and his descendants—a tall slab of gray stone upon which the Swedish runes were cut deep and clear, to last forever:

THIS IS GLOME'S VALLEY.

Paradox Gate Chronology

Extracted from: *The Gates of Time Temporal Concordance*

TIME2 EVENTS	TIME1 EVENTS
2400 B.C. Burial of Pharaoh Khafre	1KHAF4 plants L-270 slave TEF in Pyramid of Khafre
1887 Leapfrog Booster Waystop activated from Waystop I	
1899 Earliest known timer, Anya Karasova	
1908 Tunguska event in Siberia	
1909	Disappearance of Rasputin Trove from St. Petersburg, Russia
1940–72 Time of the timers, origin of unknown number of individuals naturally adept at four-dimensional autotransference	
1947 "Flying saucer" reports in U.S.	L-270 emerges in pre-Arthurian time
1951	Anchor loop L-316 bridges anachronism following "Lost Loop" final message

1949–54	Deep Hole project anachronisms concealed by U.S. military, along with UFO evidence	Kaffer obtains anomaly data, deduces origin of Whisper technology
1952	Edwin Limmer enters mainstream T2; Limmer Trust, Limmer Foundation	
1953		L-316 sacrifices itself to establish transanachronism T1 conduit; no reported survivors
1991	Second fuel war solidifies multinationalism	
1993	Emergence of sector economies, realignments of world political power	L-383 primary Whisper presence in pre-Arthurian time
1997	Dr. David Frank invents gravity light	
1998	Booster Waystop I; Anywhen, Inc.	First Whisper encounters with temporal adepts or timers
1999	Gravitational anomaly in Kansas; Siberian deep-drill findings lead to geodetic-tectonic exploration: Project Deep Hole	“Ghost sightings” of L-316 members WHIS future history attacked by Kaffer
2001	Asian Concords collapse in Sino-Arab-Slavic disputes	
2001–3	Asian wars; “Seven Days of Silence”	Merlin Base established by Whispers
2002	(est.) Timers’ “Concurrence of Privacy”	
2003	**Deep Hole incident.** Subsequent global tectonic shifts strengthen earlier theories suggesting	

a gravitic singularity in Earth's core; breakdown of most orbital comweb systems

2003–04 Verification of the Asian Abyss

2004 Global Paper Panics, power realignments. In U.S.: border mandates, regional wars; Protectorate Authority for Common Trust emerges as steward/custodian

2005 PACT enforces Edict of Encroachment

2009 Fundamentalists mobilize; deunification of states

2010–13 NSF/ISF maps tectonic shifts, first substantial evidence of relationship between Tunguska Event and Deep Hole incident; gravitic singularity theories gain in acceptance

2012 Federated Free Zones; first Revivalist uprisings

2020 Institute for Temporal Research (ITR) established in Panhandle FFZ by John Jacob Royce, pursuing Ikebata-Tolafsson bitemporal theories; research into laws and analogs governing the photogravitic spectrum

2029 Arthur's takeover of ITR	
2037–38 Arthur Rex consolidates Camelot, begins campaign against Revivalists; temporal effect focalizer (TEF) perfected	
2050 **Arthur's Anachronism**	Birth of Edwin Limmer in reverse T2
2080–2210 Rational Nationalism debates; Cutter's "All for One" address; rise of the empocracies; PACT reverts powers to Council of Commonwealths	
2388–2410 Science of genetics achieves major breakthroughs in Seattle World Symposiums	
2410 **Transpolar rift**	
2450–2600 Era of origin of Pacifica and the Pacificans	
2744 Universal Experience Bank of Pacifica sponsors World History Investigative Society (WHIS); first T1 conduit tested	
2910 Whisper expedition extends conduit upstream through T2; discovery of the Arthurian Anachronism	
2910–81 Efforts to penetrate the time storm at 2050; closed-loop tests begin	